MAP

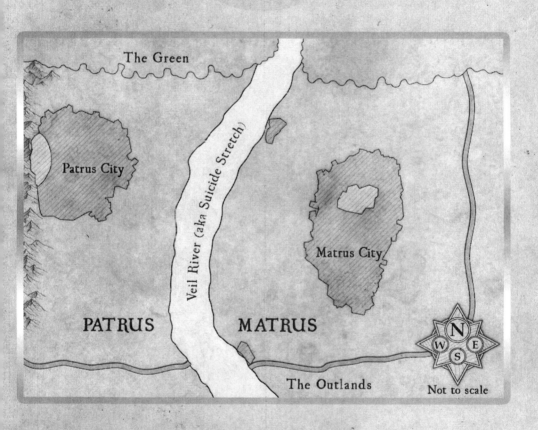

The Green

Patrus City

Veil River (aka Suicide Stretch)

Matrus City

PATRUS

MATRUS

The Outlands

N
W E
S

Not to scale

THE GENDER SECRET

THE GENDER GAME, BOOK 2

BELLA FORREST

PROLOGUE

QUEEN ELENA

I knelt in front of the throne as the crown was lowered onto my head. The crowd that filled the royal courtyard gave a half-hearted cheer. I could sense their pain and confusion. They had not been given enough time to mourn—none of us had. My mother's death had come too soon, and nobody had been prepared.

The official who had presided over my coronation placed a hand on my shoulder, squeezing softly. I looked up, and could see the unshed tears forming at the corners of her eyes, her mask crumbling. Gathering the skirts of my blood-red dress, I stood. This was not a time for tears.

It was a time for war.

"Women of Matrus," I spoke, my voice ringing out across the crowd, thanks to the microphone attached to my ceremonial gown. The crowd started to hush as all eyes fixed on me. I placed my right hand on my chest and took a step forward. "My sisters. We have been robbed." A few shouted out in agreement, but the rest of the assembly remained silent.

I took another step forward, my skirts brushing against the banister of the balcony. "We have been robbed," I repeated, nodding. "It should not be me standing before you today. It should be my mother. It should be Queen Rina." I could see the crowd agreeing in whispers that swept through the crowd like wildfire. "None of us expected that this day would come. But how could we have known? How could we have ever expected this?" I shook my head, letting my new crown glint in the sun.

Taking a deep breath, I looked out, setting my face into a mask of immutable sadness. "My mother was the truest queen Matrus has ever known. She knew when to be strong… and she knew when to show mercy. It is what I admired most in her. And I swear to you now that I will do everything in my power to be every bit the queen my mother was. I swear to you; I will be fair. I will be merciful. But most importantly, I will be *strong*." I let the word roll out over the crowd like thunder, watching the people shift under the might of my voice.

"I will search out my mother's killers, and show them

what Matrian justice is. And if there is, indeed, a Patrian element behind this dastardly plot of murder… we must take our battle to their doorstep."

The crowd stirred with tense murmurings.

I raised both hands. "I know, sisters. I know. Sparking a war is against every principle our motherland was founded on. My mother strived to maintain peace throughout her leadership, at all costs. But we all need to accept that if indeed Patrus is responsible for my mother's death, we are not the ones causing the spark… Also remember: King Maxen is different than his father King Patrick was, and thus we cannot deal with him in the same way. Maxen is a man we cannot respond to with silence!"

I pressed my fist over my heart, and then thrust my hand forward, out toward the assembly. The crowd warmed at the gesture, and soon the courtyard was awash with applause.

I was pleased by the effect my speech had on them. Gone were the mourning faces, replaced by a righteous wrath that I had fueled. It was a better response than I had hoped for. And it had set the stage for future speeches. With timing and patience, I would fuel the spark into a flame, and that flame into a fire.

I basked in their cheers for a few more moments, and then turned on my heel and left, entering the palace.

"That was your speech?" a familiar voice called to me.

I turned to find my sister, Tabitha, leaning against the door of my mother's library. She seemed pleased, which wasn't very surprising—Tabitha was always itching for a good fight.

Tabitha was the second sister, next in line for succession, and she stood out like a sore thumb compared to the other members of our family. We were all tall, but she was heavyset too, her body roped with muscles that had always set us apart in our defense classes. She was wearing black now, like she always did, but had managed to dress it up in a way that clung to her muscular figure, in a manner that was both flattering and impressive. She had a semi-sardonic look on her face—one that she always seemed to have when I was around. She also had her dagger out and was using it to clean her nails. I lifted an eyebrow at her, letting my expression do the talking.

She slid the dagger into the hidden sheath at her belt before lifting her hand, twirling her fingers around in a circle. With a sigh, I turned around slowly, allowing her to inspect my new queenly appearance. After making the circle, I folded my hands in front of me and furrowed my brows.

"So, they went with the red," Tabitha remarked. "It's

a good color, considering the theme of revenge and war." She grinned, her wide mouth revealing a pair of wicked canines.

"I knew you'd be pleased," I said, pulling my skirts open to reveal my black pants and knee-high boots underneath. I unbuttoned the clasp on the inside, and the skirt fell into a puddle on the floor. I exhaled in relief—I hated wearing skirts. "Mother was always too soft when she dealt with the Patrians. I plan to take a different course of action—one that I think your skills are perfectly suited for."

Tabitha grinned again, the predatory glint in her dark eyes intensifying. "Oh?"

I blinked at her. "Of course, sister mine. I am appointing you as the new Chief of Wardens." I allowed a smile to cross my lips as Tabitha's face contorted with anger and she spat a curse at me. We had never really gotten along. In fact, one time she hit me so hard, she fractured my jawbone—I had to have my jaw wired closed for six weeks as a result. But I returned the favor not long after by pushing her down the stairs that led to the roof. She had six broken ribs and a broken arm.

As royals, abstinence from violence wasn't enforced on us within the palace walls… at least not when there were no visitors around.

"You selfish bitch," Tabitha hissed.

I suppressed a smile. Tabitha had been petitioning me since mother's death to give her a position over the war council, except there was no war council. She wanted me to create the position just for her.

I raised a hand. Instantly, six wardens materialized— royal wardens were good at lurking in shadows.

"Careful, sister," I practically sang. "You wouldn't want to be confused with a violent Patrian sympathizer, now would you?"

I watched as Tabitha tamped down her rage—a control that I knew would cost some man terrible pain later— and kept the smile off my lips. After she calmed down, I gave her a nod. "I have a meeting with Ms. Dale in a few minutes. Please remain here until after she leaves, and I will speak to you further about the details of your position."

My sister bowed, stiffly, before I turned and swept through the library door.

I allowed myself a smile before taking my seat behind the large round desk. It felt wrong sitting here, but it also felt right. I looked over to where the wood had been sanded down and re-stained, obscuring the words that had been carved there in blood. Yet I would never forget them. They rattled around in my head like a mantra, fueling and sustaining my rage. *For the boys of Matrus,* indeed.

My mouth flattened to a hard line as I recalled the

double murder of my mother, Queen Rina, and her advisor, Mr. Jenks. Clearly, someone had found out what Mother and Mr. Jenks were doing with the boys, and they had taken exception to it.

There was a rap at the door and Ms. Dale entered and bowed. I lifted my hand, indicating she should sit in one of the chairs facing me, and she did. She was a handsome woman, aging well, and still in remarkable shape. She had been acting as a defense trainer for almost all of her life, but Ms. Dale's true occupation was one of a spy. Actually, she was *the* spy—a spider sitting on the top of a very well-placed web of informants.

"Ms. Dale," I said, meeting her unflinching brown eyes. "Tell me all about Violet Bates."

Ms. Dale took a breath in and then handed me the file she had been holding. "Violet Bates was one of my more promising students. I had been planning to recruit her for the warden's academy when she broke the law and tried to smuggle her younger brother across Veil River after he failed the screening. She slipped into delinquency soon after that, but then, when Mr. Jenks' lab was broken into, it provided an opportunity to utilize her skills for the mission to retrieve the egg—and what made her more suitable for the task was the fact that she was an orphan; relatively unknown and expendable."

I thumbed through the file, pretending to read it, but listened attentively. "I see," I said. I placed the file aside, and leaned forward, resting my elbows on the table and folding my hands. "And were you aware of her plot to assassinate my mother?"

Ms. Dale's mouth formed a grim line. "I was not. In fact, I don't believe Violet to be the killer."

"Oh, really? Why do you think that?"

"Violet's history is one of violence, certainly, but if you study the details of her infractions, it's clear that it was only when directly threatened that she did harm. She has never intentionally hurt anyone who wasn't a threat, and frankly, she didn't have good cause to murder your mother."

"Why not?"

"Because Violet wants to be with her brother more than anything in the world. Your mother was the key to that, and for Violet to murder her before getting what she wanted just wouldn't make any sense… If you're asking for my opinion, I think it's more likely that Lee Bertrand, the spy we had already planted in Patrus, is the culprit."

I refrained from rolling my eyes as I considered her statement. Lee Bertrand was a bit of a paradox, with his unorthodox birth in the middle of the Veil River. He technically had no nation of his own, but he had sworn fealty to my mother and Mr. Jenks. There was no reason to suspect him. Especially given what had happened to him. "His body was found splattered on the pavement in the courtyard," I reminded her.

She nodded, her expression guarded. "Yes, and I think it's likely that Violet killed him in self-defense."

"Then why isn't she here? Why has she fled instead of stating her innocence?"

Ms. Dale opened her mouth, and then shut it, sighing. "I don't know," she said. "That doesn't make much sense to me. I imagine that she'd come if she could, but I have no idea how she got in or out of the palace undetected. I wasn't given the details of that, as Lee was supposed to be handling the escape plan."

I sat back, eyeing the older woman thoughtfully. Ms. Dale had served Matrus faithfully for a long time, and Mother had often trusted her counsel.

"Well, the fact is, Violet Bates still has Matrian property," I said, drawing myself upright again. "So I am tasking you, Melissa Dale, with finding both her and the egg, and returning them here to sort through this… Take what supplies you need, and go."

Ms. Dale rose to her feet and bowed. Her face locked in an unreadable mask, she turned and left.

As I watched her exit, I noticed two of my other sisters—the twins, Selina and Marina—waiting outside the door. I was glad they had arrived for their meeting now. I had timed things well.

I waved my hand, beckoning them in. They approached, their movements almost synchronized. It had always creeped me out when they did that, and I imagined they were doing it now for that purpose.

"*Queen* Elena," they said, bowing as one.

"Sisters," I said, allowing a smile to peel across my face. "I will keep this brief: I want you to tail Ms. Dale, and if she leads you to Violet Bates, I want you to secure the girl and what she carries first."

Selina and Marina exchanged looks before glancing back at me.

"You do not trust Ms. Dale?" Selina asked.

I wet my lower lip. "It's not that… exactly. The issue is that until we figure out how deep this conspiracy runs, I am not going to commit only one resource to finding Violet Bates. What she carries is far too important to leave to chance; you both can appreciate that."

The sisters nodded. "We can," Marina said.

"We'll see to it," Selina confirmed.

Good. Selina and Marina had always been the most obedient of my sisters… at least, the most obedient to *me*.

As the twins turned to leave, I asked them, "Can you

tell Tabitha to come in now?" while slipping Violet's file into a drawer.

Tabitha entered the room a few seconds after the twins had exited.

"Yes?" she asked. Her tone was level and controlled, though her brown eyes appeared darker than usual.

"Will you allow me to speak without you accusing me of lying?" I asked, holding her gaze firmly.

She nodded, and I gestured for her to sit down.

"Sister, I know that you wanted to be the Minister of War, but the problem is… we are not at war." Tabitha's eyes became slits, and I held up my hand. "*Yet*," I amended. "Pronouncing you Minister of War now would only serve to indicate to King Maxen that we are declaring war, which I am not yet ready to do. As Chief of Wardens, your duties will be maintaining the walls, but also recruitment and training women, in *preparation* for the war."

My sister's face transformed as I talked, her eyes brightening and her lips beginning to curl.

Mother had always told me being Queen of Matrus was like being a clockmaker: you put the right people for the job in the right place, and let them do what they did best. My sister Tabitha was a hammer, one destined for a great battlefield. I merely gave her the opportunity to channel her abilities in such a way that would be productive.

And when the time was right, I would unleash her onto the Patrians. The world, after that, would never be the same.

I kept this thought in my mind as I picked up the phone to call King Maxen. I would offer him the pretty lies that would keep us from war… right up until the exact moment that we were ready to pounce.

CHAPTER 1

VIGGO

I sat in the detention center, my hands cuffed in front of me. I had been here for over twenty-four hours and still had no idea why I was being detained. Even the warden whom I managed to coerce into giving me status updates on the wrecked lab was clueless as to why I was being held.

I had been waiting for Violet when the explosion had gone off.

I was lucky: the initial blast had blown me back into a hallway, shielding me from the worst of the heat and debris. Others had not been so fortunate. The vision of dead men and women scattered across the floor still filled my mind's eye. But the worst were those still alive and wounded. They screamed their confusion and disbelief while staring at bisected body parts. One man was cradling his own arm to his chest, his face blank with shock.

I had done what I could to help. I had carried people out, and snapped orders to organize the few others who were capable of providing assistance.

But all the while, as I fought through that inferno in search of any remaining heartbeat, there was someone in particular I was trying to find—desperately. A young woman with long dark hair and startling gray eyes. I kept throwing myself into the building and looking for her, but returning with someone else. Each trip drained me more—emotionally more than physically. After the first hour, my thoughts turned to the worst, and I started wondering with each corpse I stepped over, which might belong to her.

And then my search had been stopped altogether; the wardens had come for me. Wardens who were supposed to be at *my* command—wardens I had *trained*—began to explain that they were taking me in for questioning. Before I could begin to make sense of the situation, one had slipped around my back and clamped handcuffs on me. *Jim Trent.* He'd never been a favorite among my colleagues.

They took me to a van parked outside the lab's perimeter, locked me in the back and escorted me to the city's primary detention facility… where I remained. After securing me in a cell, I was left without the slightest explanation.

A few wardens had walked past me since I'd arrived, but all had refused to answer a single question—except for one of the younger recruits whose name I had forgotten, but who I knew saw me as a role model. If not for him, I'd be completely without information even now. He gave me the current body count: The bombing had killed thirty-two people in the initial blast. Of the remaining survivors, most had been critically injured. Another ten had died from the severity of their wounds. The king, however, had escaped relatively unscathed.

The lad didn't know why I was being detained, and as for Violet… he had no idea.

So, I had no choice but to wait, though it was excruciating. It was the not knowing that was the worst. I would almost rather learn that Violet was dead than sit there wondering, hoping. I had no idea where in the building she had been when the blast went off—if she was anywhere near the events hall, chances were that she didn't make it. It was a wonder that the king got out alive, and that was with bodyguards assigned and trained to protect him—he rarely went anywhere without at least two of them.

A hollow feeling settled in the base of my stomach. The brief period that I'd known Violet had been a whirlwind. The evening Lee brought her to my cabin and requested for me to be her second guardian, I'd suspected I might be getting myself into more than I was willing. Violet was clearly a free-spirited and strong-minded young woman, but I never could have predicted that things would go so far so quickly, spiral so… out of control.

I still wasn't sure how I could have let that kiss happen between us. I replayed that fateful night over in my head, as I had done dozens of times since. Her hair and clothes wet and clinging to her lithe body, she'd stood in my living room just a couple of feet in front of me. Her dusky eyes had flicked to my face and before I could react, her arms had slid over my shoulders, her soft lips locking with mine. Then she'd pulled herself against me—I relived every detail now: the way her chest pressed to mine; her harried breathing; her damp-pinewood scent; the quiet moan that had escaped her throat when I had closed my lips around hers, no longer physically capable of containing the passion coursing through my veins. Every part of me had burned for her that night, and if her husband hadn't interrupted when he had, I knew that Violet and I would have done something we'd later regret.

That woman had awakened things in me I'd long thought I'd lost—emotions and impulses that I hadn't felt since Miriam. She had reminded me what it was like to feel connected to another human being; to discover a kindred spirit in a world of meaningless interactions. Violet had made me break the single rule I was professionally trained to live by—never drop your guard.

As painful as it was, I'd done the right thing by telling her that we needed to cut things off after that night. I wasn't one to make a cuckold out of any man—though I couldn't deny that a part of me had still hoped I'd be able to see her from time to time, even if we couldn't be alone together. Spotting her in the audience at a fight or visiting the lab with her husband would have done something to brighten my day, relive the few memories of what we'd once shared.

But now… now, in all likelihood, Violet was dead.

I wasn't sure where that left me.

Hollow, yes. Hollow and numb. That was what I felt now. However else her death would manifest in me would be apparent soon enough, once the shock of the attack had worn off. My brain still felt shaken from the blast.

Finally, the door to my room opened and a flint-eyed warden stepped in. I didn't recognize him, which likely meant he wasn't going to answer my questions. He slipped a key in the door, keeping his eyes on me.

"Viggo Croft," he said. "Come with me."

"Where?" I asked, standing up. At my full height, I towered over the man.

He looked a touch intimidated as he eyed me over, but said nothing—he just held out his hand toward the door. Acquiescing, I strode forward.

The warden guided me along an empty hallway and into another room, which held a table and chair. He sat me down and released my cuffs, allowing me to rub my wrists and lean back.

"What is this about?" I demanded, my eyes trained on him. He still didn't answer. Instead, he turned and left the room. But I was alone for only a few seconds before the door opened again.

By now, I felt ready to snap at whoever it was, but as the visitor stepped inside, my voice caught in my throat. It was King Maxen, clad in a deep burgundy suit. His jaw-length hair and goatee were singed, his skin perceptibly red. He gazing at me, his face contemplative and unreadable.

"Your Majesty," I murmured.

He inclined his head, his gaze never leaving mine. "Mr. Croft."

The last time I had seen the king face-to-face was

when I had been brought before King Maxen and his father, King Patrick, for sentencing after my failed attempt to cover up Miriam's crime. King Patrick had ordered me to work as a warden for four years without pay. I wasn't sure why King Maxen had come to see me now; I couldn't help but find his appearance ominous.

He moved over to the opposite chair and sat down, his posture betraying his exhaustion.

"The last twenty-four hours have been that of pure chaos, Mr. Croft," the king said, placing a folder onto the table. I looked down at it, then back up at him.

"I saw the damage," I replied hoarsely. "Who did this?"

The king tapped his fingers on the table. "Well, apparently, there are some who would have us believe that you are responsible."

I stared at him, half-believing that I'd misheard. "What?"

The king waved his hand. "No need to be concerned—we know now that you weren't. It just took us the better part of a day to realize that you were being framed… It seems that the culprits used your history against you to make it seem like your dissatisfaction with the government had brought you to a tipping point. But these terrorists got sloppy toward the end, and we were able to determine who they actually were."

My hands clenched as I leaned forward. "Who?"

"Lee and Violet Bertrand."

I froze, my mind unable to comprehend his words, much less accept them. *"What?"* I fought the urge to protest under the stern eye of the king, but the words were already forming on the tip of my tongue.

The king nodded and pushed the file in my direction. "It seems that Lee and Violet were originally sent here by Matrus, in order to steal something significant to our research. They succeeded in stealing the object. However, it turns out that one of them was even more radical than we thought—Mrs. Bertrand. It appears that, after completing the attack with her husband, she murdered not only him, but also Queen Rina and one of her advisors."

My mouth dried out. *This can't be real.* "Your Majesty," I managed, "Violet wouldn't do that. She's not—"

The king arched an eyebrow. "Yes, we discovered what an adept little actress Mrs. Bertrand is. She had everyone fooled, including you; we have recovered documents about her true nature that are a little hard to ignore." He glanced at the file. "I'll give you a few minutes to take a look, shall I?"

He stood up, his chair scraping across the floor, and

walked out. For a minute, I simply stared at the file, my brain still unable to accept the king's assertion. It wasn't possible. Violet was… not that person.

My mind suddenly flashed to the memory of her covered in the blood of the Porteque man, after she'd stabbed him to death. She had a tendency toward violence—that much I couldn't deny. But…

My hands snatched up the folder and ripped it open.

Inside, I found an assortment of files and pictures. Violet… she was not a bakery girl, like she'd said. She had been in prison for the last five years and had murdered two females. The file even included pictures of her victims. It was… gruesome, to say the least. Her first arrest had come from attempting to smuggle her brother out of Matrus and into Patrus because he had failed the screening test. It seemed that after that, she'd snapped.

I sat back, a bitter seed growing inside me. I wanted to deny the information in front of me. I searched through the file again, looking for any indication that it had been fabricated. I couldn't believe that Violet was responsible for all the death and carnage I had seen back at the lab. Yet the evidence didn't change, no matter how much I tried to will it to.

The door opened as King Maxen let himself back in, breaking me out of my thoughts. He sat down across from me. "Her history isn't pretty, is it?"

I was still struggling to process the information. It felt like I'd been hit by a ton of bricks. My brain moved slowly, unwillingly, toward the logical conclusion of these files. I shook my head. "No," I rasped.

"She fooled everyone, Mr. Croft. Not just you, but even that partner of hers. She used him to get what she wanted and then killed him without a second thought."

I nodded wordlessly, unable to speak. King Maxen allowed me a few more moments as I gazed down at the files again. Then, slowly, an icy grip began to coil around my heart, squeezing painfully tight. I could no longer deny that this was reality. The proof was before my very eyes.

The Violet I knew was a lie.

And there I had been, just minutes ago, mourning her death. Hell, I had walked through fire haplessly, pathetically, trying to find her.

She was alive. Escaped, and alive.

Rage and betrayal stabbed at me. I felt like an utter fool.

Her so-called innocence had been a lie meant to seduce me. She'd even kissed me, wrapped her body around mine like she was drowning… all lies.

My hands balled into fists.

"What is your plan?" I grated out.

The king made a show of collecting the papers, tapping them together until they were neatly stacked, and then placed them back into the file. I waited stiffly.

"I want you to find her," the king said finally.

I nodded slowly, even as I swallowed hard. It made sense to send me, I supposed. I'd had the most contact with her, and was also the best suited to track her down.

"And what do I do once I find her?" I asked.

The king gazed at me, his eyes hard and flat. "Your priority is securing this." He set a photo in front of me which depicted a silver egg. "This is integral for the continued survival of our society."

Internally, I seethed with suspicion and doubt. I couldn't care less about the rhetoric and propaganda: I knew the dark underside of Patrian life, and I wasn't about to be bought off with pretty lies. But in this moment, I couldn't bring myself to care— Violet and her betrayal were all that occupied my mind.

"I cannot stress the egg's importance enough," the king continued. "If it is lost, or if Matrus gets their hands on it, we will not be able to stand against them in the future… if it ever came to war."

The king's dark tone made me stare at him. I couldn't miss the solemnity in his worn face.

"Again," I said, "what do you want me to do with the girl?"

King Maxen leaned back. "If you can secure her and bring her back to Patrus for questioning, that is preferable. But if you cannot... kill her."

Something in my chest rebelled at the thought. The thought of killing Violet was foreign and awakened feelings I wasn't ready to process, so I pushed it down and nodded.

With that, the king rose and so did I, bowing before him.

"This will be a difficult task, Mr. Croft," he said. "But if you succeed and return the egg, you will be reinstated to your full position of Chief Coordinator of wardens, with pay intact—that will be the least the kingdom can do for your continued loyal service."

As if any of that even mattered to me anymore.

I didn't know what did matter right now—all I could think about was the immediate task ahead of me.

After watching the king leave the room, I glanced at the mirrored glass on the opposite side of the conference table, at the man who might soon have to kill a woman for her crimes.

In spite of all Violet's wrongdoings, somehow I couldn't quite meet my own gaze.

CHAPTER 2

VIOLET

I shivered as the cool air blew past and drew my dress tighter around me. The motorcycle had been traveling steadily north for the past few hours, and I had been afraid to fiddle with any of the instruments for fear of plummeting to my death. The sickening splat of Lee impacting with Queen Rina's garden path still echoed in my mind.

It had been a while since I had fled the palace, and I was still undecided on what to do. I had to make a decision, but each option seemed equally hopeless. I had no idea where the coal mines were, so trying to set a path in my brother's direction was risky, especially in a hang-gliding motorcycle that I was clueless how to operate. On the other hand, returning to Patrus to search out Viggo would only result in my death.

My chest constricted at the thought of the warden. I had betrayed him, and I didn't even know if he had survived the explosion. If he had, it was possible that he was either being blamed by Patrus, or that he knew about my involvement in it. All three possibilities tore me apart.

The words *I'm sorry* hovered on my lips, but I bit them back. What was the point of saying them now? It was too late—Viggo wasn't here, and I was.

I needed to survive.

I was frustrated, cold, and likely had been in shock for the past couple of hours. Lee's betrayal, the egg, the murders… I was drained, both physically and mentally. I needed to sleep, but I couldn't land, nor did I dare to sleep on this thing.

I reached down to the basket between my legs where I'd placed the egg and picked it up, staring at it for the umpteenth time. What could be so important about the tiny embryo encased within it (assuming that's really what it was)? What was so unique about this that people were willing to kill for it? Why had Lee done what he had done?

I had been chasing these questions around in my head for hours with no answers. Letting out a breath, I maneuvered myself on the seat and clicked the button that opened it up. Standing on the motorcycle was one of the most nerve-racking experiences I'd ever had, but I needed to put the egg somewhere safe while I figured out how to operate the machine. Careful not to knock any dials or levers, I placed the egg gently into the backpack that contained some supplies and Lee's letter. I'd already zipped the key to the egg in there—it was so small and delicate, and I'd had several terrifying moments when I was sure it was going to slip from my fingers into the foliage below.

Once the egg was secure, I closed the compartment with a click and sat down quickly. The motorcycle swung from side to side at my movements, and I clenched my hands on the seat to remain as still as possible while it stabilized. For a second, I was convinced it was going to pitch too far to the left or the right and I was going to slip off, but thankfully, it leveled out. Though that didn't stop me from feeling dizzy. I definitely did *not* like flying. My stomach did one final flip before calming down.

I settled back onto the seat, turning my mind to the future. I needed a plan, and I needed it now. I was torn between going after Viggo and explaining, or going to find my brother. After some quick thinking, I decided my brother took priority. Matrian agents would likely be after me already, and they might try to use him as leverage. I needed to find the mines and rescue him before they got to him first. After I retrieved him, I would figure out the next step.

The expanse of The Green stretched out beneath me, shafts of moonlight that escaped through the clouds illuminating the canopy. The Green looked peaceful from up here, but I knew that the whole area beneath the treetops seethed with danger. My defense teacher, Ms. Dale, had shown me that in the three days of training I had received from her before I set out on my mission to Patrus. It was certainly not a place I was excited to return to, but at least it was secluded and Lee had packed survival gear in his backpack.

I mentally went through the items within the seat compartment: There was a flashlight, four knives, five cans of the aerosol spray that seemed to repel the wildlife in The Green, a mask to keep the noxious fumes out, several cans of food, a canteen of water, a letter from Lee that was apparently addressed to himself, and photographs of the messages Lee had etched on King Maxen's vehicle and Queen Rina's library table.

My stomach took that moment to growl at me, reminding me that I hadn't eaten anything for ages. I was starving.

I looked down at the seat, biting my lip. I could open the compartment and go for a can of food, but given how shaky the aircraft had gotten last time I stood, I'd better wait.

Just then, something caught my eye—a flash of white beneath the canopy. Holding my breath and frowning, I leaned over, but the flash disappeared too quickly for me to catch what it was.

Leaning back in the seat, I looked at the controls. I was going to have to learn how to fly this thing at some point. Now was as good a time as any to start.

I knew the right throttle controlled the speed—I'd twisted it already during my escape. What I didn't know was how to make it soar higher or lower, or how to steer it.

Rubbing my fingers together, I eyed the console. There were several buttons there, none labeled. The last time I'd triggered an unknown control, the boxes that were fixed in front of and behind the aircraft had flapped open to release four corpses. Hopefully this time when I touched something it wouldn't be as dramatic.

Nervously, I ran my fingers over the console and pressed the top button. The headlight and dashboard went dark under my hand, causing my breath to hitch. I feared for a second I might have just deactivated the entire aircraft, but no—only the lights. My fingers found the button again and I pressed it, reactivating the bulbs.

I looked tentatively at the next button and clicked it. Nothing seemed to happen. Frowning, I shifted slightly in my seat and held the handlebars. They felt… looser in my hands. Before, when I had slowed it down, they were tight and rigid: the front end not seeming to swing in any one direction. Experimenting, I angled the wheel to the right.

I heard something grind beneath me, and then the aircraft shifted slightly, heading to the left. I jerked it straight, and then angled the wheel to the left. The aircraft shifted right. Looking over my shoulder, I could see a fin extending from the rear of the craft. It looked similar to a rudder on a boat, except instead of going left when the wheel went left, it did the opposite.

Weird. And also unimportant. What was important was that I could finally steer this thing, as long I remembered to turn the wheel in the opposite direction of where I wanted to go. I allowed the aircraft to continue circling left at a slow lazy pace, circling the way I had come. Periodically, I readjusted the circle, allowing it and the wind to carry me a little further back, my eyes searching for that flash of white again.

It was eerie how quiet it was up here. I stared at the canopy below, knowing it was teeming with life. Yet up here, nothing moved.

The Green was toxic. Just like the river that flowed

out of it—polluted and dangerous, anyone exposed for too long could suffer serious lesions that resulted in death. It drew my mind back to my brother, when he had fallen in the water on that fateful day I had tried, and failed, to smuggle him into Patrus. I had no way of knowing for sure if he had survived the water, but I still held hope that he was all right.

Lies, lies, lies, my mind whispered to me. It flashed to one of the pictures that sat in the backpack below my seat. Of the words Lee had carved into the windscreen of King Maxen's gold sedan before the bomb. *FOR THE MEN YOU WILL DECEIVE.* I scowled. It wasn't just men who were being deceived. Matrus was clearly doing the same thing with their citizens. Two civilizations were being lied to. I had been used, betrayed, and almost killed over this egg. I wanted the truth. I *deserved* the truth.

But I had no idea how to find it, short of returning to Matrus or Patrus. Besides, my priority was my brother now.

I looked at my compass, watching the needle swing as I circled the motorcycle in the sky.

Maybe I had imagined the flash of white. Or perhaps it was a reflection of something… maybe a body of water reflecting the moonlight.

I needed to stop looking for things that weren't there, and focus on what was. I was wasting time. But as I straightened the wheel, fixing it to the north in hope of discovering some clue about my brother, the strange flash of white caught my attention again.

Curiosity getting the better of me, I tilted the aircraft and steered toward it.

The dark canopy whizzed by underneath the carriage. I was too high for it to hit, but it was a bit disconcerting. I saw the white more clearly now as it flashed again, but I couldn't make out what it was from this distance…

A gust of wind swept up from nowhere, causing the aircraft to shake. My heart in my throat, I gripped the handlebars and adjusted my course, keeping my feet firmly planted on the floor beneath me.

The propellers groaned as the wind continued to assault the motorcycle. For a second, I rose several feet, only to drop down again, the propellers catching the air. Adrenaline flooded my body, my heart pounding in fear. My knuckles had become white from the strain of holding on.

Again the wind buffeted the aircraft, forcing it to rise and drop. I started to angle to one side, the wind pushing me and the aircraft further. My instinct was to turn into the wind—I tilted the tire sharply, and began to bank into it. It howled in my ears as I turned, shifting my hips and body. Beneath me, the motorcycle gave a deep shudder.

I kept turning hard until the wind was at my back again, and I was soaring. The ride instantly smoothed, and I exhaled a breath. It took a concentrated effort, but I relaxed my body, starting with my hands and ending with my feet.

Then something under my left foot clicked. I froze. Gears churned in the motorbike and I looked around for a long moment, my eyes wide. For several long seconds, nothing seemed to happen. I was on the verge of relaxing again, when the aircraft canopy above me snapped closed around me.

For a second, I was suspended in the air, perfectly weightless and hurtling forward. Then the motorbike pitched forward and I was falling, the ocean of treetops hurtling toward me faster than I thought possible.

CHAPTER 3

VIGGO

After retrieving my motorcycle from where the wardens had been holding it, I hurtled down the darkened streets of Patrus City at top speed. I relished the howl of the wind in my ears; it matched my mood and helped drown out any doubts I felt about the mission I'd been given.

I didn't have a lot of options when it came to recovering Violet. There was no telling where she'd gone or how she'd gotten there. Shortly after King Maxen left me, I'd realized that I only had one gambit: The tracking device that Lee had put somewhere on her. With luck, it was still active, and I'd be able to track her down using Lee's computer.

While I rode, my mind raged with questions. Why had Lee and Violet botched their own frame-up? A part of me—a very small part now— piped up that maybe Violet was behind that. *Maybe she hadn't been able to follow through on the task because of her feelings for me?*

I brushed the thought aside. It was unrealistic to think that, when she had lied to me from the very beginning. I had to stop wanting to believe that her affection for me had been genuine. It was a stupid, pathetic hope, built on loneliness and the desire to feel close to someone again.

I needed to let it go.

I twisted the throttle on the bike, urging it faster still. At this speed, it didn't take long for me to reach Lee's house. The ride was familiar to me now, anyway. Driving Violet around for all that time had made coming to this house second nature.

The triangular white and glass building loomed out of the darkness, all of its floors dark. I parked the bike across the street and stood studying it for a few minutes, looking for signs of movement.

I knew they were long gone, but it was surprising that the wardens hadn't torn the place apart yet. Then again, reflecting on the damage to the lab, they might have bigger problems to deal with. Not to mention that Lee and Violet were long gone anyway.

I approached the house. The garage wasn't locked.

Its door slid open easily, and I stepped inside, clicking on my flashlight. Two of Lee's bikes were still parked in here. I recognized the one that Violet had stolen to visit me, the long scrapes on the side from where it had fallen. It brought back an unwelcome flash of memory—Violet's lips against mine, her body trembling in my arms. I shoved it aside just as fast, ignoring the feelings that came with it.

Moving toward the back of the garage, I opened the interior door easily. Climbing the steps quietly, I headed up to the first floor. The door leading to the house was locked, but I used my shoulder and broke it down.

I heard a sound, something moving in the darkness, and froze. Reaching slowly, I pulled out my gun. My flashlight beam cut through the darkness slowly as I swung it around, and I heard the sound of something moving again, but I couldn't find its origin.

"Come out," I ordered, but nothing happened. Taking a chance, I reached over and hit the light switch on the side of the door. Immediately, the lights flared to life.

Something brown shot across the floor with a yelp, dashing under the table. Slowly, I squatted down. A dog sat under the table, its body quivering. I stowed my weapon.

"Hey," I murmured, reaching out a hand. The creature reluctantly came out, its head low and ears down. Slowly, it moved over to me, sniffing for danger. After a few seconds, it offered me a lick, its tail slowly wagging. I patted it on the head, trying to recall its name.

"Samuel," I finally said, remembering Violet had mentioned it once.

The dog gave a small bark, its tail beating against the floor.

With a sigh, I stood up and began to inspect the house. The downstairs was homey, and ultimately empty. There was no computer visible but I tore the place apart anyway, looking for anything, any clue as to where Violet would go or what her plans had been. It seemed unlikely that I would find anything like that just lying around, especially with her betraying Lee so violently, but I had to hope I'd stumble across something that would help me discover her plan.

Nothing presented itself, so I headed upstairs, Samuel following me. I moved left, into one of the bedrooms. The room itself was almost Spartan, with a small bed and wardrobe. The bed had been made. I tore off the bedding and lifted the mattress.

I instantly knew this was Violet's bed. I caught a whiff of her scent clinging to the sheets. I looked around, memorizing the details of the room. There was nothing here to indicate a long-term stay. In fact, her wardrobe was sparse—only a few outfits in the closet, no shoes, and her costume to obscure her gender.

That was it—there were no personal effects. I contemplated the implications of that. Violet had been a criminal before they had sent her here for this mission. It was reasonable to believe that she had still been treated like a criminal while she had been here, with Lee acting as her jailor. If that were true, then it also stood to reason that was why she'd killed Lee, and Queen Rina. She'd wanted to escape them.

I picked up one of her dresses from the closet. It was the one she had been wearing when I'd invited her to my fight. I ran my finger over the fabric, testing it. It was made of high-quality material. Why would Lee buy her a dress like this if she was a prisoner? It was expensive. It must have been to keep up the ruse: Lee would be expected to clothe his wife in finery.

But still, there was no lock on the door, so there had been nothing to keep her in. There had also been that evening when she had risked her life to come see me, after I had rescued her from Porteque… It was a little odd that she had been given so much freedom, and such nice things, for being a hardened criminal and murderess.

Hm. It didn't quite add up.

I placed the dress on the bed and moved out of the room, letting the questions dance around in my brain.

I moved to the other bedroom, which wasn't much larger. This was clearly Lee's room, and after a quick glance around, I crossed to his desk, turning on his computer. While it booted up, I began to sort through his papers. Most of it was business; related to the lab, a lot of scientific jargon. He had circled the word *Benuxupane* a few times.

Benuxupane. The new drug that the lab had been working on. It was a point of contention between the two regimes of Patrus and Matrus. Matrus had always supplied the pharmaceuticals for Patrus, in exchange for the produce that Patrus generated. It was one of the things that had allowed the two countries to operate peacefully in the past. But recently, King Maxen had been pushing to become more independent of Matrus, leading to heightened tension between the two countries.

Why was Lee so interested in the manufacture of Benuxupane? His bombing had certainly set the work on it backward, but why was that so important? If Lee had been acting in service of Matrus, then the bombing of the laboratory could have been an attempt to keep

Patrus dependent on Matrian drugs. But there was that weird silver egg thing that they had stolen…. What was it and what role did it play in everything?

The computer booted up, beeping for my attention. It was password-protected, but I possessed a file that allowed me to log in as an administrator—given to me by one of my more technologically savvy wardens. I plugged in my handheld and loaded the program. It took only a few seconds, and then I began to search through the files.

There was nothing on the hard drive regarding the bombing, but, luckily, this wasn't my true goal. I scrolled through the programs and found what I had come here for; clicking on one of them, I held my breath.

A map booted up, showing the streets of Patrus. Good, Lee hadn't bothered to wipe it. I used the mouse to drag the image around… but found nothing. Then I dragged the map to the east, over Matrus. It took a few seconds for the graphics to catch up to the computer, and I began to scan the streets and buildings. Still nothing.

Tapping my fingers impatiently on the desk, I dragged the map to the river and ran down the length of it. It would be difficult for Violet to hide there for long, but it might buy her some time to figure out her next move… Yet, again, there was nothing.

Frustrated, I grabbed the image, pulling it down so I could see the mountain range. I must have pulled too hard, because the next thing I knew, I was staring at the blinding green canopy of The Green.

And there, buried in its heart, was a little red dot.

I exhaled the breath I hadn't been aware that I was holding. It was Violet—it had to be. I leaned back, the chair squeaking under my weight. I felt a rush of relief, and frowned. I shouldn't be relieved to find Violet alive, it made my job much more difficult.

Then again… it would be nice to see her again, if only to shake her and demand answers from her. My stomach knotted at the thought, and I resisted putting my fist through a wall in anger. This girl had no right to make me feel so conflicted. I pushed the feelings aside and focused on the task at hand, knowing that logic, more than any confusing tangle of emotions, would help me now.

I downloaded the program to my portable; my mind already whirling. Violet had taken refuge in The Green. It was, in one sense, smart—the toxic environment and dangerous creatures were a massive deterrent to most people. But it was also risky—if she didn't have the tools to survive, or the knowledge, she could be dead in a matter of hours.

The program finished downloading, and I unhooked it, slipping it into my pocket. I had an idea how to get up there.

I left the bedroom, my mind already ticking off everything that I would need for The Green. But as I crossed the hallway and headed for the stairs, a sound at the front door halted me.

Peering down, I saw a man entering, stepping past the door I had broken. Etched into the skin beneath his right eye was a dark triangular tattoo. He was a Porteque gang member. The group had kidnapped Violet in an attempt to re-educate her in the proper role of being a woman, and had been planning on murdering her. His eyes shot up to me before I could step back.

We froze for an instant, staring at each other. I reached for my gun and he did the same.

Then two gunshots exploded, shattering the silence of the house.

CHAPTER 4

VIOLET

The motorbike and I crashed through the treetops, hitting branch after branch. I had time to cover my face, but then something hit my head, sending shockwaves through my brain and knocking me out.

I awoke a short while later—at least, I thought it was a short while—hanging upside down, my lungs on fire. I opened my eyes, the latent adrenaline lending itself to awareness, and looked down. I was suspended probably seventy feet from the ground. I grew dizzy looking down, and focused my attention on a tree branch as waves of nausea ran through me.

It got a little better, but it didn't help the breathlessness that was coming from the lack of air. I became aware of the wheezing sounds I was making, and realized I needed the mask in the seat of the motorbike. I risked a glimpse of the ground, scanning it for wreckage, but it wasn't there.

Then I heard something creak above me, and tucked my chin to my chest, looking upward. The motorbike was only a few feet above where I was snagged on one side, cradled by branches. My ankle was caught in the handlebars. I dropped my head and looked around. There were several branches to my left that I could try to grab hold of if I swung myself in that direction.

As I moved, I cursed myself for being an idiot and getting distracted in the first place. Now my one means of transportation was wasted, and I was stuck in The Green. A tremor of fear went through me at the realization. I had some basic working knowledge of the place, but I wasn't sure if I was equipped to handle it.

A wave of darkness crossed my vision. I knew I was running out of time. Without thinking, I started to swing. I could hear the branch above me groan, and I shuddered, but kept rocking, my hands reaching for the branch.

I touched it, just a brush of fingers, and then fell back, pushing my body into an arc. The branch above me groaned again, but I kept my focus as I swung back toward the branch, my hands outstretched. I dug my nails into the moss and bark, arresting my swing. Above me came a disconcerting crack.

Slowly, I pulled myself closer, until I could reach the branch with my other hand. Using it to stabilize myself, I readjusted my grip. The muscles in my arms and legs were screaming in protest at the physical exertion and lack of oxygen. Shakily, I wrapped my arms around the branch, and then tried to lift my hips to extract my foot from where it was lodged. It didn't budge. Gritting my teeth, I pulled my leg as hard as I could.

The motorbike shifted a little with a small whine, and then an even louder crack sounded as the branch holding the motorbike broke. I held on to the branch I was clinging to with all my might. I felt the handlebars drag against my ankle and then slip away as it began to fall. There were more sounds of tree branches breaking below it, and I felt the tree shudder from impact.

After the noise had stopped, I dared to open my eyes. Branches had again stopped the motorbike, about thirty feet below me. It looked more secure, as it was being held by three branches, not two.

I took another breath, and then gagged, the lack of oxygen causing the reflex. I was already dizzy, and now my ankle hurt from where the motorbike had clipped it.

I started moving, as waves of vertigo ripped through me. Closing my eyes helped, but not much—not to mention climbing down blind was a really bad idea.

Scrambling down the branch was not easy, but by some mercy, I managed it. Once I made it to the trunk, I gradually lowered my legs down to the branch below, keeping my weight off my damaged ankle.

The moss was spongy beneath my hands and feet. It was also slick. I should have moved more slowly, but time was running out for me. Each breath I took made me more and more light-headed. I had to get to the motorbike, and I had to get there now.

I climbed more swiftly downward. Luckily, the branches on this tree were thick, and there were many of them. I finally reached the branch that suspended the motorcycle, and gingerly put my weight onto it.

Sweat was trickling down my forehead, and I felt the sharp pains in my joints and rib cage. The skin on my hands was shredded. I struggled to breathe; the sounds coming from my lungs were weaker and wheezier. I was at the end of my strength. Disregarding caution, I scrambled along the branch to the motorbike.

It was on its side, but the tree held it tight. With shaking fingers, I stretched my body out, reaching for the trigger to the seat on the floorboard. I could feel my balance shifting radically, and I jerked back, catching myself before I fell. I took a deep breath of the toxic air, fixed my gaze on what I needed to hit, and then reached out and slapped the button.

To my relief, the seat popped open. I scrambled closer to it, reaching in and grabbing the bag. My breathing shallower than ever, my vision blacked out. I felt with my hands instead, and, after what seemed like an eternity, I jerked the mask out of the bag, and sealed it to my face.

Greedily, I sucked lungful after lungful of filtered air. I heaved my exhausted body back to the tree trunk and braced my back against it, allowing myself to relax and breathe for a few minutes, giving my oxygen-deprived body a chance to recuperate.

After five minutes, I opened my eyes. I was no longer blind and felt more alert, though my entire body felt like a bruise. All I could do was keep moving. I checked the contents of the backpack to make sure I hadn't dropped anything, and then, after making sure the egg was securely inside, I closed the zipper and slung it over my shoulder. The left side of my body screamed in protest; I was sure that I had broken a rib.

Exhaling into the mask, I began to slowly work my way down. It was much easier now that I wasn't starved of oxygen, but my dress still made me go slower than I would have liked. To make matters worse, the small amount of moonlight being filtered in from the canopy was disappearing. It had all but vanished by the time I reached the bottom, but I had memorized the placement of the last two branches, and luckily my spatial reasoning and depth perception were decent. As soon as my feet crunched to the ground, I immediately swung the bag around, my finger searching blindly for the flashlight. The sounds of The Green seemed louder in the dark, each hiss and animal cry sounding like it was coming from directly behind me.

My fingers found the cold grated metal of the flashlight, and I turned it on as I pulled it out, shining the light all around.

Immediately, the sounds around me lessened as the shier nocturnal creatures moved away from the light. My knees gave way with relief and exhaustion and I dropped to the ground, rolling until the tree was against my back.

I could feel sleep trying to claim me, the earlier exhaustion of the whole Lee nightmare coupled with the physical exhaustion of getting down the tree both working together to make my body feel disjointed, like a poorly stitched doll.

I fought it tooth and nail, reaching into the bag clumsily, and pulling things out, scattering several items across the mossy ground. I saw the silver egg roll by. My eyelids drooping, I clumsily reached to grab it, tucking it into my lap while my other hand groped for the aerosol container.

It seemed to take forever for me to compress the canister, and even after I did so, all I did was make a few half-hearted passes with it over the ground around me and the trunk behind me, before my muscles went slack, and I was pulled into unconsciousness.

I woke some time later, my body jerking upright, the hair on the back of my neck standing on end. It was still dark, and I was still tired, but something had forced me to wake up. I picked up the flashlight with shaking hands, and scanned the clearing. What had roused me? *Did I hear something?*

The ever-prevalent mist clung to the ground, roiling about. I could only see a few feet in front of me, and every shadow cast by the flashlight was causing me to jump, my worry deepening.

My heart was pounding so hard; I could feel it in my throat. There was something out there, something that I wasn't seeing, and my mind was screaming for me to run. But I forced myself to keep still, to steady my breathing.

For a second, I thought about the Benuxupane in the bag—the white pills that would keep me from feeling my emotions, but I disregarded the idea. My instincts were warning me of danger. If I took another dose of King Maxen's pills, it might soothe me too much.

So, I forced myself to be calm, focusing on slowing my haggard breaths while continuing to scan the mist.

It took a minute for me to respire normally and once I did, I became aware of what had woken me up. A low buzzing sound… a sound that seemed to be growing louder. Closer. Panic surged in me again, as I realized that the red flies were coming.

CHAPTER 5

VIGGO

I whirled around the bannister as I fired. The motion caused my shot to go astray, but I avoided the bullet that lodged itself in the wall behind me by doing so. The Porteque man fired a few more shots, and I squatted down, counting his bullets. He was three down.

I heard him scrambling across the floor, likely toward the kitchen to take cover by the cabinets. I crept down a few more stairs until I could see into the kitchen, and risked a glance to confirm his destination. Then I leveled my gun, waiting—patience and cover were the two things stressed during gun training.

The second I saw a flash of his black cap, I squeezed the trigger. He ducked down before the bullet hit, causing it to shoot into the glass counter behind him and cover him with shards. I heard him curse, and remained still, my arms outstretched, waiting for him to reappear.

Just then, the front door flew open to my left. I ducked back just in time to avoid bullets fired from two men appearing in the doorway.

"Are you all right?" one of them shouted, and I heard the man in the kitchen grunt in the affirmative.

I was outnumbered and outgunned. I had the advantage of an elevated position, but I needed to decide on my best strategy.

I chose to bluff first. "I am a warden of King Maxen on special assignment," I boomed down. "There are more wardens coming. If you don't relinquish your arms, they will shoot you down."

One of the men in the doorway laughed. "No they're not," he called up. "I watched as you arrived here, and in the twenty minutes you've been here, ain't nobody showed. You're lying."

I cursed internally.

"What do you want?" I asked, already sensing the answer.

"We're here for that bitch who calls herself a woman. She's a murderer!" There was a sound of flesh hitting flesh, followed by a curse and some harsh whispers. I grinned grimly, realizing that one of them had said a little too much. I waited for the whispers to settle down.

"That's why I'm here too," I said. "You're right, she is a murderer, and I'm bringing her to justice." It irritated me that my chest constricted as I said the words—I pushed it aside. *She is a murderer. Get used to it.*

There was a long pause. "Is that right?" the man from the kitchen shouted.

I paused, wondering if any of these men had been present, and seen my face, when I'd rescued Violet from Porteque. If they had, they would likely think I was lying to protect her, though I had no real intention of calling a truce with the men of Porteque. Patrus was harsh on women, but not as harsh as these men were: They would torture any woman they deemed "unwomanly" until they broke them. At least in Patrus, women were given a quick death. With the Porteque gang, they were the living dead, their agony lasting for years.

I had no qualms about lying to these bastards, or telling them the truth to get them to stick their heads out so I could kill them. I was not a murderer by nature, but I had seen some of the rescued victims of their "re-education" program, and in this case, I was willing to make an exception.

"Yeah," I shouted back.

The man in the kitchen laughed, a cruel sound. "I wish I could believe that, but I recognize you. You rescued her after she murdered my brother, and you let her get away with it!"

With that declaration, he fired, the bullets hitting the wall next to me, spraying me with plaster and chunks of wall. I raised a hand, protecting my eyes. This was not going well. *Time for a new plan.*

I moved back down the hallway swiftly, heading into Lee's bedroom. I shut the door, locked it, and pushed the heavy dresser against it for good measure. It would buy me some time, but not much.

Darting to the window, I ducked down low, and then glanced out quickly over the backyard, looking to see if they had posted a guard in the street beyond it. It seemed deserted, but lights were beginning to come on from the other houses.

I debated what to do—if the neighbors had heard the gunshots, which was likely, they were already calling the wardens to inform them of the trouble, but there was no way that they would get here in time to assist me.

I began stripping the bed. I had never actually tied bedsheets together to form a rope, but I was fairly good with knots. I quickly began tying the ends together, making a makeshift rope. I was three stories up, but falling even one story was better than falling three. It took no time for me to tie them together and anchor them using the bedframe.

I was a heavy guy, but luckily the bedframe was heavy, too. It would hopefully support my weight on the descent. I tossed the bundle of sheets out the window, just as the doorknob began to rattle.

"Got him! He's in here," came an excited voice. I fired my gun in the direction of the door, not meaning to hit anyone, but spook them.

"Nobody's home," I called dryly as I grabbed the sheets, wrapping them around my arm and around my waist, in a makeshift rappelling line.

I straddled the window sill, keeping one leg over it as I slowly tested my weight on the line. My heart was pounding as I did, because if the knots failed or my hand slipped, I would fall face first into the asphalt below. There was a slamming sound against the door, and I smiled grimly. The sheets were holding my weight. By the time they got the door opened, I would be at the bottom.

I took a deep breath and removed my other leg from where it was hooked over the sill. Bracing my feet against the wall, I started to let myself down a few inches when an urgent whine grabbed my attention.

Looking up, I saw Samuel, his front paws scrambling

on the window sill. He must have been hiding in one corner of the room. He was shaking, his soft brown eyes wide and full of panic. He whined again, trying to climb up on the sill.

For a second I hung there, just staring at the canine while my mind churned on what to do. Then, with a low groan, I climbed back up.

The door was thudding harder now, and I could hear the scraping of the dresser's legs on the floor as each impact pushed it back.

"If you get me killed, then I am revoking your man's best friend card," I muttered as I grabbed the dog and tucked him under my arm. I started to leave, and then, remembering, I pulled my gun and fired two rounds into the computer on the desk. I heard the doorknob break as I tucked the gun back into the holster. Quickly, I swung out of the window, one hand on the sheets, my other arm trying to keep a hold on the dog.

Rappelling this way was difficult, especially because the dog was struggling against me. "Stop it," I hissed, repositioning him over my shoulder.

The dog gave a high pitched whimper, but I ignored it, as I focused on using one hand and both legs to lower myself down to the ground. I wanted to move faster, but one wrong move and we would both drop. It was hard, but I had to be patient.

I neared the bottom, my shoulder aching from the strain. The makeshift rope swung about five feet above the driveway. If I could make it to the end, my feet would be touching the ground no problem.

Just then, I heard a commotion coming from the third floor. Looking up, I saw a head poke out of the window, and felt a tug on the rope. I knew they weren't pulling me back in. Glancing down, I gauged the distance, took a deep breath, and let go.

The sensation of falling had always been disconcerting to me. It was the sudden weightlessness that overcame you, where the only indication that you were falling was the air racing past your ears.

I bent my knees to absorb the impact, but it was still harder than I wanted, and I fell to the side, remembering to cradle the dog to my chest to avoid him getting injured.

"He jumped," shouted one of the men.

I snatched my gun from the holster, and fired at the head that poked out from the window. He slumped, my aim true, and I heard the remaining two men curse, dragging his limp form back through the window.

I took the opportunity to escape. Standing up, I raced to my bike. I was relieved to see it untouched. I opened up a large side bag and the dog gave a yelp of excitement, his tail slapping against my ribs. I tucked the dog in, clipping it closed so that his head remained out— it would be uncomfortable for him, given his size, but it would have to do.

I jumped on the bike and gunned it. Gunshots exploded behind me and I crouched low, making myself as flat as possible. This helped streamline the bike, but also made me a harder target. Bullets whizzed by me, and I grimaced. There wasn't anyone on the street, thankfully, but even a ricochet through a window could kill. I couldn't stop to check though. I could only hope that the other wardens arrived in time to catch them.

Irritation filled me as I realized I was basically running away. It wasn't who I was, even with the odds against me. The fact that these men were still on the loose, doing as they pleased, sickened me, and I was letting them go free. It was almost enough to make me turn back. Almost.

I had bigger things to focus on. Namely, a girl with dark hair and gray eyes who had been haunting me since the day I met her. A girl who had murdered dozens of people and left me to be hanged. My grip tightened on the throttle in anger, and I had to take a deep breath to relax it.

I looked over at the dog, his mouth open and tongue lolling out, my mind planning my next course of action.

After a few minutes of riding, I pulled over to the side of the road and slipped out my handheld. I kept my gaze on the street behind me, just in case the Porteque men were pursuing me. The first call I made was to headquarters, alerting them to the presence of the men at Lee's address. They curtly informed me that they were aware and that the wardens were on their way.

I made a second call. I waited patiently and then began explaining what I had learned, and gave a list of what I needed for the trip ahead. After the call was done, I patted Samuel on the head, then gunned the bike, taking off toward Veil River.

CHAPTER 6

VIOLET

I froze, the buzzing of the red flies overwhelming my senses. Every time I breathed through the mask, it made the sound disappear for a second, causing the hair on my body to stand on end. I held my breath, listening for the noise, trying to discern the direction they were coming from.

The rest of the sounds in The Green seemed to have dulled, as if all the creatures knew the red flies were out on a hunt. My mind fumbled to remember what Ms. Dale had done on that first day we spent in The Green, but my brain felt thick as a brick.

The buzzing sound was definitely growing louder; moving closer to me. My heart beat quickening, I stumbled backward, away from the noise. My foot struck something, sending it spinning away from me. I managed to get the flashlight on it a few seconds before it disappeared into the mist, illuminating the silver aerosol can as it rolled across the mossy ground.

The aerosol can. I was so stupid. Of course, the aerosol can.

I scrambled after it, searching for it on the ground. The buzzing grew more persistent, but I focused. The can would help keep them away from me. I just needed to find a small space to squeeze into so that they couldn't engulf me.

I heard something shriek from the direction of the buzzing, and stilled. My hands shaking, I cursed beneath my breath. I needed to get it together. Never in my life had I felt so helpless and frustrated. My anxiety was palpable.

I thought again about the Benuxupane pills in the bag. I had taken them only once, and they had managed to suppress my emotions. Maybe I really should take them again.

No, I told myself firmly, my fists clenched. If anything, they were responsible for how I was behaving right now. I remembered Lee mentioning something about one of the side effects being anxiety. Maybe it was responsible for the fact that I couldn't seem to think straight right now.

I scanned the ground, and found the silver can

wedged under a root. I shook it—it was half full.

I hurried to where my bag was, taking extra care to make sure everything was back in place. I nearly kicked myself when I saw the other four canisters in the bag. I had known they were in there, but with the panic that seemed to be arresting my senses, I could only seem to focus on one thing at a time.

I took a deep breath, and tried to calm my mind, picturing the steps of what I needed to do to hide. First, I needed to finish packing the bag.

I did it quickly, in spite of my shaking hands. I sucked in a deep breath of air through the mask.

Second, I needed to find a hole. I began to scan the tree that I'd been sleeping against. The roots were massive, but I didn't notice anywhere I could curl up and hide.

The sense of panic threatened to overwhelm me again, as I felt tears forming in my eyes. Crying in a mask was never a good idea, as moisture in there would cause it to fog and obscure vision, so I took yet another deep breath and blinked back the tears.

I started talking to myself, which helped me to focus.

"Okay, you just need to find a hollow log. That's good. Just use your flashlight and look around. There's plenty of vegetation here, so you'll find something very soon."

Focusing on my words helped push the anxiety aside. I felt my chest loosening, and my muscles unclenching. The shaking in my hands stopped. I moved quickly, talking as I did so, until I spotted a hollow log.

I felt my lips start to form a smile, when something caught my eye. I adjusted the flashlight, focusing on it, and almost screamed.

Twenty feet in front of me, rippling out like a wall, was the swarm of red flies, hovering in unison. Their crimson bodies shimmered, and it might have looked beautiful, if it wasn't so terrifying. It was hard to make out an individual red fly. They darted in and out of the swarm too fast to distinguish. From this distance, I could feel the buzzing of their wings, the sound vibrating along my skin and in my bones.

I took a step to the left, toward the log, and I watched as the swarm rippled, adjusting itself to me. The log was maybe five or six feet behind me. I licked my lips and took another slow step back.

The swarm exploded, little red blurs shooting toward me like bullets. Unable to control my shriek, I dropped my flashlight and ran. My legs tore across the mossy ground, eating up the distance in a matter of seconds. I could feel the air behind me growing denser as the swarm closed in.

Without even thinking, I dove in headfirst. It felt like it took me minutes to roll over, canister in hand, and spray, but in reality, it was seconds. I heard the splat of the red flies as they impacted on the log. I continued to spray the aerosol container in front of the hole, keeping them out. Through the spray, I could see the red bodies trying to push their way in, only to jerk away as they made contact with the haze.

I wasn't sure how long I sat there, spraying the aerosol container at the hole. The red fly swarm sat just outside, buzzing around. Occasionally, it would try to press in, but the spray held it back. It was growing lighter in my hand with all the continuous spraying, so I blindly reached for the bag with my other hand.

I wished I hadn't dropped the flashlight. Occasionally, as the swarm buzzed against the log, there would be a gap and I could see the light shining through from where the flashlight sat on the ground. But beyond that, I couldn't see anything. I didn't even know how big this log was inside, and I was too afraid to try and feel it out. So I sat, arms around my knees, spraying the hole, my legs cramping and back aching.

I found the bag, and changed aerosol containers. My finger on my left hand had become stiff from compressing the spray nozzle, so I flexed my hand, spraying with the other. I really wanted to stretch out. I really wanted to sleep, but I knew I couldn't. If I did, I would die.

And for what, some deranged psychopath, some stupid egg, and some game of political power? I wanted my brother. I wanted Viggo. And I wanted to live a life free from violence and fear. I just had no idea how I could do it.

I remembered when I was younger, and Tim and I were lying in bed, reading a story. In it, a woman was lost in a forest. Her sisters had been captured by an evil man, intent on selling them in Patrus. The woman had run from him, and had barely escaped. She cried in the forest, bemoaning the fact that she didn't fight the man, and that she would never see her sisters again. She was crying so hard, that she didn't notice the old woman who had come to kneel next to her. The old woman explained that her own daughters had been taken by the same man, and that she was on her way to kill him. She asked if the younger woman would like to help, and together, they found the man, killed him, and freed the sisters.

There was a lot more in the story in between, but the old woman was a sort of legend in Matrus. She had no name, and no great power, save that of knowledge. She was exactly what I needed—a guide. I knew it was childish of me to want that, but I allowed myself to dream of the story, if only for a moment.

I was so embroiled in my thoughts, that it took me a minute to realize that the forest had gone silent. Sitting up straight, I stared out of the hole, and saw nothing but the light shining in from the flashlight.

I didn't dare stop compressing the aerosol container. For all I knew, it was a trap. I waited for what seemed like eternity. My legs and arms were starting to tingle from being held in that one position, but I ignored it— or at least, I tried to. It started at my ankles, and began working its way up my shins and to my knees. I didn't dare move my legs to stretch them out, but the prickling sensation was starting to irritate me. So, I reached down and began rubbing my legs with my free hand. As I smoothed down the fabric of my dress, I froze as I felt something roil under my hand.

Quivering, I removed my hand, and began to draw up my skirt, the sound of fabric sliding across my skin filling the small space of the log. It spilled over my knee and I clapped a hand over my mouth to keep from screaming at the long black centipede clinging to my leg.

I became aware of other movements around me, and felt the brush of thousands of sharp little legs. Something shifted behind me, disturbing my hair, and I felt the weight of a hard body pressing into my scalp.

I screamed and scrambled out of the hole, jerking my bag around me. Three centipedes hit the ground as I shook my body and head frantically, trying to dislodge the creatures. I shuddered, crying openly now as I continued to shake myself, my mind and body convinced there were more on me. I ran hands over my arms and hair, trying to make sure they were all clear. Revulsion welled up in me at the thought of any of those insects on me, their tiny little legs pricking into my flesh, crawling over me. I couldn't seem to stop shaking, and had to take the mask off a few times to wipe my face and the glass lenses as cold tears spilled down my cheeks. I realized I was having a panic attack. I closed my eyes and focused on my breathing, trying to convince myself that they were gone.

It took several minutes for it to work. I was equal parts repulsed and frustrated. I had made up my mind about what to do—finally—and now I was stuck in the last place in the world I needed to be. Alone.

I suddenly found myself wishing that Viggo was there. He'd know what to do better than I would. Suddenly inspired, I pulled a memory of him into my mind, and used it to ground myself, by imagining every line of his face, from the curl of his lashes to the strong cut of his chin.

Eventually, I started to calm down. Methodically, I

began checking my body again, when I felt something on my upper thigh start burning. Looking down, I saw a centipede clinging on to my dress, biting through the fabric with its massive black pincer mouth. Gasping, I grabbed the squirming body with my hand, ripping it off me and throwing it as hard as I could.

I grabbed my backpack, shaking it to make sure it was clear, picked up the flashlight, and began limping away, the wound in my leg throbbing. I searched for another hidey hole, and found one quickly. This time, I sprayed the hollow, using the remaining contents in the second container. Insects swarmed out, and I flinched as a couple of centipedes slithered past, but after a few minutes, I was convinced it was clear.

I slipped inside, fighting wave after wave of panic. My breathing was labored, but I tried to focus on anything but the centipedes. I dumped the contents of my bag on the floor, and began to rummage about. Lee had packed some spare clothes, and I slipped the shirt on, buttoning up the front. It was large, but serviceable. I ripped up the dress into long strips, and then grabbed the canteen. Gritting my teeth, I poured some over the wound, watching as blood and yellow fluid ran down my leg. I wiped it off with one cloth, and then repeated the action several times before I realized I couldn't spare any more water.

Then I wrapped my leg up with a piece of cloth, hoping to stop the bleeding. I slipped on Lee's pants, making a belt out of one of the strips of fabric, and then leaned back, my head pounding.

As I lay there, I realized that I was in serious trouble. Chances were that the centipedes were venomous. Everything in The Green seemed to kill, and if I didn't find medical help soon, I was quite certain I would die.

CHAPTER 7

VIGGO

"**V**iggo, *don't leave me! Please don't leave me here!*"

I jerked awake, trying to flee the sound of Violet's call ringing in my ears. My forehead impacted on the low ceiling, pain exploding. I cursed, rubbing the spot, my foggy mind and accelerated heart rate making me forget where I was for a second.

The gentle rocking back and forth reminded me, and I groaned, laying back in the bunk. I couldn't remember most of the nightmare, just the sound of women crying, and Violet begging me not to leave her. I was covered in a cold sweat from the intensity of it, my shirt clinging to me.

I felt something cold and soggy press against my hand, working its way in so it could nuzzle my palm. Looking over, I saw Samuel gazing at me with his big brown eyes. I patted the dog on the head softly. It was oddly comforting to do so, and it helped chase the nightmares away.

I sat there for a few minutes, forcing the panic and fear away, clearing my mind for the task ahead. Sitting up, I quickly changed my shirt and pants, exchanging them for more durable clothing, capable of handling the extreme dangers of The Green. Shrugging on my coat, I whistled for the dog, and headed up the stairs to the deck of the boat.

The boat belonged to Alejandro Simmons, who stood behind the wheel, peering ahead down the river as the engines pushed us ahead. Alejandro was older, possibly around fifty, and had been navigating the toxic river that divided Patrus and Matrus for nearly thirty years. According to him, he had won the boat in a bet. According to his wife, however, Alejandro had cheated.

Regardless, Alejandro was the only person in Patrus who was willing to brave the toxic waters and navigate the boat upstream to The Green. Actually, Alejandro collected samples from The Green and delivered them to scientists in Patrus to be studied. He was probably an expert on everything in The Green, and had organized several expeditions into the toxic environment.

I had met him when I was in training to become a warden. A part of our induction included a module on how to survive in The Green, and Alejandro had been the instructor. Truthfully, I liked the old man, even if he was a bit crazy.

"Hey yo, boy!" Alejandro crowed. "Glad to see you're awake. You had me worried there for a bit."

I frowned. "What do you mean? I've only been asleep for a few hours."

"Try twelve, my friend."

Pulling out my handheld, I scanned for the time. *Whoa.* Sure enough, he was right. I'd been out for twelve hours. It made sense, I supposed, considering the last forty-eight hours had been basically sleepless. I checked to make sure Violet's beacon was still active— it was—and then shut it off.

"You should've woken me," I said, gruffly, moving to stand next to him.

"I ain't your keeper, boy," replied Alejandro. "Truth be told, when a man sleeps that deep, it means he's got problems… Likely lady ones."

I stood silent, staring at him. Not many people could meet me in the eye for long, but Alejandro did.

"It might help you to talk about it," he said, arching a bushy white eyebrow.

I refrained from rolling my eyes, but leaned against the rail, crossing my arms. "There isn't anything to say."

"Start with her name."

I gave a quick huff. "Nothing to say, old man," I repeated.

"I ever tell you how I met my wife?"

"Yes," I reminded him sardonically. "Repeatedly."

Alejandro smiled under his beard, the white and brown hairs of his beard parting. "Actually, I'm sure I have. But I might have left out a detail or two. Something that might be relevant to your situation…"

I sighed, knowing that Alejandro was going to keep bringing it up until I let him tell it. "What are the details then?" I muttered.

Alejandro turned the wheel slightly, his eyes fixed on the horizon. "The first is, well, she was already engaged when I met her. To my best friend."

I shrugged my shoulders and nodded. It wasn't that surprising, and it wasn't illegal to steal another man's woman before they were married. It was typically the reason why men married their women so quickly, within days of the engagement. Once they were married, she was his property in the eyes of the law. That was another reason why I had been intent on cutting things off with Violet after our night of indiscretion.

"All right, what's the second?" I asked.

"She killed him," he said flatly, his face forward.

I froze, his words hitting me like a punch. "What happened?"

Alejandro sighed and turned a little to face me. "He was beating her. And my Jenny… she just couldn't take it anymore. She stabbed him."

"How did she not get hanged?"

He gave me a look, his face grim. "I lied," he said simply.

I couldn't believe it. My friend had just confessed to covering up a murder. He was a criminal.

Then again, so was I. I had done the exact same thing… for two women. He'd just done it better.

"You went in as a neutral witness," I said, my tone level.

He shrugged. "It wasn't hard. My family and I lived next door to Marty. Jenny would come over for dinner sometimes, and I could hear them through the walls. I wanted to call the wardens, but…" He trailed off. He had been stuck between his best friend and a woman, and male best friends always won in Patrus, or at least, were supposed to.

"I heard something crash, and raced over to find her, covered with blood. Her blood, his blood. I saw it in her eyes… she knew what she had done, and she knew she was going to swing for it. But I took her hands, and I held her close, and I promised I would help her."

His words twisted the knife of a wound long past. I could remember saying the same words to my wife. But I had failed her.

"I haven't seen you in two years, Viggo. You just fell off the face of the planet. You let us visit you at first, after Miriam… but then you just put us off. Until you show up, asking for a ride to The Green. You at least owe me some explanation. I want to make sure what you're doing… well, that it isn't going to make you worse."

After Miriam. The words were hollow in my ears. I had lost her.

And now here I was chasing after Violet, a part of me—to my aggravation—still wanting to protect her, the greater part of me wishing I had never met her.

"I'll be fine, Alejandro," I said quietly.

Alejandro stared at me for a long second, and then sighed. "As you say, boy… Might want to go get your gear ready. We're nearing the drop point."

I looked over and saw the fences marking the territory of The Green gliding past on the bank. Grabbing my mask, I slipped it on, and started going through my pack. I had all of the gear to survive tucked away in a bag, but it was second nature for me to check and double check.

One by one, I pulled out the items and laid them on

the bed. I had five aerosol containers, five days of rations, a water canteen that was capable of pulling water out of the air, my gun, an assortment of pills and ointments to help with animal attacks, a polymer blanket, a lighter, a leash for the dog, an extra set of clothes, and a pair of cuffs. I set them aside to pack last.

I heard Alejandro stomping around above deck, and finished packing. Slinging the pack over my shoulder, I went back on deck. The river was rushing past, the speed picking up. I looked at Alejandro, who was standing at the helm with Samuel, holding the wheel in place.

"Is it always like this?"

Alejandro nodded. "For this stretch. The river banks close into a choke hole, and water moves out faster. It'll pass once we're through."

I looked ahead at the churning water, nodding. Alejandro knew his business, and I knew mine.

"Quiz time, boy." Holding back a sigh, I grabbed the rail and nodded. "What happens if you attract a red fly swarm?"

"Find a hole, flush it out, and use the aerosols to keep them out," I recited.

"Good. What happens if you get entangled in orange vine?"

"Don't panic, and don't cut it. The sap inside is

flammable when exposed to the atmosphere. Track the vine to where it connects to the main plant, and cut out the nodule. It will release."

Alejandro nodded. "What if you come across a wild boar?"

"Don't run. It will chase you. Back away slowly and do not make eye contact."

"Good. Did you bring all the medications for the venom and burns?"

I nodded. "Yup. It's all in here," I said, patting my bag.

Alejandro nodded, throttling up the engine. I grabbed Samuel's collar and braced myself against the rail. It was unlikely that we'd sink, but I didn't want the dog to lose his balance and get knocked overboard.

"Why are you taking the dog?" Alejandro shouted over the engine, his eyes scanning the panels.

I shrugged. "He might be able to help scent my target," I called back.

We fell silent as Alejandro navigated the rapids. I'd never actually seen him in his element before, but he handled himself and the boat well, and after a few minutes of bouncing around, we were clear. I released Samuel's collar, keeping an eye on him as I moved closer to Alejandro, scanning the river. I could see the transition point between The Green and the rest of the world, a black scar cutting through the land.

"I'm going to drop you up ahead," Alejandro said, pulling the throttle back on the engine. "You're far enough out of the way that you shouldn't encounter any patrols, but be careful—tensions are going to be high after the death of Queen Rina."

I nodded, and held out my hand, shaking his with a firm grip. "Thanks, Alejandro," I said, and he nodded.

"You're a good man, Viggo. You just need to get back into the world."

I didn't respond, because there was really nothing to say. I watched as we approached the bank of the river on the Matrian side. When we were a few feet away, I reached down and picked up Samuel, holding him tight to my chest.

I took a few steps back to get a running start, and then leapt the gap between boat and land. If I miscalculated, I could have fallen in. I landed squarely on my feet, my knees buckling to absorb the impact. I put Samuel down, hooking a leash to him, and turned.

Alejandro was waving at me. "I'll be back in one week," he yelled. "If you can make it upstream five kilometers, there's a tree that fords the river. Use that to cross to the Patrus side, and I'll meet you there. If not, signal me on this side with your flashlight."

I waved a hand over my head, acknowledging his message.

"Oh! And be careful of the mist ghosts!"

For as long as I'd known him, Alejandro had insisted there was something else living in the mist, something not quite human, and not quite animal. Yet no one else had ever seen it.

Rotating my shoulders under my pack, I pulled the handheld out, and fixed Violet's position.

"C'mon Samuel," I muttered grimly. "Time to go find Violet."

CHAPTER 8

VIOLET

I woke up, instantly alert. Once more, the sounds of the forest had fallen silent, alerting my brain to some imminent danger. It was daytime, or as close to day as it could be in The Green. Muted rays of light trying to penetrate the dense canopy cast the forest in deep dark shadows, bisected by small slivers of light.

I shivered, peering out of my shelter. I looked around slowly, trying to draw as little attention to myself as possible. There was less mist today, so I could see further than normal, but nothing moved. It was like the entire forest was holding its breath.

Then came a long keening sound, soft and low. It was difficult to pinpoint the direction it came from. I slowly reached into my bag, and pulled out the gun. My heart was pounding, but I was in better control of my emotional state than yesterday. It seemed that the Benuxupane had finally worn off.

I gripped the gun tightly, just like Ms. Dale had once shown me, and continued to scan the undergrowth, my eyes trying to pierce the gloom, looking for any telltale sign of danger.

The groan came again, long and urgent, replacing the silence of the forest with its haunting song. It was beautiful and terrifying at the same time.

Adjusting my grip on the gun, I used my free hand to help myself up. The bite on my thigh throbbed, but I ignored it. I rested my hip against the trunk of the tree, and continued to scan the forest. Whatever it was, it was well hidden.

I took an experimental step forward, my muscles tense in anticipation. A tree branch snapped under my foot.

A flurry of movement exploded from the undergrowth to my left, and I dropped to one knee, my gun up. I heard the sound of cracking branches and leaves being pushed out of the way. It took me a moment to realize that whatever it was, it was moving away from me.

I exhaled the breath I had been holding, my muscles sagging in relief. I hadn't been able to make out what it was, but I was surprised that it chose to flee instead of attack. Given how the forest had fallen silent at its presence, I had expected something predatory, like the red flies.

Maybe I had scared it. Humans weren't common in The Green, and if it hadn't encountered them before, it could have fled as an act of self-preservation. It was a puzzle, but for the meantime, I was safe.

I couldn't be sure how much time had passed since I'd fallen asleep. I lowered myself back down into a sitting position, and began going through the bag.

Now that my adrenaline was fading, I became aware of how much pain I was actually in. My ribs ached with each breath I took, and I had an acute headache. All of my joints were throbbing, and, in spite of the humid heat, I was shivering, which meant I had a fever.

A fever was bad. I needed to re-evaluate my plans on rescuing my brother. Chances were that I would die trying to make it to him. I needed help.

I forced myself to drink six long gulps of water from the canteen, then opened one of the cans of food, using my fingers to eat the green gel inside. I recognized what it was: It was a protein gel, filled with vitamins and nutrients, but basically tasteless. Which was good—my stomach was already heaving from the water.

After I finished, I started sorting through what I had left. It was hard to focus. Nausea coursed through me, forcing me to stop a couple times, sucking in air to try and calm it down. I concentrated on sifting through my supplies while I considered my next move. Getting organized helped me focus.

I strung the key to the egg on a piece of fabric and tied it around my neck. I put the gun into one of my pockets, and slipped the clips into my back pocket.

Then I started to put everything back in the bag, but paused when I picked up Lee's letter, my eyes reading his words again, considering them.

Lee talked about us being pawns, and maybe I had been one. But even a pawn could capture a queen. Maybe there was a way I could do everything I wanted, using the egg. I breathed out, letting the thought roll around in my head.

Then the dizziness was back, and my stomach writhed. I couldn't hold it in. Leaning over, I had the good sense to rip off my mask before my stomach started heaving, pushing out all the food and water in my stomach onto the mossy ground of the forest. It took several minutes before my stomach was empty, and when I finished, I wiped my face off, and pulled the mask back on, sucking air through the filter. I leaned back heavily on my knees, ignoring the compulsion to lie down.

With shaking hands, I untied my makeshift belt and

slid Lee's pants down over my hip until my bandage came into view. I untied it, removing it from the bite.

The skin around the bite was red and inflamed. Looking at it, I felt the wound throb, sending tendrils of pain up and down my leg. I touched the skin around the wound. It was hot. I pushed down a little bit, and bright yellow fluid leaked from the puncture marks.

A wave of disgust coursed through me, and I had to turn my head to keep from vomiting again.

It was definitely venomous. All of my symptoms were clear indications and it had become obvious to me now that I had two options, both of them equally dangerous for different reasons.

I needed medicine. I might be forced to make a sharp change of plan.

Both Patrus and Matrus would likely have what I need, but they wouldn't just give it to me. The instant I turned up in either place, I would be seized as either a terrorist or a murderer.

I thought of the egg. That was potentially my ticket. Both sides wanted it, and I had it. I could use it to barter for treatment, and possibly immunity. I just had to decide which place to make my deal with.

If I chose Patrus, I ran the risk of them not honoring their deal. In fact, I doubted very much that King Maxen would take kindly to a woman having anything over him. He was a proud Patrian male. If I showed up and demanded treatment in exchange for the egg, he would likely take it from me, and kill me anyway.

Then again, if I went to Patrus, maybe I could locate Viggo and ask him to help me. If he was still alive…

I pushed the thought of Viggo being dead from my mind. But even if I did find him, there was no guarantee he'd help me. Depending on how many holes Patrus had discovered in Lee's and my tracks, Viggo might be in prison, soon to be executed.

If that was the case, maybe I could use the egg to save him and me. I pulled the object out of the bag, watching the light reflect on its silver surface.

I wanted to hope that would be the case, but I knew in reality that it would never happen. King Maxen wouldn't allow me or Viggo to go free, nor would he lift a finger to help me.

Returning to Matrus made sense. The Matrians would be more reasonable with me since I was a woman, and would likely honor their deal. Not to mention, the only evidence that they had on me was from when I touched Queen Rina's shoulder in the office, after her death.

I had Lee's letter of confession—that would help to exonerate my name. And I still had the egg, which I could barter. If I was smart about it, I could clear my name and claim my brother, and maybe get transport down south of Veil River to The Outlands in search of somewhere for both of us to live.

I shuddered as a quiver of fear raced down my spine. That was a desperate thought.

No one knew what was in The Outlands. Several expeditions had been sent throughout history, with not a single person making it back. There had even been an unprecedented cooperative effort made with King Maxen's father, King Patrick, and Queen Rina, to send a group comprised of both Matrians and Patrians. They had been given the most powerful transmitter both countries could produce, enough food and water for months, and weapons. For a week, transmissions were coming through regularly, and reports were printed for citizens to track. Then transmissions went dead, with no more reports coming in.

Eventually, both sides had given up hope of return. Some believed that the Patrians had turned on the Matrians, killed them, and wound up dying themselves. Then again, I was certain that the Patrians were sure that it was the reverse. Either way, it didn't matter. No one returned from The Outlands.

Still, I had limited options. Given the time I'd already spent in The Green, it was clear that this place was death. The Outlands were an uncertainty. What was certain, was that I could never again live in Matrus or Patrus. As a pawn, I was a liability—they couldn't let me live long enough to potentially expose them, even if I didn't know the full extent of the egg's purpose and intended use. Not to mention, they had physical evidence that I was present at the crime. Combined with Lee's dead body, it would be rather condemning to the Matrian government that I, alone, was responsible.

However, given that no one returned from The Outlands, it was an option that I was sure the Matrians would accept, since it certainly meant death for me and my brother. Still—a slim opportunity for survival was better than none.

I put the egg back in the bag. The best, obvious first destination was Matrus. I would hide the egg somewhere in The Green, find a warden, and introduce myself. I would explain that I had something that the queen wanted, and that I wouldn't give her the location until I had been treated, my brother returned to me, and provided transport to The Outlands.

If the new queen wanted the egg, it would work out. Perhaps I could even give them Lee's letter as evidence clearing my name. I wasn't sure if they'd believe me, but it was worth a shot.

I retrieved Lee's letter, folded it up, and tucked it into one of my pockets. I stood up slowly and then picked up the bag, slinging it over my shoulder.

I used my knife to cut a branch off a tree. Stripping the smaller branches off, I weighed the stick in my hand. It was almost as tall as I was, which was good. I was going to need a walking stick for this hike. Resting against it, I realized I was already sweating from that small bit of exertion. I was running out of time.

I pulled out the compass, spinning it until the needle pointed north. Then I oriented myself in the opposite direction, and began heading south. I was going to have to move quickly or I would die out here. Taking a deep breath, I began to walk, doing my best to ignore my aches and pains with each step I took. With a little luck, Matrus was only a day away. I could travel that far in a day, I thought, as I pushed into the forest.

A tiny voice inside me whispered that I could also die before the day was over.

I ignored it.

CHAPTER 9

VIGGO

I woke up to the feeling of a heavy weight on my chest. Ungluing my eyelids, I was met with Samuel's brown eyes. The dog had been a bag of nerves since we had entered The Green. His fur had been standing on edge for half a day, and each sound of the forest caused him to whine and move closer to me. Now he seemed calmer, although that could be because he had burrowed in close to me. It was too hot to have a dog sleeping next to me, but every time I tried to move him, he would just get up and return to his original position. Eventually, I had given up.

We had traveled as late as possible last night, setting up camp last minute. I knew from Alejandro that the most dangerous creatures in The Green were nocturnal. It was risky to move at that time and would attract a lot of unwanted attention.

I sat up, pushing Samuel off me. The polymer blanket I had strung up was still undisturbed, but I didn't know what might be waiting for me on the other side. I pulled it aside slowly. The area around the campsite was clear.

I quickly broke everything down, taking only a few minutes to eat a cold breakfast and drink some water. I offered some food to Samuel, who ate greedily.

"Better fill up," I murmured, patting his head. "We won't be resting again for a while." The dog seemed to understand, and finished everything I put in front of him. I'd make sure to give him water when we moved, but I didn't want to stop at all, if possible.

I pulled out my handheld. Violet's dot had frozen last night, but now it was moving again. I studied it for a few minutes, analyzing the direction she was heading in. It was clear she was making a beeline south, in a straight line. If I cut east fast enough, I would be able to intercept her by tomorrow morning. I'd have to check in a few times to confirm that she maintained her direction, but until then, I needed to preserve the handheld's battery.

Standing up, I checked my gun and shouldered the backpack.

"Come on, boy," I said to the dog, patting my thigh. He immediately sprang up from where he was lying and began to follow.

Hiking through The Green was challenging, and heading in a straight line instead of picking a path was particularly dangerous as there were creatures that were easily disturbed hidden in the foliage. The forest was alive with sounds, which was a good sign. It was when everything went silent that signaled a predator in the area.

As I hiked, I found my thoughts returning to Violet—the woman who continued to haunt me, even after I'd learned of her deceit.

Tomorrow morning was closer than I liked. I was both ready to see her, but also not. She had lied to me, betrayed me, and tried to set me up to cover her crimes. But she had also kissed me, enveloped herself around my body and held me like I was the only thing she needed in the world. She made me feel unsteady, not in control of myself, and I hated it.

I was angry. That much was certain. A part of me wanted to shake her for using me. Throw her in a prison so I would never see her face again.

But I couldn't deny that I was also worried. Violet was a tough, resourceful woman. However, The Green was dangerous, with any number of things that could kill her in an instant. I was certain she had some skills in surviving the dangers out here, but even Alejandro wouldn't tempt his luck by remaining here too long, and he was an expert.

A flash of silver caught my eye, and I turned, pulling out my gun. I could hear something rustling in the bushes ahead of me. Beside me, Samuel crouched low to the ground, a trickle of a growl escaping his mouth. I tensed as I became aware of the forest growing silent.

Samuel and I remained still for a long moment. The rustling appeared to be moving away from us. We held our position until the sound had gone. Once the forest was noisy again, I holstered my gun. I took my canteen out of my pocket. I pulled my mask off, took several long drinks, and then replaced the mask. I offered water to Sam using the food tin from earlier. He drank it greedily.

I watched the dog, finding myself envying his ability to survive without a mask. Most animals could—it was only humans who would die when exposed to the polluted air. Scientists theorized that animals both in The Green and for miles surrounding it had adapted to the area's contamination because their lifespans were shorter, and it was likely that they were exposed to the toxins for many generations. While many animals had died from the pollution, a percentage of them developed an immunity, which they had passed down to their offspring.

According to the scientists, eventually humans would develop an immunity to it as well, given time. It sounded like some sort of hopeful propaganda to me, one that gave people hope that eventually, they would be able to leave their safe haven and re-enter the world… whatever the world was.

I didn't share their opinion. What use was it to hope that one day we could leave? The Green was deadly and The Outlands a mystery that no one had been able to answer. People thrived and survived in Matrus and Patrus. Life there was better than certain death.

After Samuel was finished with his drink, I put the canteen away and checked the compass, comparing it with the handheld. Violet was still heading south. I clicked it off and tucked it into my pocket.

I started walking, my mind trying to work out why Violet was heading the way she was. She had to be using a compass—her trajectory was too accurate to be merely wandering the forest. Was she purposefully heading back to Matrus, and if so, why? She was a wanted criminal there, too.

Unless she was heading for something or someone else. If she was part of a terrorist group, The Green would be a perfect place to have a rendezvous.

That actually made the most sense to me—it was likely that Violet was working with a terrorist cell. There weren't many in Patrus and Matrus. The Porteque group was the largest one in operation, but there were a few others of note.

The Unification Coalition was the most innocuous. In fact, calling them a terrorist cell was ridiculous, as the only thing they did was protest the treatment of the minority gender in both countries. They published manifestos that spouted that gender-specific laws only served to hurt both countries, and urged both Matrus and Patrus to unify under the idea that all people were meant to live equally, no matter what their gender.

Suffice it to say, they were pretty unpopular on both sides. Both governments had no interest in changing the policies that allowed them to stay in power. I knew I certainly would not be treated well in Matrus. I was far too aggressive for their society.

After the Unification Coalition, there was a Matrian group simply known as the Mothers. I didn't know much about them—nobody did. In fact, if it weren't for a bombing of a Matrian lab, it wouldn't even be known to exist. The facility had been raided, but nothing stolen. Nobody was even hurt in the blast. No one was sure why they had targeted that place. The only evidence that supported their existence was a single word on the wall—WHERE?

It was the newspapers themselves who named them the Mothers, after someone wrote a letter pretending to be a part of the group. It had turned out to be a hoax, the woman in question arrested and later deemed to be unbalanced, but the name had stuck.

Of those three options, none of them seemed likely to be behind any of Violet's actions. I had to wonder if somehow, there was a new group of malcontents, one even more dangerous than the others.

Then what could she be up to? She wouldn't be working alone, would she? If so, for what reason?

Samuel interrupted my thoughts with a soggy nose to my palm. I looked down, and realized that his hackles were standing on end. Irritated that I had yet again let my guard down thinking about Violet, I pulled the gun and looked around.

Everything seemed fine—in fact the forest was practically vibrating with sound. The mist roiled across the ground, clinging to everything it touched.

Then, as if someone flipped a switch, all sounds stopped. I felt the hairs on my neck standing on end, and I froze. I was in the middle of a clearing, with no discernible cover around me. I was exposed.

I looked at Samuel. His focus was completely in one direction. Trusting his instincts, I turned that way, dropping to one knee and leveling my gun.

The mist could play tricks on the mind. It shifted and moved, casting shadows that made it appear like something was back there, moving. I remained calm, knowing that if I fired my gun at a shadow, I might attract the attention of whatever was concealed in the wall of mist.

Suddenly, there came a long hooting sound, low and urgent, thrumming through the clearing. I almost squeezed the trigger, I was so surprised.

Samuel quivered at the noise, whimpering softly.

The hooting came again and again after a few intervals of silence. I remained still and steady. I had never heard of this phenomenon before. It could be wind for all I knew, but something told me that there was something dangerous on the other side of the mist.

Samuel and I remained frozen for several minutes. My shoulders were starting to ache from holding my arms up for so long. I had good muscle control, but no matter how strong a person was, they wouldn't be able to hold a position like this forever.

Suddenly, there was a creaking sound from above, from something moving in the canopy. I started to look up, when the bushes I was trained on moved. I froze, sweat trickling down my neck.

I heard the rustling moving away, and I frowned. Whatever it was, it was not attacking, but moving away. I took a few steps after it, pushing through the dense undergrowth, trying to make it out. The movement stopped, and for a second, the mist thinned, casting a shadow.

It was large, barely distinguishable, but I froze as I could make out one significant detail. *It was standing on two legs.*

Suddenly recalling Alejandro's words, I wanted to move on from the area as quickly as possible. Alejandro had told me that "mist ghosts" existed, but I'd never believed him. Now, I wasn't entirely sure what I had seen, but it had been tall, as tall as me, and large.

And, given that the forest reacted to it like a predator, it might change its mind and come back. I had no intention of becoming a meal. Samuel and I would make a wide circle around, as it was right in our path. It was better to be delayed than to walk into a trap.

Behind us, the silence persisted, and I felt as if thousands of eyes were watching me. I kept my gun in my hand as we moved as quickly and quietly as possible away from the area.

It took several hours for me to stop checking over my shoulder.

CHAPTER 10

VIOLET

Everything ached, from the top of my head to my toes. Each step I took was agony, and I wasn't sweating, which was a bad sign. Shivering, I leaned on my makeshift walking cane, and pulled the canteen from my pocket, sucking down the cool water. This was the third time I had drained it, and each time, to my amazement, it had filled up again. It must have been designed to draw moisture from the atmosphere somehow.

I wiped my mouth, coughing. I shifted my bag, grimacing at how heavy it felt on my shoulders, checked my compass, and then started moving.

I wasn't moving quietly. I knew it, and I hated it. Each step I made was obnoxiously loud, even to me, and I was on the verge of delirium. The bite wounds on my thigh continued throbbing, as if reminding me that the centipede had won. Or, at least, would win, very soon.

Ignoring my macabre thoughts, I pressed on. Cutting the walking stick had been a good idea on my part. It was perfect for pushing brush aside as I passed by. I was leaving a trail, but I figured it didn't really matter—as animals were going to be following my scent anyway. And if anyone was looking for me… well, I wouldn't be around for much longer, so let them find me.

I stopped my depressing line of thought yet again, not willing to agree with the part of me so eager to surrender. I wasn't ready to give up yet.

I pressed forward, the leaves rattling all around me. The steps seemed to merge together as I focused solely on the ground in front of me. I stumbled and tripped constantly, but I picked myself back up, and kept going.

Talking to myself helped, a little bit. I kept urging my body on. It was hard. Each step felt like I had run a mile without stopping.

In a small clearing, I paused to take another break. I allowed myself the luxury of sitting down, but only to check my wound. The area around the bite was no longer red, but purple and swollen. The entire area was about as big as my fist. Liquid welled from the punctures with that same yellow pus tinged scarlet with my blood.

Crap.

I ripped another piece of my dress. What I was about to do was going to hurt, a lot, but I needed to drain the wound. Taking a deep breath, I started to squeeze the wound, forcing the infectious fluid out.

The agony was tremendous, like someone was shoving red hot pokers into my thigh and wiggling them around.

I managed to choke back my scream, but after I finished, I collapsed, dizzy from the pain. It took me a few minutes for it to pass, but when it did, I managed to rinse the wound off and wrap it with a new rag. The old one, I tossed on the ground.

It was tempting to stay there. The moss and debris covering the ground was soft, and I was so very tired. But I couldn't let myself—I knew that once I closed my eyes, it would be impossible to get back up. So I forced myself to stand, using the walking stick to help keep my balance. I groaned as the weight of the bag hit me, and I almost collapsed again.

It was the egg. *That blasted egg.* It was weighing me down. I had to reconsider trekking through the forest with it, but I was worried hiding it this far into The

Green would mean that it could never be recovered. I had to be smart about where I hid it, if I was going to leave it anywhere at all.

My mind wasn't feeling particularly up to the task. It was difficult to hold a thought long enough to continue it. I took a long drag of water, and resolved to eat some of the food. Maybe it would help.

I pulled a tin out of the bag and cracked it open. The protein gel was so unappetizing, I felt my stomach tighten in protest, trying to force it out before it even went in. But I needed to eat. I was burning calories with each step I took, not to mention the fever I had. My body was already in starvation mode, and it would only get worse.

I closed my eyes and forced some of the gel into my mouth. The texture made chewing unnecessary, so I just swallowed it, forcing it down past the lump in my esophagus.

Once I finished the tin, I put it back in the bag, and took a deep calming breath. It helped me focus.

I pulled out the egg. The size and shape of it was distinct. If I hid it on the southerly route I was taking, I could use the compass to get me back. Provided I knew where to start from. However, there was no guarantee that I would choose the right path. And with how slowly I was moving, gauging the hiking time was out.

I needed to create a landmark that only I could recognize, but be vague enough that everyone else would overlook it.

My time was running out. I could already feel my stomach rejecting the protein gel. I concentrated on my breathing, trying to push past it.

I needed a hole, somewhere safe and dark. I could cover it with moss, and then block it with a rock. Then, I could use the cloth from my dress and hang it in the area, so I knew I was in the right place. But how to hide the rock?

The more I thought about it, the more I realized it was hopeless. There was no way I was going to be able to backtrack my way in a forest this dense. I had to carry it.

I tucked it back into the bag, my body movements leaden and weak. I shouldered the pack, and started walking again. My vision was growing gray. Not rapidly, but I noticed blurriness just at the edges of my peripheral vision.

I stumbled as a stick rolled under my foot, my ankle folding. I jerked my weight back, trying to avoid falling, but I overcompensated. My body impacted with the ground, but it took my brain a moment to register.

I groaned, and started to sit up, when a flash of silver caught my attention. Turning my head to the left, I saw a massive coil flex, the scales shimmering as it moved. Tracking the coil, I found the head looming up over me.

I gasped.

The snake stared at me, the beady eyes black and unexpressive. Its head was as big as my torso, much bigger than the one Ms. Dale scared away. Its tongue flicked out, pink and forked, tasting the air. I was aware of the sound of it breathing, like air escaping a tire. The coils tightened, and it reared back.

I rolled out of the way in time for its head to impact the ground with a snap. Adrenaline was flowing through me, cutting through the fog and pain. I continued to roll on my side, and then tucked my body. My muscle memory was working for me for once, and I managed to roll so I was up on one knee. I drew the gun from my pocket, sighting down the barrel.

The python hissed at me, the coils spooling up again. I exhaled, and squeezed the trigger, unloading the entire clip into its open mouth. I was glad the target area was so large, because even though the adrenaline was helping, I wasn't sure I would have been able to hit a smaller mark.

The snake thrashed, blood pouring from the twelve bullet holes in its head and mouth. For a second, I thought that somehow, even with all of those bullets, I had missed the vital organs. I started to reload the clip when it suddenly collapsed, the coils slackening.

I exhaled, my breathing hard. Leaning over, I tore off my mask, and immediately emptied the contents of my stomach onto the ground. The adrenaline was receding, leaving me even more tired than when I had started. Yet again, I was faced with the option of just lying there and going to sleep.

I wasn't sure how I kept getting back up. It was almost mechanical at this point. My body was beyond exhausted, but it was like it didn't know how to do anything else but walk.

Picking myself up, I staggered under the weight of my bag, but remained upright. I picked up my stick, and then continued moving south. I double checked my compass, just to make sure I was reading it correctly.

I walked until I thought my vision had gone dark. It took me a while to realize the sun had set. I took out my flashlight, and began stumbling around, looking for a place to sleep. Eventually, I found two massive roots to a tree sticking out of the ground, providing cover on both sides. I sprayed it with the aerosol can, watching the moss wilt and die under it. I managed to place the pack gently on the ground, and then I allowed myself the luxury of collapsing.

I rolled over, so I was lying on my back. I was thirsty

again, always thirsty, so I tried to work my canteen out of my pocket. I couldn't even feel my fingers, so it took me what felt like an eternity to get it out. Rolling over to my side, I managed to pry it open, and tilt it so that the cool water trickled past my lips.

I immediately vomited it up. I tried again, drinking a smaller amount, with the same result. After the third attempt, once I finished heaving, I gave up, and rolled over on my back.

Once again, the Benuxupane filled my thoughts. It wasn't because of fear, or grief, or pain, or even the guilt that I thought of it. Those feelings were there, but they were buried under something greater. Something more terrifying and upsetting.

I wanted the Benuxupane because I knew I was finally giving up. I could feel the icy darkness of sleep waiting just behind my eyes. Every time I shut them, I could hear the beating of great wings, ready to pick me up and carry me off to wherever the dead go. I didn't want to feel myself surrender to death. I didn't want to experience the feeling of being beaten. It was a point of pride at this point, but this final act was mine and mine alone.

Reaching out, I felt around on the ground, searching for the strap of the bag. I couldn't roll over at this point—I didn't have the energy to burn anymore. So I reached, until I felt the canvas fabric in my hands. I pulled it over, finding one final burst of energy to pull it until it rested against my stomach.

My vision was almost completely faded at this point, the darkness creeping in. I reached in the bag, my fingers seeking the vial of pills.

Then darkness claimed me and I was falling away from the world, into a pit of black.

CHAPTER 11

VIGGO

I pushed through the undergrowth, my eyes glued to the handheld. I knew I should be paying more attention to the environment around me, but, dammit, I was worried about Violet.

I had been monitoring her last night, and when she had stopped moving, so had I. I calculated how long it would be before I intercepted her before going to sleep. By my calculations, it would be three hours.

When I woke up, she was still stationary. She had probably just woken up as well, and was breaking camp. I fed Samuel breakfast, ate some food myself, and then broke down camp. Then I started walking east. After an hour, I checked the handheld and her location was still fixed, and unmoving.

I paused, wiping the sweat off my brow. It wasn't late

yet, but she should be moving by now. I checked my compass, and changed my direction slightly, anticipating a new rendezvous point.

I traveled the new direction for half an hour, when the voice in my head won out, and I clicked the handheld back on. She was still not moving.

I realized that there were only a few reasons for her to stop moving. The first was that she had met up with whoever her allies were. That might mean a change of direction, or even loss of the signal.

The second reason, the one that made my chest clench, was that she had been attacked, and was dying.

I exhaled sharply, a curse bursting out of my mouth. Samuel yipped in surprise, his large eyes watching me intently.

"Sorry, boy. That wasn't meant for you," I said, offering my hand.

He sniffed it, his tail wagging slowly. He gave my fingers a little lick—I had spent the larger part of the day training him not to leap on me and lick my face—and then sat down on his haunches, waiting.

No matter what her reason for remaining stationary, I knew I had to travel fast. I studied the map and her location for a few seconds, fixed my compass so that the arrow was pointing north, and then began pushing through the undergrowth.

It was slow going. There weren't a lot of natural paths bisecting this part of The Green. Which could be a good thing—no trails meant no predators. Or at least, limited predators.

I came upon a massive log, and decided to scramble over it. I picked up Samuel and helped him up, then climbed up myself. The drop on the other side was a bit steeper than the side I had climbed up on, but I dropped down, not bothering to secure a rope to myself.

Luckily, I landed perfectly, and then I called Samuel, who, after a moment of hesitation, leapt off the log into my arms. I set him back down, fixed my compass, and continued.

I was taking risks and I knew it. I needed to slow down, but a part of me feared that if I did, I would find her dead. I tried to convince myself that I wanted her to be alive because I wanted answers from her. I wanted to know why she had chosen me for her duplicity. I wanted to know why she had wormed her way under my skin. I wanted to know why the hell she had kissed me.

My logic reasoned that she couldn't give me answers if she was dead.

But my heart was beating to a different rationale— one that said it wanted to find her, to make sure she was safe. That if I lost her, I'd never see her smile at me again, or see her frown when she objected to something about Patrian society. I'd never hear her laugh. I'd never feel her lips.

My heart felt that if she died, I'd never feel happiness again.

I growled, sending Samuel skittering again. *Ugh! Get it together, man!*

The minutes ticked by, melting into hours as I moved. I paused periodically, giving water to Samuel and taking some as well, the compulsion to start running toward my destination thrumming through my veins.

Eventually, the urge to run won out, and I tore through the undergrowth, my legs pumping, leaping over bushes and logs, Samuel keeping up next to me. I knew that we were generating too much noise, but I was beyond caring. Anything in this death trap that got between me and my goal would be sorry.

Luckily, nothing did. I slipped the handheld out of my pocket as I ran, using it for reference as I closed the difference. I crashed into a clearing, my dot practically on top of her dot, and stalled, my heart pounding.

Gazing around, I could see the mist was more concentrated here, obscuring my vision. I scanned the ground, searching frantically, when Samuel's yip alerted me.

Turning, I saw the dog shoot off, and I followed blindly, having the good sense to pull my gun. Samuel guided me around a root, and then I saw her.

She was lying on the ground next to a pile of dried vomit. Her skin was extremely pale. Samuel immediately rushed to her, licking her face, trying to get her up. I was close behind him, pushing him aside.

Violet's pulse was rapid under my fingers, her breathing wheezing and shallow. I slid my hands under her back, pulling her up, and her head lolled side to side, limp. Placing her in between my legs so I could better control her body, I lifted her eyelids and shone a light in her eyes, but her pupils didn't respond.

I quickly set to unbuttoning her shirt, my mind racing. She had been poisoned, but by something she ate or a venomous creature, I couldn't tell. I reached the last button, and then I froze. Undressing her while she was helpless… it felt wrong. Granted, I had seen her in next to nothing, but still, I felt a little odd about exposing her like this.

I overrode it. Her life was more important.

Pulling open her shirt, I inspected her skin for bite marks. Finding none, I pulled her shirt back on over her shoulders, and then moved to her pants.

All of a sudden, Violet started to seize in my arms, her body jerking like a broken marionette doll. I wrapped my arms and legs firmly around her. The fit lasted for several seconds, and when it was over, she had white goo pouring from her mouth.

I quickly shucked off her pants, and immediately saw the makeshift bandage encircling her thigh. I removed it quickly. Her upper thigh was swollen, black, and writhing. I recognized that she had been bitten by one of the great black centipedes. I laid her down on the ground on her side and placed a knee on her hip, so she couldn't jerk away.

Removing my knife from my belt, I quickly sliced the wound open, using the blackened puncture marks as a guide. Violet twitched, but remained unconscious.

Yellow pus and dark blood spilled from the wound. I grabbed my canteen, and rinsed it out, until I could see the orange placenta-like encasement that held the infant centipedes.

All of the centipedes in The Green were venomous, but the greater black centipede's venom was more insidious if the symptoms weren't recognized. The venom was at work, dissolving Violet's muscle tissue and pumping poison into her veins. Meanwhile, the nutrients created by the venom of the sac seeped back through, feeding the growing life inside.

I used my knife and punctured the sac. Translucent centipedes about the size of my thumb slid out of the case, dripping down her thigh and onto the ground. I used the bandage to wipe them off, throwing them as far away as possible. Gently, I grabbed the edges of the egg sack, and pulled it out, taking care not to rip it.

Once it was out, I opened my bag, pulling out my medical kit. I quickly mixed an antiseptic powder packet with some water and spread it over her wound. It dried and hardened quickly, fixing her tissue in place.

As it dried, I found the necessary two pills that would help her system process the venom and extricate it from her body. I forced them into her mouth, poured water down her throat, and stroked her neck until she swallowed them.

I continued to pour water down her throat, working liquid into her, and I kept her in my arms. I told myself it was so I could monitor her better. If she vomited while she was unconscious, she could choke, so I needed to be there to make sure she didn't.

But deep down, I knew I had her there because I needed to feel her against me. I kept checking her pulse to make sure she was still alive. I fought the urge to talk to her, because I knew the words that would spill out of my mouth would be a mixture of platitudes, begging her not to die, coupled with vicious accusations.

Several hours passed before I felt comfortable letting her go. Her pulse was beating strong and regularly, and color was returning to her cheeks. I forced some more water and medicine into her mouth, replaced her mask, and then laid her down, wrapping her in my polymer blanket. I put some distance between us and sat down, staring at her. She twisted fitfully in her sleep, wresting her hand out of the blanket as if to fend off a blow.

My jaw clenched. How could a creature so dangerous seem so helpless at the same time? Violet was a walking contradiction. It was like there were two Violets—the Violet that was a threat to everyone around her, and the Violet that was a threat to herself.

I ran a hand across my face. I had been nursing Violet for hours, and the run had taken a lot out of me. I was exhausted. Samuel yipped, and crawled over me, whining softly, his tail thumping on the ground, reminding me that it was dinner time.

I opened up a tin, gave him half, and then ate the other half. In the fading light of the sun, I saw Violet's bag lying toppled over from where I had kicked it in my haste to get to her. Some of the items were out—a few aerosol cans and some food items were scattered across the ground.

Moving over to it, I began to rifle through it and immediately recognized the silver case as the egg. I picked it up, examining its surface. I found a keyhole, and I looked at Violet, and the key she had tied around her neck. It was tempting to open, but then again—I had no idea what was inside, and I didn't relish the idea of accidentally setting off some sort of bomb.

I set it aside, and began to rummage around. Everything else was for survival, although her bag was missing several important things, like medicine that could save her life. I heard something rattle as I went to set the bag aside. Frowning, I reached into the bottom and felt the cool press of glass under my fingers. I pulled it out, and examined it. It was a vial with several white pills. The vial wasn't labeled. I contemplated it for a few seconds, and then repacked the bag, placing three empty aerosol containers to one side.

Then, I removed Violet's blanket and went through her pockets. I found her gun, an extra clip, and a few slips of paper, which I removed. I covered her back up, and then clicked on my flashlight. There were two pictures—one of Queen Rina and a blond-haired man, both sitting with their throats slit, and the words "FOR THE BOYS OF MATRUS" carved into the desk that sat between them. In the other, I recognized King Maxen's car, and the words "FOR THE MEN YOU WILL DECEIVE" scratched into the tinted windshield.

I unfolded the paper. It was a letter from Lee Bertrand, addressed to someone called Desmond. Sitting back, I began to read.

CHAPTER 12

VIOLET

I was standing on a precipice, staring down into the velvet darkness. It felt like a dream, but maybe that was what death felt like—a dream that no one could ever wake from.

I kept waiting for something to happen, but I just stood there, staring down, waiting. I kept hearing things in the darkness, but I couldn't make them out. I knew I should be afraid—in fact a part of me was. But another part of me was curious.

Taking a deep breath, I stepped forward. Everything shifted under my feet as I did, and suddenly I was standing in the hall of my old house. My mother was standing in front of me, her face a mask of disapproval. "Again, Violet?" she asked, her eyes sad.

I looked down at the back of my hands. They were

bloody and torn. I looked back up at my mom who was now walking away, her back to me. She was leaving me.

"I'm sorry, Mommy," I cried, trying to run after her. It was like my legs were stuck in honey. The faster I ran, the slower I went. "Mommy," I yelled, reaching for her.

She didn't look back as she entered a door, closing it in my face. "I'm sorry," I said against the door, tears running down my cheeks. "Please come back. Please... come back."

I stood there, my face and hands on the door, crying, begging her to return.

"Violet?" came a small tremulous voice next to me. I turned, and there was Tim, my little brother, his eyes wide. He held out his hand to me, and I reached for it. I held it for a second, his skin warm and vibrant under my touch.

Then he was slipping, falling into the toxic waters of the river. I screamed, reaching for him, the river bank lifting me away from him. He stared up at me, his eyes black and dark, before he disappeared into the swirling depths. I tried to jump in after him, when strong hands grabbed me, carrying me away.

I clawed at the earth, my nails digging furrows into the dark soil. "No!" I screamed, kicking my legs. I broke free, and started to run toward the edge. I dove off the side, intent on rescuing my brother, when the landscape shifted beneath me.

I watched as the canopy of The Green rushed in. I raised my hands, still screaming, my body tensing for the impending impact.

"What are you doing?" said a gruff voice.

I was standing in the middle of a clearing, and in front of me stood… Viggo. He looked handsome, his face cleanly shaved, his eyes earthy green, and his hair falling to the sides of his face. I wanted to touch him.

I took a step forward, and stopped, looking down. I was wearing the dress I wore to Lee's and my wedding. I met Viggo's eyes and he shook his head.

"You betrayed me," he said, his voice raw.

"No, I –"

"You're toxic, Violet. You hurt everyone you love."

"No!"

"I never want to see you again."

"Please–"

I watched as vines dropped from the trees, covering Viggo. He stared at me, his eyes filled with rage and pain and betrayal. I tried to rush to him, but the vines had wrapped around my legs, holding me in place. I looked down, and watched in horror as they morphed, turning black, scales forming and legs erupting from their surface.

The centipedes writhed against my legs, heaving as more and more piled in around me. "Viggo," I cried.

He continued to stare at me, as the vines started to cut into his skin, cutting long lines that welled with blood and poured down his face. "You are toxic," he said.

I watched as the vines constricted, forming scales of their own, until he was wrapped in the coils of a silver python. I heard the snap of bones and screamed, trying to push through the centipedes to get to him. His eyes bulged in their sockets. One of the python heads hissed, opening its mouth to swallow him whole. I closed my eyes, hot tears dripping down my cheeks.

I collapsed on the ground, the centipedes gone. "Don't go," I cried.

"You did this, Violet," said a voice behind me. I kept my eyes closed as I felt the clammy touch of a hand on my back. "You did this to me."

I forced myself to look up into Lee's eyes. His face was misshapen, his bones broken. He moved around me in jerking steps. "You killed me," he hissed.

"You killed me," echoed Viggo's voice.

"You killed me," came my mother's voice.

"You killed me," said my brother.

I screamed, clamping my hands over my ears as they chanted all around me. Vertigo assailed me as I felt the whole world shift. I could hear more voices chanting with them. Queen Rina, Alastair Jenks, the two girls I'd killed in Matrus, and the man from the Porteque gang who I had stabbed—all of them screaming at me.

I tried to explain, tried to deny, tried to justify, but their voices only grew louder. They all surrounded me, screaming "You, you, you," over and over again as they died, but didn't die.

I screamed until my voice was hoarse, until the tears stopped pouring from my eyes, until they all fell down. Sudden silence filled the air, until Lee began to move. He sat up, his broken bones creaking and snapping under the weight of his body. He picked up the silver egg between us, and advanced on me.

I backed away, but somehow he was faster than me. He slammed the egg into my chest, forcing it in through my skin. I screamed again as agony spread through me. Light began to shine from the hole as he forced it inside of me. "Together forever," he leered.

Strong hands grabbed me suddenly, and I jerked against them.

"Violet!" came a soft urgent voice. The tightness in my chest intensified, and I struggled harder. I felt my fist connect with something, heard someone cursing, and I jerked awake.

I curled around myself, my stomach queasy and my hands shaking. I couldn't shake the dream; the images I saw. I was panting, my heart sick with guilt even over the deaths I wasn't the cause of, when the hands returned, touching me gently.

I jerked away, suddenly surprised, and looked up. It was… Viggo. Leaning over me, his rugged, stubbled face a mixture of concern and anger.

I cried out, covering my eyes, not willing to see him torn apart again. He grabbed my hands, pulling them away, and shaking me.

"Violet," he hissed, his eyes intense.

I shook my head, denying his existence. "I can't watch it again, I can't. Please don't make me!"

Viggo stared at me, teeth clenched hard, a muscle in his jaw pulsating. Finally, he yanked me into his arms and lap, holding me close. I curled up into a ball and clenched my eyes tight. I felt him stroking my hair. I was aware of him speaking to me, but the nightmare still clung to me too tightly. I kept waiting for him to die. For me to kill him.

Eventually, however, I accepted that he was real. The press of his strong hands on my back, rubbing my tense muscles, weren't another figment of my imagination. He was here. It was his strong heartbeat next to my cheek, his rough jaw pressing against the top of my head, and his calm and even breathing filling my ears.

Confusion flooded through me.

"Viggo," I whispered, suddenly aware of how parched I was.

"Yes?" he said, his chest rumbling.

"How are you here?" I breathed, lifting my hand to his shoulder.

He shrugged me off, and sat me on the ground. I was too weak to hold myself up, so he propped me up against the tree root. I looked around, blinking sluggishly. "This is a dream," I said, aware of my voice slurring.

"No, Violet, it isn't," Viggo replied curtly as he picked up a canteen.

I tilted my head up to him, so I could look at him as he loomed over me. He pulled my mask off, and I gasped, weakly trying to reach for it.

Viggo is trying to kill me, I thought. *I deserve it,* a tiny voice added.

He deftly avoided my hands and lifted the canteen to my lips. I opened my mouth to protest, and he tilted the canteen, pouring cool water down my throat. I didn't understand, so I coughed, water going down the wrong way.

He swore, kneeling down next to me, jerking me forward and whacking me on the back. I hacked until the feeling passed. He replaced the mask for a few seconds so I could suck in some air.

"You're trying to kill me," I croaked.

He gave a *tsk* of annoyance. "If I wanted you dead, I would have let you die from your bite."

Groggily, I looked over at my leg. "It was venomous," I said.

"I know."

"Thirsty," I said, feeling the rush of blackness returning.

He sighed, and slipped my mask off again, placing the canteen against my mouth. I was ready this time, and I drank the water as it poured in, my throat remembering what my mind couldn't seem to. After a while, he took the canteen away and replaced the mask.

My stomach full of water, I felt my eyelids drift close. I forced them open, suddenly panicked. "Don't let me sleep," I whispered to Viggo, grabbing his arm.

He gently removed it, and shook his head. "You need to sleep, Violet. It's the best medicine."

"But they're waiting for me! You're waiting for me. I killed you. I killed others. Please…"

Viggo blinked, and sat down next to me. "*Who* did you kill, Violet?"

"Everyone," I explained. "I mean, I didn't kill all of them, but I did four of them. I'm responsible for four deaths! I-I can't face them. They won't let me explain. I'm sorry," I choked, "I'm so, so sorry."

I felt Viggo's Adam's apple bob as he swallowed hard. "Okay," he said tightly, after a pause. "I will hold you, and if you start to have nightmares, I promise to wake you. All right?"

I couldn't even respond; the darkness was taking me again. I struggled against it, fighting with all my might. Then I felt his arm come around me, holding me. It was like a weight that kept me centered, a shield that kept me safe from the people who haunted me. I exhaled in relief, and surrendered myself to sleep, confident that the nightmares wouldn't find me as long as Viggo was there.

CHAPTER 13

VIGGO

I sat on one of the roots, the tree trunk to my back and the pistol on my lap, waiting for Violet to wake up. She was curled up around Samuel, who hadn't left her side since we found her. It had been twenty-four hours since then, and another twelve since her nightmare.

I had only been able to sleep a few hours myself; it was too dangerous for both of us to be unconscious.

It gave me time to think. There was something more going on here, but I wasn't quite sure what it was. I reached into my pocket, and pulled out Lee's letter. From what it stated there, it was clear that Violet had no idea what his true intentions were. In fact, it appeared that Lee had played her.

However, this didn't change the fact that she had to have been aware of the bombs in the laboratory. That she had played a part in setting me up. Though at some point, Lee had started to have difficulty with controlling her. That brought a small smirk to my mouth: The idea anyone could control Violet was laughable. She was far too headstrong.

Lee had mentioned giving her pills—did he do it to make her more compliant? If so, when did he start giving them to her? What kind of pills were they? Were they the same ones I had found in her bag? If so, would giving them to her make her more inclined to answer my questions when she woke up?

So many questions, and the source of any answers lay unconscious a few feet away from me. I ran a hand through my hair and sighed again.

Lee was behind the attacks. And now he was dead. Did Violet kill him? If so, was it in self-defense, or born of a desire to take the egg for herself?

I looked at the egg. I still hadn't tried to open it—I wasn't sure I wanted to know what was inside. I knew that I had been fed a lie by King Maxen now, who had said the egg was Patrian property, but it was clear from the letter that it had been stolen by Patrus from Matrus. And, given how desperately both countries wanted it, I actually found myself agreeing with Lee—maybe it was better that neither found it.

I had no illusions about the depths of depravity both

countries would drop to in the name of the "greater good." Whatever was in that case was dangerous— dangerous enough to kill for and spelled nothing but trouble for both nations. A part of me was seriously tempted to hike over to the river and toss it in so that no one could have it.

Violet stirred and I set aside my thoughts, watching her. She was looking much better, albeit haggard and dirty. She gave a deep sigh and then continued to sleep, and I frowned, returning to my thoughts.

The egg, created by Matrus, stolen by Patrus, stolen back by Lee and Violet. Only, Lee had then betrayed Queen Rina, killed her and her advisor, and fled the palace. He'd planned to kill Violet as well, or for her to take the blame for the murder at least, but somehow she had stopped him. Then she'd headed to The Green… Why? She had the egg. All she had to do was go back and explain, right? Especially if she could use the egg as leverage.

Then again, Violet had been on the wrong side of the law for a long time. Maybe she just didn't trust the government anymore, and planned to do something else with the egg. Although what that could be, I had no clue.

Also, who was Desmond, the person the letter was addressed to? Whoever he was, it was clear that he and

Lee were close. Maybe he was part of a terrorist faction? Lee was an anarchist against both countries, but would he go as far as to join a terrorist group?

It wouldn't surprise me if he would.

"Viggo?"

Violet reclaimed my attention. She was sitting up, looking at me, her eyes wide behind her mask. An immediate flash of anger slid into me. *How dare she look so innocent,* I thought with disgust, my mind turning back to the bombing.

I leapt off the root, my legs bent to absorb the impact. "Mrs. Bertrand," I drawled sardonically, offering her a little bow.

She grew pale and flinched. "Don't call me that," she whispered.

"Oh? Why not? It might have been a ruse, but you were legally married, after all."

Violet shook her head. "It was for the mission," she said hoarsely.

"You mean the mission where you planted bombs and killed people?" I asked. I was being intentionally cruel, but my anger needed an outlet, and the source of my anger was here in front of me.

"I didn't want all those people to die," she rasped. "Lee planted extra bombs that I didn't even know about until it was too late. I had no *choice*. You have to believe me."

"*Believe* you? After you set me up to go down for your crime?"

Tears were starting to form in her eyes. "I tried to talk Lee out of it! I swear I tried. I was trapped."

I scoffed at her. "Like I should believe you. I've seen your file, Violet. I know about all the people you hurt or killed before you even started this mission."

Violet swallowed, tears still spilling from her gray eyes. "I know," she said. "I'm a murderer… and even those I don't murder who are involved with me end up dying. The queen, Alastair, Lee, the girl in school and in the prison… everyone who touches me dies."

I frowned, unprepared for her response. She continued, staring at her hands. "I'm toxic. I'm poison. Y-You need to stay away from me!"

I shook my head. "Oh no, Violet. I'm here to bring you back to answer for your crimes."

Violet stood up, her knees shaky. "I'm not going back with you," she exclaimed. "I may be responsible for those lab deaths, but I didn't actually commit them. I've been a pawn in someone else's game for too long. I'm not going back."

"The hell you aren't," I growled.

She took a step back, raising her arm. "Don't, Viggo! Please, don't."

I examined her. She was trembling, probably still weak from the venom and the lack of food. I hesitated, feeling a thread of disgust worm in through my anger. I was scaring her.

Instantly, I wanted to kneel down in front of her and comfort her. She looked so afraid, it was hard for me to believe that it wasn't an act. I turned around for a second, collecting myself. My anger was overriding me. I needed to slow down and gain some perspective.

There was a long silence between us, and finally, I broke it, turning back around toward her. "Sit down. You need to eat something."

I was surprised that she actually sat and I moved over to my backpack, pulling out a few tins. I used grabbing them as a distraction, so I could slip a pair of cuffs into my pocket without her noticing. She'd balk if she saw them, and I was not in the mood to overpower a girl who was recovering from the brink of death.

I handed her one of the tins, which she snatched out of my hands. I watched with a mixture of revulsion and fascination at how quickly she gobbled it down. I knew she'd be hungry waking up, but not that hungry. She asked for another one, but I shook my head. "Wait for that to settle. We have a limited supply and I want to make sure you're not going to vomit it up before I give you the next one."

I handed her the water and watched her take long pulls from it. Once again, I took it away from her before she was willing to stop. She accepted it though and, after wiping her mouth, she lowered the mask back to her face.

"Thank you," she said. I nodded, setting the water canteen on the ground in front of me. Samuel decided to remind her that he was there, by placing his head in her lap. She made a cooing sound, and began rubbing his head. He squirmed into her lap, his tongue lolling, and I felt an irrational surge of jealousy toward the dog.

"How did you find me?" she asked as she rubbed Samuel's belly.

"Tracker technology," I replied.

"What? Via the tracker Lee put on me?" She frowned hard. "He said he removed that software from his computer."

"It seems your husband couldn't be bothered."

She flinched. "Please don't call him that."

"Why not?" I taunted. "You were married."

Violet narrowed her gray eyes as she looked at me. "I understand that you're angry with me for my part in the bombing, and setting you up, but there is no need to be cruel, Viggo." Her tone was icy. "Be angry, don't be cruel."

I considered her words and knew she was right. I tried to convince myself that I didn't care if she found me cruel, but it didn't work. I did care.

That was the whole damn problem.

"Fine," I said begrudgingly. She inclined her head to me in a wordless thank you, and I tipped mine back at her. "So, explain to me what happened."

Violet's eyes met mine, her face guarded. "Well, it seems like you know a great deal. I'm guessing you read Lee's letter?" I nodded. She pressed her lips together in a thin line. "Well, I had no idea about most of it. The bombs, yes, but I didn't know so many people would get hurt. I never realized how good at lying he was."

"Who's Desmond?" I asked.

Violet shrugged. "That's Lee's middle name. Do you know Lee's story?"

I shook my head.

"Lee's mother was from Matrus," she explained, "his father from Patrus, and he was born on a boat in the middle of Veil River. His mother gave him the middle name of Desmond. I think he was writing to himself."

I frowned, mulling that over. "You think he had two personalities?"

"It's the only thing I can think of—I think he went insane and was trying to punish the two countries that wouldn't accept him."

"But they did accept him," I said. "Matrus trusted him to spy for them, and Patrus obviously believed his patriotism. He could've done anything for either of them."

"He felt like a pawn, Viggo. I get that feeling, even if I don't agree with what he did." She cast me a sidelong glance. "So should you," she added softly.

My jaw clenched at her declaration. I ignored her small jab, focusing on the task at hand. "Why did you come here, Violet?"

She sighed, and rubbed the back of her neck. "Lee and I... well, when I discovered he had killed the queen and Mr. Jenks, I went to confront him. He was already taking off on that stupid flying motorcycle, so I... I grabbed on. We fought, and then he tried to drag me off. I upset his balance and he fell. I killed him. After that... I just sort of... I don't know. I was in shock. I had read his letter, and opened the egg, and –"

"You opened the egg?" I interrupted.

She nodded, pulling out the key that hung around her throat. "Yeah."

I stood up, holding out my hand for the key. Violet eyed me warily, her gray eyes searching mine. Eventually, she folded, and untied the cloth securing it to her neck.

I walked over to the silver case, and fit the key to the

hole. There was a hissing sound, and then it opened. I stared at the orange colored case, and at the small, barely formed embryo for a long moment, and then turned to Violet, who shrugged.

After several seconds of examining the strange embryo and the container, I pulled the key, sealing it up. Violet looked at me expectantly when I approached, and I returned the key to her, not wanting her to end her story prematurely.

She took the two ends of her makeshift necklace in her hands and began securing it to her neck while she continued, "Anyway, Lee was heading north, and I didn't know how to fly the damn thing. I crashed into The Green, got bitten by a centipede and… well… you know the rest."

"Why were you heading back south?"

Violet shrugged. "I figured… I figured out the bite was venomous and I decided to bargain the egg with Matrus for a cure. And for my brother."

"And if you hadn't been bitten?"

She tilted her chin up. "I would've carried on north. To find my brother."

I had heard enough. It was a pretty convenient story, but it was just that—a story. There were enough elements of truth to it to make it believable, but I wasn't hearing them. She had betrayed me, and cost innocent people their lives, no matter what her regrets were.

I stood up and crossed over to her, ignoring the feeling of how wrong I was in doing what I was about to do. I'd been sent out here to retrieve her and the egg, and that was what I was going to accomplish. It was far easier than dwelling on what she had told me right then.

"Violet Bates Bertrand, you are under arrest on the authority of King Maxen of Patrus," I announced, slipping the cuffs on her wrists before she could stop me.

CHAPTER 14

VIOLET

The rope stretched between my cuffed hands and Viggo's hand like a leash as we walked. Sweat poured down my skin in rivulets, and I was practically gasping for air as he marched me through The Green like a dog. Samuel gave a yip, bounding between us, reminding me that I was being treated worse than a dog.

Suddenly furious, I gave a vicious tug of the rope. Viggo's grip was strong, so I barely moved his arm from where he clutched it. He turned, and from under his mask I could see the muscle in his jaw twitching. For a second, I wanted to punch him in that exact spot.

Since slipping the handcuffs on me, Viggo hadn't said two words to me. Oh, I had struggled after he put the cuffs on me. I had tried to run, tried to fight, but I was still weak from the venom that had laid me out.

There was no way I was getting away from him in this condition.

I was still baffled by his sudden change in demeanor. He had seemed to be listening to me as I told my story. I tried to keep it short and succinct, and he had still arrested me! He was still dragging me back to Patrus, where a noose would be waiting for me in the public gallows.

I was struck by how unfair the situation was. That feeling had intensified as the day went on, until I was practically seething with rage, like a teapot about to blow. I wondered if I had been a man, if Viggo would believe me. I dismissed the thought as soon as it came to me. The only reason Viggo was so mad was because I had kissed him.

Viggo tugged the rope, urging me to move. Defiantly, I tugged it back, my limbs shaking from the exertion from walking for the last two hours. Samuel ran through my legs and then lay down, panting, his eyes on Viggo.

Viggo took a long, hard look at us. Spitting out a curse, he walked the distance between us, pulling something out of his pocket and thrusting it into my hands. Looking down, I saw the canteen. Parched, I opened it. It was hard with my hands bound together, but I managed. Then, as I lifted the canteen up, I realized that it was next to impossible to take off my mask. If I did it while holding the canteen, all the water would spill out of it. If I did it with the canteen closed, I would be holding my breath for a long time in a toxic atmosphere.

Frowning, I looked at Viggo. I was going to have to ask him to help me and I really didn't want to. My pride wouldn't allow it—especially since he was acting like a domineering and arrogant… well… Patrian.

Defiantly, I replaced the cap, and tossed it back to him. He caught it out of the air deftly, frowning at me. I gave him my best rebellious face, even though my throat was desperate for water. He shrugged and began walking again.

This was the extent of our communication. He tugged the rope and I staggered on, cursing myself and him for being idiots.

I needed the water if I was going to get away from him. I needed to keep my strength up. Not taking it was only hurting me, not him.

Get it together, Vi, I told myself as I stepped over a log.

The wound on my leg twitched as I stretched too far to get over the log, and I gave an involuntary gasp at the twinge of pain as I felt the skin stretch under the bandage.

Viggo was immediately there, his green eyes blazing behind the clear plastic of his mask.

"What happened?" he demanded, his hands reaching out to steady me.

I gaped at him, as he uttered the first words he'd spoken to me for hours. It was tempting to ignore him like he'd been ignoring me, but I was too concerned about my wound. I put aside my pride.

"My leg, I might have…"

He immediately reached down and started unbuttoning my pants. Eyes wide, I jerked back out of his hands.

"What are you doing?"

Viggo gave a sigh, like his patience was being tried. "It's not exactly the time to be prudish. I need to see your thigh. That means the pants come down."

It was irrational, I knew, but I did not want Viggo taking my pants off. The fact that he had already done so while I was unconscious was upsetting. The logical part of my brain knew that it needed to be done, but the emotional part was unwilling to bend.

"No," I said, shaking my head. Viggo's face grew determined, and I took another step back. "Viggo, I said *no*."

He advanced, his face a mask of grim determination. My heart started to pound as he stalked toward me like a predator. I knew I should be afraid, but the sight of him moving toward me like that made me feel… excited.

That scared me more than anything.

Without meaning to, I held up my hands to fend him off, turning my face away. "Please Viggo," I said, my voice coming out high-pitched and shaky. Samuel suddenly appeared between us, his fur on end and a growl trickling between his lips.

He stopped a few feet away from me. I risked a glance at him, and I saw him looking down at the dog, and then his clenched hands. He looked up at me, and I could see the uncertainty in his eyes. I was trembling, unwanted tears forming in my eyes.

Viggo's face softened—that was the only way I could describe it. It was like watching a massive storm melt away into a beautiful sunset.

"I'm sorry, Violet," he said, his voice thick. "I shouldn't have…"

I nodded, unable to force words out of the huge lump in my throat.

He took a step closer, his hands up with palms out. "I really do need to check your wound," he said carefully, his voice calm and even. For a moment, I wondered if this was how humans sounded to wounded animals, until I remembered, I *was* a wounded animal.

I exhaled sharply, and inhaled, remembering how the simple act of breathing had helped calm me for the past few days, and nodded to him.

He let me unbutton my own pants. It was difficult,

but it gave me a sense of control over the situation. Then he helped me slip them over my hip, pulling them down to the wound on my thigh. He went to one knee, examining the bandage, his fingers pressing on the edge to make sure it was still sealed.

There was something intimate about him being down there, his face inches away from my thigh, but I pushed it aside. I fixed my eyes on anything else. Samuel came up from the other side, and I reached down to pet him. It was awkward, but it kept me from seeing how exposed and vulnerable I was to Viggo.

He inspected the bandage for a few more seconds, and then helped me slip my pants on. All and all, the inspection lasted less than two minutes. It had felt like longer. I was allowed to button my pants back up, and re-tie my makeshift knot.

We stood there awkwardly for a few seconds longer and then Viggo handed me the canteen. I looked at him, but there was no challenge in his eyes. I opened the canteen, and when I wordlessly nodded that I was ready, he lifted the mask off my face. I drank the water quickly, trying not to breathe too much. Once I was finished, he replaced the mask and I closed the canteen, handing it back to him.

He removed his own mask and took a long swig, and then poured some in his cupped hand, offering it to Samuel.

After our water break was finished, he straightened up.

"C'mon," he muttered, picking up the rope from where he had dropped it on the ground. "We need to keep moving."

I frowned, but started walking behind him. As we walked, my mind churned over what to do with Viggo. I had tried for honesty, but it was clear he didn't believe me. But then he had shown genuine care for me.

His behavior was contradictory and confusing, and it was very frustrating to try to understand, especially since he wasn't talking to me. The truth was that I was angry. Furious really. I had never expected to see Viggo again, but now that he was here, with the truth in front of him… I didn't even know what he was thinking.

I'd taken all that I could stand. I planted my feet and stopped as we neared the slope of a dip in the forest. Viggo didn't notice my pause, initially, until the rope swinging between us pulled taut. I held my ground, pulling back against it. He spun, irritation across his features.

"Why are you stopping?" he demanded.

"I want to talk," I replied in a manner that I hoped sounded calm and collected.

"You've said enough, Violet."

"I've only told you the truth, *Viggo*."

He rolled his eyes and closed the distance between us

until he was looming over me. I kept my face expressionless, which was hard considering how imposing his size really was.

"The truth," he said mockingly. "And what am I supposed to believe? The crazy story that Lee betrayed his country even though he had no reason to?"

"You read his letter—"

"Or a girl who's a criminal? Who betrayed *me!*" he barreled on, his face in a sneer. "Which one is more believable to you, Violet? What is the more likely scenario?"

I narrowed my eyes at him. "You arrogant, egotistical, misogynistic... Patrian," I spat. "Trained to believe that every word coming out of a woman's mouth is a lie or a manipulation."

"This has nothing to do with the fact you are a woman..."

"Oh, doesn't it?" I breathed out sharply. "What are you really mad about, Viggo—that I wasn't who I said I was, *or that I kissed you*?"

A muscle in his jaw started ticking, and I watched his green eyes becoming hard and dangerous.

"I'm so glad you brought up that kiss," he said, his voice low and bordering on menacing. "Because I was wondering about that." I froze, my heart palpitating in anticipation. "I was wondering how a woman got so cold that she could kiss a man the night before she planned to lure him to his death. Did you kiss Lee like that?"

An icy anger throbbed through my veins, and before I could stop myself, my foot contacted with Viggo's knee. He wasn't expecting that, and he was forced backward, dipping toward the slope.

I turned to run, when his strong arm wrapped around my waist, dragging me with him in a fall. The next thing I knew, we were rolling over the edge, a tangle of limbs. His arm was like a vice around my stomach as we bounced down the hill, until we rolled to a stop.

I scrambled to my feet, feeling jostled and confused. Viggo seemed worse, struggling to his hands and feet, his back to me. Without hesitating, I leapt on his back, slipping my bound wrists over his head and wrapping my arms around his neck, squeezing. He made a surprised sound, his hands going over my forearms to try and pull me off. I had leverage though, and the superior position.

Viggo tried to jerk me over his shoulder, but I wrapped my legs around him, holding firm. I was careful not to choke off all his air—I was angry, yes, but I didn't want to hurt him.

It turned out that was a mistake on my part. He managed to work a few fingers under my arm, and, in a feat of incredible strength, he pulled my arm straight out. I released one leg I had wrapped around his waist, and planted it in the back of his knee. He buckled, dropping down.

Viggo managed to pull me around to the front of him, using my freed limbs as an opportunity to unbalance me. He used his moment to try to push me into the ground, but I rolled with it, curling my back and using my knees to push his weight over mine. I landed on top of him, my hands trapped behind his head, his body under my body.

We paused there for a moment, staring at each other, when Viggo reached up, grabbing me gently by the back of the neck, and pulling me flat against his chest. His other arm wrapped around the back of my shoulders, and I felt his chest rise in a deep, heaving sigh.

"I missed you, Violet," he breathed, holding me closer.

"I missed you too," I admitted, savoring the feel of his arms around me. I pulled away, looking him desperately in the eye. "Viggo, please. You have to believe me. I didn't kiss you because it was part of the plan. I kissed you because I… I couldn't stop myself. I kissed you because I *wanted* to. I didn't want to carry out Lee's plan. He gave me this pill, and it made it so I couldn't feel anything."

"It's times like this that I really hate these masks," he muttered.

I looked at him inquisitively.

"I could kiss you to shut you up," he added with a small grin.

I smiled, but it was bittersweet. "Do you believe me?"

Viggo gave a heaving sigh, his chest contracting under me so I could feel his heartbeat, strong and steady, where our torsos touched. He reached up, moving a lock of my hair off the visor. "We should go," he said, avoiding my question. But I could see it in his eyes, the suspicion that I was playing him.

I sighed and placed my head against his chest, wishing that I could do something to make him believe me.

"What are you going to do with me?" I asked.

There was a long pause. "You have to go back, Violet. There's no other way."

I sat up, shaking my head. "They'll kill me," I whispered as I pulled my cuffed hands from behind his head.

He reached up and held my face, or rather the helmet. "I'll protect you," he whispered, his eyes sincere.

I shook my head at him, tears pricking at my eyes. "You can't. You couldn't even protect your wife." I flinched as I said it, but now was not the time to mince words.

Viggo flinched too, and I hated myself for even saying those words, no matter how honest they were. But I could see it in his eyes—as much as he wanted to believe he could keep me safe, the truth was that neither of us could control what would happen if we returned to our homelands.

Viggo opened his mouth to reply, when something grabbed me, yanking me off him and into the air.

CHAPTER 15

VIGGO

I bolted frantically after Violet, my legs pumping like pistons as I tore after her. Samuel raced alongside me, his body surging in and out of the undergrowth. Violet's shouts were disappearing in the distance, and I could no longer see her or her captor in the canopy.

What the hell?

Running, I pulled the handheld from my pocket, and pulled up Violet's signal. I felt relief wash over me as it focused in on her dot, moving away from me rapidly. I kept the handheld on, and pushed after her, leaping over downed logs and weaving among trees.

Sweat was pouring down my face as I ran, and my breath was coming in ragged gasps. I was in good shape, but I wasn't going to be able to run like this forever. I needed to pace myself if I was going to have any energy to deal with whatever had grabbed her and ripped her away from me.

And if whatever it was hurt her… a surge of panic hit me, giving me a burst of energy that I poured into speed.

I tried to wrap my head around what I had seen grab Violet, but everything had happened so fast. It had swung through the trees, using vines to carry her away.

My heart lurched at the thought of some unknown creature. If it bit her, and was venomous, I doubted any of the medicines I had brought would save her. Not to mention she was still weak from her last bite. She might not last long.

Though if whatever took her was going to eat her, it wouldn't waste time. It was likely dragging her back to its lair.

Fear fueled another burst of speed in me, and I raced through the trees, barely having time to register them before having to react. My pace was relentless, even Samuel was having trouble keeping up.

I continued to run, leaping and dodging obstacles. The problem with running so fast, however, is that unless the environment was perfectly level and flat, it would eventually force me to slow down.

Which is essentially what happened—only it didn't slow me down—it flat out stopped me. I miscalculated a step, and when the spongy ground gave more than I expected, and I went flying through the air into a chasm. I fell, maybe ten feet, before hitting the ground.

I lay there for a second, sucking in air and staring up at the sky. The chasm wasn't big, probably five or six feet wide, but it was long. I took inventory of my body, making sure nothing was broken, when the ground at my back heaved.

Surprised, I shifted on my side, and froze as I realized that there were coils after coils of writhing serpentine bodies under my hand. Huge silver pythons, to be exact, writhing in a massive ball that had just happened to break my fall.

The ball shifted, jerking me off balance, and I realized that it was a mating ball. This was incredibly dangerous. I needed to get out before they managed to trap me inside. Just then, I noticed the handheld perched precariously on one of the coils a few feet away. I scrambled over to it, the undulating mass quivering under my feet. The handheld tipped on an angle, then fell in between two coils.

Without thinking, I leapt on one and jammed my arm between the two up to my shoulder. My fingers stretched blindly into the void of space, and I felt the brush of scales against my fingers. Behind me, I heard a hostile hiss, and I froze. I kept reaching, my other hand fumbling in the front of my pants for my pistol. The hissing intensified, and I could feel the python's cool breath on my back.

I leapt to the side at the last possible moment, and fired at the snake's head. The first bullet went wild, but I adjusted my aim, and unloaded the clip into the wide ebony eye. The snake collapsed. I felt the familiar touch of my handheld with my other hand, grabbing it and snatching it out before I lost it.

Above me, Samuel was barking. I risked a glance up, and saw that there was a tree that had collapsed, forming a bridge. One of the branches was only a few feet over my head. Running as best I could as the mass of hissing snakes shuddered beneath my feet, I planted one foot on the side of the chasm, using it to push off and leap toward the branch.

I caught it, and began pulling myself up. The hissing below me was loud in my ears, but I ignored it, focusing instead on my tenuous grasp as I pulled myself up the tree. Once I was on top of the log, I crossed quickly over to Samuel, and knelt down next to the dog.

I wiped the sweat off my brow, and pulled the handheld out of my pocket. Violet's dot had stopped. I paused, waiting to see what would happen. Then, the dot began to head back toward me.

Violet had escaped whatever had grabbed her, but I

needed to hurry to her in case it was chasing her.

We took off running, heading toward the dot as it headed toward us. She was still several kilometers away, but that was nothing, provided I paced myself.

I had already formed a stitch in my side from the mad dash earlier. While it was important to get to Violet, I knew I wouldn't get there if I kept tearing through the forest like a mad man. I checked the handheld again as I jogged, correcting my position slightly. Violet's dot was moving much quicker now, and I was worried she was being chased.

As our two dots neared each other, I slowed down, pulling my gun. I topped a crest, which dipped down into a deep valley. The mist was thicker here, more difficult to see in. I pulled my gun and ordered Samuel to heel. The dog pressed in tightly to my leg as I slowly entered the mist.

It coiled on the ground and in the air, touching everything it could. As I walked, it parted under my feet, forming little eddies in the mist that swirled violently before slowly settling back down, clinging to the earth like a white blanket.

The mist that hung in the air was thinner, almost like gauze had been pulled over my eyes. I saw something moving in front of me. At first, I thought it was Violet, and I opened my mouth to call her over, when the mist parted partially.

A woman stood, her feet shoulder-width apart, a gun in her hand pointed at the ground. She seemed to be watching something ahead of her. She had brown hair, was slightly taller than Violet, and wearing some sort of black outfit that was skin tight. Her back was to me, and she hadn't noticed me. I held my hand in front of Samuel, an order for him to stay, and held my gun loosely in my hand.

Who was she, and what was she doing in The Green? Could she be a Matrian scientist, gathering up samples for study? If so, she was in really deep—Alejandro never let anyone stray farther away than a day's walk from the boat or camp. Anything more than that risked certain death, in his eyes.

I turned my gaze to where she was staring. The mist hung in the air, casting shadows. Eventually, it roiled as something moved through it. I heard her before I saw her, the sound of her crashing through the undergrowth at her full running speed. Something was definitely chasing her.

The woman moved, pulling her gun up, training it on Violet. I swung my gun around, my heart in my throat. Whoever she was, she was going to hurt Violet.

She squeezed off a shot before I managed to shoot mine. I heard the sound of Violet crumpling on the ground, her body collapsing.

CHAPTER 16

VIOLET

The weightlessness of being lifted away and hauled into the trees ended with a sickening jerk as we landed on a tree branch. I struggled to breathe as the arm wrapped around my waist held me tight, constricting my rib cage.

I was facing down, the ground at least forty feet below me. I started to say something, when suddenly we were airborne again, plummeting toward the ground at nauseating speed. I flinched in anticipation of the impact with the ground when we were hit with another jerk, and started to swing through the air.

I realized that whoever or whatever it was that had grabbed me was using the vines to travel, swinging through gaps in the canopy. I opened my eyes, beholding the ground whizzing past my nose, and decided to shut my eyes again.

Still, the weightlessness persisted, sending the familiar sensation of vertigo racing through me. I felt my stomach clench, and had to concentrate on my breathing to keep from vomiting.

I was well aware of the creature next to me, but too dizzy to open my eyes to inspect it. Its breathing was heavy, like it was becoming more and more winded with each swing.

I heard the creak of a branch under our weight, and I held my breath, anticipating the next leap into nothingness, but after a few seconds, I realized that it had stopped to catch its breath. I was still being held by my waist, face down. To carry this much dead weight with just one arm meant that whatever this thing was, it was incredibly strong. It made me even more apprehensive about opening my eyes.

Yet curiosity was coursing through me. I remembered the strange shadow I had seen with Ms. Dale during our training, and how it had appeared to be the shape of a human. This thing, this creature, was clearly bipedal. Could it be some sort of ... mutation?

I needed to know. Slowly, I cracked open an eye. The ground sat nearly fifty feet below, and the branch we were on was swaying in the wind and under our weight. Immediately, the nausea returned full force, and I gagged a few times in my mask.

Suddenly, the arm around me loosened slightly, and I found it much easier to breathe. I tilted my head to the left and was met with two massive legs, knees slightly bent to maintain balance. The skin was an incandescent black that seemed to both sparkle, and blend in with the environment as it moved. It was bizarre to look at, but as I examined it closer, I began to notice partitions in the black skin that reminded me of the scales on a reptile or snake.

Immediately, a man with a snake's head formed in my imagination, turning my blood cold.

I needed to escape, but despite it loosening its arm around me, it was still holding me in a vice-like grip. I needed for it to loosen up a little bit more. But if I tried anything now, I would end up dead or worse. I had to be patient.

The legs tensed next to me, and the next thing I knew, we were soaring again. Once more, it felt like I had left my stomach behind me, as we dove off the branch in an arc. Then, I heard the snap of the vine catching our weight, felt our fall hit the bottom of the arc before swinging us back up.

That was it, I realized instinctually. There was a point where the vine arrested our fall, and if I could time it right, I might be able to get him to drop me right after. As long as the ground wasn't too far below, I'd survive. Then I'd have to find a place to hide.

My heart sank as I realized the only thing I had on me was my compass. Without a gun or an aerosol canister, I wouldn't be able to hide, let alone survive. I needed to figure out how to get back.

My mind raced, and I carefully reached my trapped arm into my pocket, pulling out the compass. I kept my grip firm on it, well aware that if I dropped it, then I was well and truly dead.

It was hard focusing on the small face of the compass. It took several passes on vines before I could orient it correctly, and then a few more to confirm that whatever the creature was that was holding me was heading in a fixed direction. I sensed that wherever it was taking me was a place that I would never escape from.

I slid the compass back into my pocket, and waited for an opportunity.

I was getting used to predicting the movements of the swing, and gauging the distance to the ground and between arcs. I could tell that the creature was preparing its next swing, as it angled toward a group of vines hanging from the trees. Now was the time.

I went completely limp, allowing my limbs to flop around. As I predicted, the creature gave a grunt of strain, as my weight threw it completely off balance. We were nearing the bottom of the swing when I planted my elbow into its torso. I felt the hard plane of muscles give under the force, heard it grunt, and felt its arms release me. I was aware of it slipping from the vine, but I didn't risk a full glance at it.

Instead, I jerked my hands out in front of me, my hands grasping for another vine as I fell. I snagged a vine with one hand, squeezing it tight. I managed to get my other hand around it, and I gripped the vine hard, hissing in pain as it began to cut into my skin. I slid down several feet before I finally slowed to a stop.

I had closed my eyes after grabbing the vines, and it took me a few seconds before I could open them. When I did, I started laughing hysterically—I was dangling a foot from the ground.

I lowered a shaky leg to the ground, and then the other, eventually releasing my grip on the vines. I grimaced as I opened my hand, blood pouring from ugly cuts bisecting my hand. All of the joints and muscles in my hand ached from the force I had squeezed the vine, but overall, I gauged the damage to be superficial.

Breathing deeply, I took a second to rip off some fabric from my shirt and tie it around my hands. At the rate I was going, I was going to run out of clothes to wear in a matter of days. It struck me again how hopeless it was to even think about surviving out here—everything tried to kill you.

I grabbed the compass and set my direction so that I would hopefully intersect with Viggo. For a second, I considered heading in another direction, away from him. His reluctance to believe me had really hurt, much deeper than I could have imagined. I knew I had hurt him deeply, but his insistence on taking me back to Patrus was only condemning me to death. At least out here, I had a better chance.

Suddenly, something behind me snapped, and I turned. Something shifted in the shadows under the canopy.

I didn't hesitate—I just started running. Hurt or not, Viggo had all the weapons and supplies, as well as the egg. I would need those before I could even think about escaping him.

My heart sank into my belly at the thought of leaving him again. I pushed it aside, and focused on running.

I loved running. I used to run all the time when I was younger, before everything had happened. Before Tim had failed the test and Mom had died. I had never felt comfortable confined to the track either. The streets of Matrus were my running grounds.

But running through the forest was hard—there are a thousand things that can slow a person down or trip them. I ducked branches and dodged trees that sprang up in my way. I spun and twisted, flying across the mossy ground, my feet and arms pumping, hair flying.

It was difficult at first, learning how to breathe through the mask, but after a few minutes, I got the hang of it, taking care to exhale out of my mouth, and down away from my visor so as not to fog it.

I could hear something chasing me. It crashed through the undergrowth behind me, but I felt confident that once I got up to speed, I could get away. When I ran full out, I felt like I could fly.

Trees began to whiz by as I ramped up my speed. Trickles of sweat ran down my skin, but I kept my breathing even and measured.

I came over a crest, taking measured steps as I plummeted down. I could still hear whatever it was chasing me, but I didn't look back. I kept my gaze forward, hoping I was still heading in the correct direction. I was not taking any breaks to check. Once I lost this thing, I would have to focus on finding Viggo.

The mist was growing thick, making it harder to see. I was forced to slow my speed to a trot in order to not plow headfirst into a tree. As I slowed, I became aware of the lack of sound coming from the forest. The hair on my neck stood on end, and I felt, rather than heard, something behind me, nearing me again.

I bolted once more. I caught a glimpse of something coming over the opposite side of the ridge, and I cut toward it, hoping that whatever it was would either be helpful or keep whatever was chasing me distracted while I got away.

Several things happened at once, but at the same time, everything seemed to slow to a stop.

I was aware of something brushing past my hair, causing me to jerk my head to one side.

Then my ankle folded under me as I took a misstep and tripped.

As I began to tumble through the air, I heard the distinct sound of gunfire filling the clearing.

Following that, a line of fire suddenly exploded on my ribcage, making breathing extremely difficult.

Then time caught up with me. I had a glimpse of Viggo's face as I fell, the ground rushing up to greet me. As I fell, I felt a brief moment of confusion at Viggo's ability to defy gravity and be upside down, and then I hit the dirt, the pain in my chest intensifying unbearably as I skidded across the mossy ground.

CHAPTER 17

VIGGO

Violet's name was on my lips as I squeezed the trigger. Red blood erupted from the woman, arcing in the air and splattering on the ground, but I was already racing to Violet's still form.

My heart was pounding so hard I could feel it in my throat. Samuel reached her long before I did, his tail wagging, his tongue licking her fingers. I skidded to a stop, dropping to my knees next to her.

She was lying on her stomach, her face toward me. Her limbs were askew, one leg straight down, the other tucked up, both arms over her head. Her eyes were closed, and I couldn't tell if she was breathing.

I studied her back, and didn't see any blood. My mind raced, recounting my training. If she was hit from the front, and there was no blood coming from her back, that meant that the bullet was still lodged inside her. I would have to be very careful in turning her over—I didn't want to accidentally move the bullet and do more damage.

I reached for a shoulder, and then let go in surprise as Violet's eyes popped open. "Viggo?" she mumbled, her gaze confused.

"Don't move," I said. "You've been shot."

She frowned at me. "No I haven't," she said, starting to push herself up.

I placed a hand on her upper shoulders, pushing her gently down, cursing the interaction for fear of the bullet still lodged inside her. "Violet!"

Giving a sharp huff, she craned her neck around. "Viggo, I'm fine," she insisted, pushing against me.

"Stay down!"

She pushed harder, and then managed to turn on her hip, slipping out from under my hand. She pushed me with both her hands, offsetting my balance. I landed hard on my side, staring at Violet as she stood up, dusting off her pants and her shirt. As she did, I saw that there was no bullet hole. I exhaled in relief.

Violet squinted behind her mask, her gaze darting around, and I stood up. She seemed on guard, her eyes searching the mist. It took me a second, but I picked up on the fact that the forest had fallen deathly still. I quickly undid her cuffs and placed her gun in her hands. "I'm sorry for leaving you unarmed," I said as her hand closed over the butt of the gun.

She gave me a side glance, but didn't respond, her gray eyes darting all around.

"It was right behind me," she said after a moment. We had pressed our backs together, and were moving in a slow circle. I nodded, keeping my focus alert. Samuel had seemed to pick up what was going on, and was circling our legs, keeping close to us.

The silence stretched on and on, both of us very aware of the impending danger. I kept my hands loose, my breathing even as we moved. I could hear Violet still panting behind me, her breathing loud and sharp in my ears.

"You okay?"

I felt her nod. "Yeah. I just got a sharp cramp in my side."

"Not enough potassium," I replied, and she gave a little *tsk*.

"I know that. Luckily, I've got a great excuse."

"Oh yeah," I replied, turning my gaze to the canopy. "What's that?"

"This jerk of a warden wasn't feeding me properly."

I chuckled. "This jerk of a warden just saved your life again."

Violet scoffed. "I don't need you to save my life, Viggo. Besides, I was doing just fine by myself."

"Sure you were," I drawled sarcastically. "I'm pretty sure that I've saved your life four times now."

"No you haven't."

"Shall I count?"

"I'd rather you didn't."

"Because you know I'm right?"

"No," she denied.

I suppressed a smile. The banter was helping keep us calm. Getting under Violet's skin was just a perk.

"First, the Porteque gang," I said. "Second, the centipedes, which I think I should count twice, once for the venom, and the second for the eggs they laid in there."

"They laid eggs in me?" Violet gasped. I could feel her shuddering behind me, and immediately regretted making her aware of that.

"You know what... never mind. It doesn't matter how many times I've saved your life. All that matters is..."

I trailed off, realizing that Violet's back was no longer pressed against mine. I whirled, and found her a few feet of way, squatting down and staring at a spot on the ground.

Cautiously keeping my eyes on the trees, I peered

over her shoulder. There was some sort of blackish liquid soaking into the ground.

"I think you hit it," Violet whispered, staring at the spot.

"Not me, I shot…"

I trailed off. In my haste to get to Violet, I had paid little attention to the woman I had shot. I moved back toward the spot she had collapsed.

Just then, a bird's cry filled the forest, and just as quickly as the silence had started, it disappeared under a cacophony of noise. I felt the tension leaving me. Whatever had been chasing Violet was clearly gone.

I hurried over to the massive tree, my eyes searching the ground for her. The woman was still lying face down on the ground. Blood was seeping from the wound in her shoulder. I turned her over, to find her still breathing, with an exit wound on the other side.

The woman was older, with fine lines around her eyes and mouth. She was probably around forty, with short brown hair. It was clear she kept in impeccable shape—her body was fit and muscular.

Violet pushed in behind me. "Oh my God! That's Ms. Dale," she exclaimed, immediately dropping to her knees next to the woman.

I frowned. "Who is Ms. Dale?"

Violet had begun applying pressure to her wound.

"Give me something to stop the bleeding," she said, tilting her face up at me.

I hesitated. Whoever this woman was, she was dangerous. It was very possible that she had been sent into The Green to retrieve Violet and the egg.

"Violet, you realize this woman—"

Violet nodded. "Yes, I realize that she is probably here to do what you were going to do, only for the Matrians instead of the Patrians. It doesn't matter—Ms. Dale was kind to me once. I am not going to let her bleed out and die here. Besides… this seems to be the week that everyone wants a piece of me."

She said that last bit with such depreciating bleak humor, that I resisted the urge to pull her into a hug. I wanted to promise her that everything was going to be all right, when I knew perfectly well that I couldn't guarantee that.

I sighed and set my bag down, before going through it for supplies. I didn't have much left. There were no more instant bandages, and only one blood patch. I had plenty of anti-toxin and anti-venom pills, but beyond that, not much.

"Vi—" I said.

"What?" she snapped. "You shot her, and all she was doing was trying to save my life."

I sighed. "We have no idea what she was trying to—"

Violet arched an eyebrow at me, her mouth flattening

into a thin line. "This is the woman who taught me to shoot, Viggo. She taught me how to defend myself. They picked *her* to train me for that stupid mission. She is an expert markswoman. She didn't miss me. She was aiming for the thing chasing me."

The conviction pouring off Violet's voice gave me pause, but her drive was one based on emotion, which had no place in the setting we found ourselves in.

"Giving up our limited supplies to help her is risky. We need them so we can guarantee our own survival—"

"Viggo Croft," she hissed, lifting her hands so I could see the blood covering them. "You shot this woman who was only trying to help me. You and I are both aware of the reason she is here, and you need to get this survival mindset out of your head, and return to the land of being a decent human being."

Her words hit me like a sledgehammer. I was behaving coldly, prioritizing our lives as more important than hers. I had decided that she was the "them" in "us versus them", and that her life was expendable.

In that moment, I was suddenly grateful to Violet. Compassion burned in her like a beacon, and I couldn't help but be attracted to it like a moth to a flame. Since my wife had died, I had cut off almost everyone I had known. It was easier that way—easier not to feel. How misguided I was: The feelings didn't go away. I had just buried them under a veneer of calm. I had become so distanced from humanity, so apart from it, that I had forgotten that life was precious.

It didn't mean I was going to trust the older brunette lying on the ground. It just meant that I was going to do my best to help her.

I nodded to Violet and began passing her what she needed. She applied the cotton bandage, but blood was quickly seeping through it. I wrapped a piece of blue fabric around the cotton, and then applied the patch to help her replenish blood.

Afterward, I took a moment to inspect Violet's hands. They were scraped up. I made her open and close them a few times. They weren't broken. I also took a moment to inspect her thigh.

"We'll probably be able to take the bandage off in another day or two," I said, as she pulled her pants back over her hip. She nodded. She'd been pretty quiet throughout the entire ordeal. "What's wrong?"

She shook her head, her gaze on Ms. Dale's unconscious form. She looked pensive, like she was thinking about something.

"What is it?"

"Why her?" she asked, nodding her head to indicate Ms. Dale.

"I don't understand."

"She's not a warden. She's just a self-defense teacher. So why did they send her to find me?" She reached down, gripping the egg with both hands and pulling it out of my bag. "Viggo… we need to figure out what this thing is, and why everyone wants it."

I hesitated, my mind racing. That was a tall order, considering that we had no idea where to begin. Not to mention, it would likely require us to go to Matrus, a place that wasn't exactly welcoming to people like me.

Violet turned to look up at me, her gray eyes searching mine for an answer. Before I could respond to her, Samuel gave a warning bark.

I looked at him, and his body was tense, his ears up. He gave another bark, looking at us, practically vibrating with energy. I could tell that he was on the verge of bolting, but resisting that urge so he could warn us. Violet and I started to pull out our weapons, when I heard something else…

A high pitched sound was permeating through the trees and into the clearing. It was so faint at first that it was hard to hear, but it grew, until the buzzing was a roar in our ears.

Violet and I exchanged glances, and looked down at ourselves. We were covered in blood, and Ms. Dale was still bleeding. There was no way we had escaped the incoming predators' notice.

Without uttering a word, we began gathering our things, urgency lending speed to us. I hauled Ms. Dale over one shoulder, while Violet shouldered my bag. She pressed one aerosol can in my hand, and pulled the two remaining ones out of her pocket.

"Run," she whispered urgently, and together, we started running, knowing that the red flies were not far behind.

CHAPTER 18

VIOLET

As we fled, I couldn't help but think about Viggo's assumption regarding Ms. Dale. There was no other explanation for it. She was there for me, to collect me and bring me back to Matrus. I knew what would happen from there: I'd be convicted of regicide. It didn't matter how much evidence I provided to prove that Lee was the killer. He was dead, which meant no one could exact revenge upon him.

Yet, as far as I knew, Ms. Dale was just a defense teacher. Every year, she would recommend her best students for training with the wardens, some would be accepted, some wouldn't. That was it. She'd lived in the same neighborhood as I did, went to the same stores, did the same chores. She didn't have kids, which was not uncommon for some women—they chose their careers over children—and I had never seen her in any type of relationship with anyone outside the parents and students.

So why would they send her? Was it because she knew me? Or was she more deeply involved than I had thought? I contemplated all of these questions as I watched her bouncing on Viggo's shoulder. I knew it was unlikely that I would ever get all the answers I craved, but I couldn't help but ask them.

I felt like a fly trapped in a massive web, but I could only see a few of the strands that had trapped me. I kept trying to escape so I could see more, but I was caught too tightly, and the spider was settling in over me, about to devour me. Everything that kept happening to me reminded me that a noose was waiting for me, and it seemed like I would never escape.

Although, being in The Green also reminded me that sometimes things just happen. There were things that I could control, and things that I couldn't. It was a waste of energy to worry about the questions, especially with death constantly waiting.

I knew that this was one of those things that we couldn't survive. The swarm of flies were drawn to blood, like bees to pollen. Viggo and I were covered in it, thanks to my insistence on helping Ms. Dale. In spite of our help, her wound was still seeping blood—I could see it dripping on the ground behind us.

As long as she bled, the red flies would find us. No amount of spray in the container would keep us safe and I was exhausted—I felt a bone-deep weariness that made everything around me seem slower. The past four days were all starting to add up and tax my system. Running on fear and adrenaline could only sustain me for so long. After a while, my body would be unable to produce more, and I would crash hard, my body shutting down against my will.

I couldn't think about that, no matter how inevitable it seemed. I had to focus on the task at hand—finding a way to shelter us from the threat of the red flies. I looked up and realized I was falling behind, so I fixed my eyes on Viggo, trying to find the energy to keep up.

My body, however, had other ideas. The stitch in my side from earlier flared up, and as I tried to run faster, it pulled tighter, knocking the air out of my lungs. I had to stop.

"Viggo," I gasped, staggering to a halt.

He paused, and turned. Sweat was pouring from his forehead, making his hair stick to the sides of his face and his mask. His shirt was drenched, his chest heaving as he gasped for air.

We were silent for a second—the buzzing had faded slightly, but we knew that wouldn't be for long.

"I'm not sure we can do this," Viggo breathed, shifting Ms. Dale's unconscious form to his other shoulder.

I nodded in agreement. "We need to hide."

He shook his head. "We can't. Once the red flies sense blood, they hunt out their victim with unerring accuracy. It doesn't take them long to find their prey once they have that taste."

"But if we find a log…"

"A friend of mine is an expert at this. He's tested their response time. It took them three hours to hunt down prey that was over ten kilometers away."

I absorbed the information, my stomach shrinking. "So what can we do?"

Viggo handed me a canteen, and I drank a few sips, not wanting water sloshing around in my belly as we ran. He did the same, and closed the lid.

"I'm not sure," he finally said, but I could see the answer in his eyes.

Abandon Ms. Dale, and run for it.

I would be lying if I said that I hadn't considered the possibility. Once they had her, the swarm would likely ignore us for long enough to escape. We could flee while they drank her dry.

My stomach turned at the thought. No matter what happened, I wasn't leaving anyone behind.

Viggo seemed to notice the determination stamped on my face, because he sighed. "We'll keep an eye out. If we see something we can seal up with the blanket in my bag, we'll try, all right?"

I nodded. Viggo whistled to Samuel, who had been standing next to him, panting the entire time. I watched as both of them started to move again, heading up the hill.

I took a moment to collect myself, and then followed behind them at a light jog.

The sun was setting, creating long dark shadows on the ground. I put one of the aerosol containers in my pocket and pulled out my flashlight, shining it. It did little to illuminate our paths as we ran, but it was better than nothing.

The forest flew by me, and I tried to keep my breathing even. My ears were trying to pick up the high-pitched keening of the flies over the sounds of our footsteps and panting, but since we fled the glen where we had found her, there was nothing. It was almost eerie, like the forest was holding its breath to see what would happen.

I kept trying to find places for us to hide, but it was hard. In the several times I had needed to hide in a log or a hollow, they had seemed plentiful. But this part of the forest was denying us any spark of hope.

I cut over to the first log I spotted, using the flashlight to illuminate the area. I inspected it quickly, but my heart sank. It had multiple holes along its length, likely left behind by some wood boring insect. Viggo's blanket was too small for it to cover everything.

We started running again, and I kept my eyes peeled. I eventually saw a tree with a hollow spot in the center. The top half of the tree had collapsed, leaving the top part of the trunk a jagged ruin, with wooden slivers jutting up. I dashed over it, ahead of Viggo, and shined my flashlight inside. The hollow was a little more than a crack—there would be room for one of us to hide, but no more. I sighed, and resumed running.

The third place was one of those trees where the roots erupted from the ground like walls. I thought we could string the blanket up between two of them, and seal it off from detection, but the roots were spread too far apart, even at the base. There was no way it would work.

I felt my final sliver of hope diminish as the last trickle of light disappeared from the canopy.

Viggo had stopped to drink more water, and I jogged up next to him before stopping. Fire was raging under my skin as the muscles in my legs burned. I placed my hands on my knees to keep from collapsing, sucking in air through the mask.

"Vi—" Viggo said, his voice soft.

I shook my head. "No," I insisted, knowing what he was going to say.

He sighed and placed a hand on my shoulder. "You are my priority," he said, simply.

I gazed into his green eyes for a long moment. I was on the verge of saying *okay*, of agreeing to leave Ms. Dale there, when Samuel barked.

Turning the light on him, I saw him facing the way we'd come, his ears up and his body low. He was quivering in fear.

I heard it seconds later. The buzzing from the swarms I had heard before were nothing compared to this. It was the sound of a massive body of water crashing on the earth—angry and loud. I turned my flashlight, and saw flashes of red making a beeline for us. We had paused for too long.

"Run," I shouted, turning on my heel. Viggo had already started running with me. I was relieved to see that he was carrying Ms. Dale, but in a few minutes, it might not matter.

Once again, I was going to be responsible for the deaths of the people I cared about. But I wasn't ready to give up yet.

I ran behind Viggo, keeping up with him as fear fueled our legs to move fast. I kept a canister of aerosol ready, just in case.

The buzzing drew nearer, and as the light from my flashlight bounced over the ground, I saw a flash of crimson. It hit me in the chest.

I looked down in time to see it shoving its needle nose into the flesh of my skin. I slapped it, feeling its body crunch under my hand, its crushed body spurting the blood it had just absorbed all over my shirt and chest. I noticed more coalescing, and could see that one was on the back of Viggo's neck. I quickly used the aerosol container, and sprayed it.

It fell off, but more were coming.

The insidious thing about red flies, I realized, was that you could hardly feel their bite. Another one landed on me, using its six long legs to clamp down on my skin. For all I knew, there were already a hundred on my back, draining me dry.

I smashed that one, and began spraying the aerosol can behind me, trying to ward them away. It helped, a little. I raced up so that I was running alongside Viggo, spraying us both with the can.

"Here," I shouted over the cacophony of noise. I thrust the flashlight into his hand and pulled out the other aerosol.

I began spraying both of us in a frenzy. Wave after wave of red flies swooped in to bite us, but they veered off whenever I was spraying the mist. I was keeping them away by doing it, but it was only a temporary measure—I would run out of spray long before they lost interest in us.

Viggo was faltering under Ms. Dale's weight. I could tell from how he was running. He was winded, and constantly trying to shift her weight around so that they wouldn't trip, but he couldn't keep it up for much longer.

Then the flashlight beam cut across some trees, and I saw a blinding flash of white peeking through the green and brown fronds. It was hard to see, like the trees and leaves were there intentionally, keeping it hidden.

As my mind raced, the light again cut across it, stunning my eyes with its brightness. I remembered the flash of white that I had seen from the canopy, before I had crashed. And now again here.

From the air, I hadn't really been able to make it out. Down here… it seemed uniform. Consistently the same. The white was unnatural and foreign, way out of place for The Green. My mind was scrambling to try and identify it.

Whatever it was, it was worth checking out. I grabbed Viggo's arm, shouting for him to follow, and then cut toward it. I pushed through the dense undergrowth and when I emerged on the other side, I almost stopped moving when I realized what it was. Excitement coursed through me, and I yelled for Viggo again.

It was a building.

CHAPTER 19

VIGGO

Running while carrying a woman is no easy feat, even for someone in as good a shape as I was. Running for your life while carrying a woman was an impossible task. I wasn't even sure how I was accomplishing it at this point. It was like I had flipped a switch in my mind that had turned off everything essential, except what I needed to run. It felt mechanical, like I was a robot, only capable of running, yet it freed my mind to think about some things.

I hated suggesting that we leave Ms. Dale behind. It was a practical suggestion, but it still didn't sit right with me. I knew that Violet had, and likely was, still considering it. I understood her hesitation, I shared it with her. I wasn't eager to have someone's death on my hands.

I imagine it was worse for Violet. She had seen so much death the past few days, and been responsible for more than a few. I could tell that her decision to rescue Ms. Dale was a bit of a selfish one, for multiple reasons.

The first was that the two women shared an emotional connection. Violet was downplaying it, but I had picked up on it when she had talked about her. There was an affection there, which made sense, considering Ms. Dale had clearly been a mentor for Violet.

The death that had been haunting Violet for a while was also playing a major role in her decision. I could see the guilt and regret in her eyes when she talked about the deaths of the last few days—she hadn't wanted anyone to die—she felt responsible. Because of that, it was like she was trying to prove to herself, and the world, that she could actually save someone. I wasn't sure that Violet was aware of that drive, but it was readily apparent to me.

But I could also tell that Violet wasn't only considering her emotions in saving Ms. Dale. There was a logical reasoning behind it. Violet had questions, and Ms. Dale could have some answers. It was all about surviving until she could get those answers.

I couldn't blame Violet for being selfish: I had questions as well. The mysterious egg that was the focus of all this, and Lee's letter… It was nagging at me, like an unfinished puzzle with missing pieces. I guessed that was why I decided to become a warden. A lot of people, when they saw my size and fighting prowess, assumed I became a warden for the more violent aspect of it, but I liked solving things, and was more intrigued about understanding the why and the how, than beating down the who.

Truth be told, I only liked fighting in the ring. I liked the rules and the structure of it. Causing harm to someone was better if they knew that they had signed up for it, as twisted as that sounds. There was an expectation in cage fighting, a knowledge shared by both competitors, that someone would get hurt, and we accepted it.

Most people who committed crimes or did illegal things did it with the hope of not hurting others. In fact, they tried everything to avoid it. Most crimes were non-violent, so there was a certain expectation that their arrest, if it came, would be non-violent as well. This wasn't always the case, but it made me uncomfortable to inflict violence upon them when they didn't accept that as a reality of their crime. It didn't stop me from doing my job, of course, but it did keep me from being aggressive toward criminals who hadn't hurt anyone physically when they committed their crime.

Of course, if they met me with violence, then I had no problem showing them exactly how violent I could be…

Violet's hand on my shoulder jerked my mind back to reality. I had been running on auto-pilot, but now I felt blood pouring from multiple bite wounds on my neck and arm—Violet had been doing her best to keep the red flies off of me, but they'd still gotten through.

I glanced over at her. She was pointing off to the left, and shouting something. I realized that I was having problems understanding her—likely the blood loss and exhaustion were messing with my senses.

She shouted something again, her lips forming words that seemed foreign to me. I blinked, trying to clear the cobwebs from my head and focus on the now.

"Viggo!" Violet said, her hand squeezing my arm tightly.

"Yeah!" I responded.

"Flashlight!"

I held out the flashlight, which she took, replacing it with an aerosol can. I immediately began spraying it over me and Ms. Dale, letting the cool mist envelop us. I could feel the sting on my skin as some of the droplets made contact with open wounds. I knew there were a lot more we couldn't see.

Violet took off in the direction she had pointed, and

I followed. It seemed like she was moving toward the densest part of the foliage. I wanted to shout at her to stop, because running through that would be dangerous. Then I realized, the density of it would help provide cover from the massive swarm that was threatening to envelop us. It would help diffuse their numbers, and if they collided with a tree or branch hard enough, they would die.

I admired her sharpness as I pushed through the leaves. Using the forest as a shield was dangerous, and we had to slow down our pace considerably, but still, it would probably help more than it hurt.

I had barely started running in the thicket, when suddenly I was out of it again, a giant white structure looming up in front of me. I pivoted, making a hard left, and I heard the soft plops as the red flies chasing me hit the wall at breakneck speeds.

A path was carved out around the structure, and I followed Violet's bobbing flashlight beam, chasing after her. How had she known this was here? It was exactly what we needed—but it was such an odd find that it almost seemed surreal.

There were no windows, and I could tell the structure was made of concrete. The path around it had been carved out from the wilderness, but as I ran, I could see that the surrounding plant life remained. In fact, it seemed like it had been cultivated, which was smart. It was perfectly hidden, buried deep in The Green.

It wasn't very big, either. I rounded the corner after about twenty feet, and came to another wall about forty feet long. Violet was already turning the corner to the next part, and I pounded after her, Ms. Dale flopping against my back.

The red flies were back, buzzing around me. I compressed the nozzle to the spray, keeping them off us, but it slowed me down a little. I could hear Violet shouting from ahead.

I staggered around the corner, my breathing now coming in ever shorter bursts. Violet rushed toward me, excitement lit upon her features.

"There's a door," she shouted. I nodded, and struggled to put one foot in front of the other. My legs were shaky. I could see the silver entrance ahead, but my vision was becoming blurred.

As Violet continued spraying me, I felt the sting from a dozen new bites. I realized that they had been on me, biting me all along. Blood was also dripping from several bites on Ms. Dale. We were slathered in the stuff.

Violet grabbed me, trying to pull me after her. I watched the excitement morph into concern, and realized I was growing dizzy. I felt like I was lying on my back, trying to watch people who were upside down.

Then I remembered Samuel. "The dog," I rasped. "Where is he?"

Violet shook me, and said something again. I stared at her blankly. Blood was pouring from her now, and I realized that I was holding her back. Samuel would be okay—he was a resourceful dog. If he had been smart, he would have fled into the jungle away from us. Violet, however, wouldn't abandon us to save herself.

Looking into those gray eyes, I did the only thing I could to save her life.

"Go," I said, pulling Ms. Dale off my shoulder and thrusting her into Violet's arms. She staggered under the other woman's sudden weight, but I was already stumbling away from her.

I heard Violet shouting, presumably my name, as I moved out of the reach of the aerosol spray. Immediately, the red flies swarmed me. I couldn't feel their bites, but I could feel thousands of wings beating across my skin as they pelted against me.

I sank to my knees, struggling to smash as many as I could. Their bodies burst under my hands, as I released even more blood from their bodies into the air, encouraging the feeding frenzy. I couldn't hear Violet over the sound of the red flies, so I had to hope that she took the opportunity I had created for her to make it to the door.

I felt my body start to give out. I began to fall over, the dizziness and exhaustion overwhelming my will to remain upright.

But something caught me before I could hit the ground. I looked up, and there was Violet, one hand on the back of my neck, her fist full of the collar of my shirt. I watched as she struggled to pull me with one hand, her hand using the other to spray the aerosol can over us.

I felt a surge of anger at her for disregarding my noble self-sacrifice. I was literally sacrificing my life for hers, and she was still risking her neck to save me.

Ironically enough, that anger helped fuel my exhausted limbs. I clung to it, using it to stand up, and start staggering to the door. Behind me, I heard Violet spraying the aerosol container, keeping the swarm at bay. The aerosol can was failing, I could make out the hissing sound of it cutting in and out.

I didn't look back, knowing if I did I wouldn't make it to the door. I staggered over the threshold, tripping over Ms. Dale's unconscious body as I did so. I managed to catch myself, but I sat down hard, the dizziness making my vision grow dark.

I heard Violet shutting the massive airlock door behind us. Several red flies got in, swarming over Ms. Dale.

Violet was bleeding from several spots, blood trickling down her neck and arms. She stepped over Ms. Dale, her movements disjointed. I could only watch as she reached the other side of the small room.

I wasn't sure what her intention was, but it became clear to me as she hit a red button that was glowing dimly on the other wall. Immediately, a white gas started pouring from the ceiling, covering us all.

And then everything went black.

CHAPTER 20

VIOLET

I pulled the airlock door closed, my tired muscles straining against the weight of it. It took effort, and I was rapidly running out of energy. But we were so close to surviving, I just needed to close the door.

I succeeded, but several of the red flies had gotten in. I swiped at my arms, dislodging them, but I could make out more of the red creatures on Ms. Dale and Viggo. Viggo had collapsed on the other side of the room.

I felt a surge of anger toward him and his pig-headed need to sacrifice himself for me. It was irritating that he felt this need to save my life all the time, which had been what had fueled me to completely disregard his sacrifice and rescue him. I made a mental note to talk to him about that later—if we survived.

I staggered over Ms. Dale's body toward the opposite

wall. My limbs felt like jelly, my legs were quivering with each step I took. I could tell by the glazed look in Viggo's eyes that he was in a similar state. His face was pale; his lips had lost all color. The blood staining his clothes looked almost black under the dim lighting.

I saw the glowing red button like a beacon and suddenly remembered where I had seen something like this before: At one of the work camps, there had been a quarantine room like this, to help remove hazardous waste and biological hazards from the workers.

Placing all of my hope in the button, I pressed it, and then allowed myself the luxury of collapsing. I wasn't sure what would happen next, but I couldn't kill the remaining red flies in here. If I missed even one, or passed out before I could kill them all, we were finished.

As a white gas poured from the ceiling, I heard a hiss, and my eardrums tightened. I realized the room had become pressurized. I swallowed, forcing my ears to pop.

I watched as the gas filled the chamber, obscuring everything. I heard the buzzing of the red flies as they endeavored to escape it, but there was nowhere to go. I could hear and feel their bodies falling, one by one, until the buzzing was gone.

I wasn't sure how long the gas persisted, but the important thing was that our masks filtered out whatever had killed the red flies. Although, given the state of Viggo and Ms. Dale, the waiting would likely also cause their death. I twisted my head, looking up to the button. There was something new flashing just underneath.

I pushed myself to my knees and looked at it. There was a sequence of numbers counting down in flashing yellow. I watched as the numbers counted down from sixty, tension growing in my back. What if there was some sort of passcode I had to enter before the chamber vaporized the gas or something? I looked around for some sort of key pad or panel, running my fingers across the wall for any sign of it, but couldn't find anything except the button and the timer. I went to the door, struggling against the massive wheel that was there, but it was jammed into place.

I turned back to the timer as it hit zero. There was a soft hissing sound, and I opened my eyes. The gas that had flooded the chambers was being sucked out. The panel under the button was now counting down again, this time from thirty. I waited this time, watching it closely.

The white gas had completely dissipated in thirty seconds, and the panel turned green, flashing the word "Clear" across it.

Tentatively, I placed my hand on the wheel, but

instead of finding resistance, it seemed to spin eagerly this time. I opened it gently, expecting to see people on the other side. Instead, it opened up to a concrete room about twenty feet wide and ten feet deep, with glass lockers containing white suits in them. There were also metal lockers on one wall, with names posted on them. I looked at them, but they were obviously surnames with no indication as to their gender, giving me no clues as to who owned this place.

This was some sort of research facility. It was unclear if it was a Matrian or Patrian facility, but given that it was on the Matrian side of the river, it seemed most likely to be Matrian.

I looked over at Viggo, who seemed to be bouncing in and out of consciousness. Taking a breath, I reached up and removed the mask with a pop. I took an experimental breath of air, and was rewarded for it.

I immediately pulled Viggo's mask off, and then Ms. Dale's. I looked around for Samuel, but he wasn't with us. I bit my lip, worried for the dog. It was tempting to pull Ms. Dale and Viggo into the chamber and take one of the suits to go look for him.

That was until I realized how much Ms. Dale was bleeding. She had more bites then Viggo and I put together. I needed to tend to them first, and then go look for Samuel. That meant finding medical supplies.

I hesitated—this facility was clearly being used by people, or at least it had been. But where were they? Surely, they had some sort of security presence. Whoever they were—they wouldn't come to The Green and create this facility only to hide from intruders, right?

It was eerie. I pulled the gun out of my pocket and checked the magazine. The clip was full. I slammed it back into the hilt, and stepped into the secondary chamber. There was a door opposite of me, so I crossed to it and started to open it.

"Violet?" came Viggo's hoarse voice from behind me.

I paused, and went back to him. His eyes were glazed and he seemed disoriented. I pulled the canteen from his pocket and placed it on his lips, pouring some into his mouth. He took several long sips.

"We're inside," I said as he drank. "I'm going to see if I can find any medical supplies for you and Ms. Dale. Wait here."

I set the canteen in his hand. Viggo reached for me, trying to stop me, but I deftly avoided his grasp, and headed back to the hatch across from the airlock.

It was difficult to ignore my own weakness. I wasn't even sure how I was still going at this point. The door was heavy, and it took every scrap of effort to open it, but I eventually got it open.

Panting, I leaned against it, feeling it push against me. As I crossed the threshold, it swung closed, sealing me in.

That was an interesting feature—the doors closed themselves. It must be for security purposes. There were similar doors at one of the work camps I had been assigned to. It was in case of fires—the doors were always closed in case of a fire. It would seal people in to die, but it would keep the rest of the facility safe from the flames.

The next room was a hallway. Ensconced lights filled the room with a sickly yellow glow, but the light didn't hurt my eyes. The hallway stretched for another ten feet, ending at another door. I leaned against the wall heavily as I made my way to it.

The wheel practically turned itself, reminding me that there were likely people about, and I pushed it open slowly, stepping over the threshold and letting it fall closed behind me. This room was another hallway, but with doors and windows lining the walls. Moving forward, I began looking through the windows. The rooms behind them were filled with a mixture of lab equipment and medical equipment.

I didn't know much about either, but most things seemed to be for scanning or blood samples, though the last room was set up like a hospital ward.

Twisting the hand wheel, I opened it up, the smell of antiseptic flooding my nostrils. There were two massive cabinets off to the side. I focused on them.

I pulled on the cabinet doors, but they were locked. Frowning, I moved over to the desk and began searching through the drawers, looking for keys. Luck seemed to be on my side, because I found several of them on a ring in the second drawer, set neatly in a bowl in the corner. I snatched them up, and began inserting them into the lock.

It took a few keys, but finally I unlocked them. I started grabbing things I recognized, placing them in a bedpan that had been sitting on the bed. Alcohol swabs, blood patches, band aids all went in. I wasn't sure if the bite from a red fly was venomous as well, and there were several vials of liquids I didn't recognize.

Viggo would know better than me about those, I figured, as I collected more things. I grabbed a saline bag for Ms. Dale. I wasn't sure how it worked, I just knew it was something you did at hospitals. I just hoped I could wake Viggo up for long enough to guide me in stabilizing her.

I tucked the keys into my pocket and scooped the bedpan of supplies up from the bed.

For a second, I paused, staring at the bed. It was so tempting to just lay down and close my eyes for a minute. I felt the need to rest like a heavy weight pressing down on me, like a warm blanket.

I shook my head, taking a deep breath. I could rest later, once I had saved everyone's lives.

Grinning at the thought, I staggered out in the hallway. I wanted to laugh, it was so preposterous. I was going to save Viggo's life. I had saved Viggo's life for once. Now, he couldn't make his stupid teasing comments about all the times he saved me, because I had saved him too.

After I actually finished the saving. And got some sleep. And saved Samuel. And explored this strange building. And discovered the secret of the egg. Then I'd do it.

I started chuckling at my absurd mental checklist—it was impossible—just like the fact that I was alive at this very moment. That I had finally succeeded in saving people, not killing them. I laughed so hard that tears streamed down my eyes, until I realized I was crying.

My hands were shaking and I was shuddering with each breath. It was all hitting me at once—everything. For the last four days—less than a week—I had endured a trial and a half of pain, betrayal, emotional upheaval, and fought for my life and the lives of others. I was tired beyond words, emotionally drained, and mentally exhausted.

I deserved the tears that were flooding down my cheeks. I had earned them in blood and sweat, and by defying the odds. I had defied death itself and won, at least for the moment.

I sat down and cried, well aware that Viggo and Ms. Dale were waiting for me in the air locked room. The thought of it sent waves of panic through me, which in turn made me feel guilty. I rationalized that I wasn't panicking because they were depending on me, although that didn't help. No, I was panicking because of how tired I was.

Sleep deprivation was a difficult thing for the mind to handle. My brain needed sleep so that I could function, and because of the lack of sleep, I was breaking down, and I knew it. I just needed to hold it together until I could get Viggo up. He could take care of Ms. Dale and himself.

I felt the tears continuing to fall, my eyes raw, but I picked myself up anyway. I felt dead and empty as I made my way back.

Viggo was leaning against the wall on the other side of the door, his expression relieved as he looked at me. I tried to feel relieved too, but I couldn't. Wordlessly, I held out the supplies while hot tears slipped from my eyes and down my cheeks.

CHAPTER 21

VIGGO

Violet was breaking down, and I didn't blame her. When she opened the door with tears running down her face, holding out a bedpan of medical supplies, I ignored them completely, and pulled her to my chest, wrapping my arms around her.

Her shoulders shook as she sobbed, her tears collecting on the front of my chest. I stroked her hair, letting her cry it out. I held her for several minutes, the sounds of her choking sobs filling the small room.

"I shouldn't be crying," Violet breathed against me, as her tears started to subside. "We still have work to do."

I placed a finger under her chin, tipping her head back so she was looking at me. Her eyes were like twin storm clouds, threatening to spill over again. Deep dark bags had formed under her eyes, and her face was streaked with blood and grime.

She had never looked more beautiful. Without thinking, I dipped my head and pressed my mouth against hers. For a second, she was still, frozen under my mouth, and then she softened, her lips parting. She wrapped her arms around my shoulders, pulling her body flush against mine. I cupped her face and her neck, feeling her pulse beating strong under my fingertips.

After savoring her for a long moment, I broke the kiss, and rested my forehead against hers.

"We're alive," I whispered, using my thumb to stroke away her tears. "You saved us all, Violet. We're safe."

"I lost Samuel," she wheezed.

I shook my head. "Samuel is smart, and better equipped to survive. We'll find him."

She nodded, sucking her bottom lip between her teeth. "I'm so tired, Viggo," she whispered, and I could see the exhaustion was more than just physical. She needed to rest.

"Okay. Tell you what. Help me move Ms. Dale to a bed. I'll patch both of us while you get a little sleep, okay?"

She hesitated, her eyes searching mine. "What about you? You need to sleep too."

I nodded. "We'll sleep in shifts." I had no intention of waking her up, of course. She could forgive me this one little white lie.

Violet needed sleep more than I did. She was on the verge of mental breakdown, and we couldn't afford for her to have one, not at this juncture. Besides, I was worried about her. I wanted her to feel safe and secure, and get some much-needed rest. I didn't mind suffering for that.

Violet nodded, and then paused again. "This place… we have no idea where the people are or when they'll be back. We need to search it. Do you think it's a Matrian facility, given that it's on Matrus' side of the river?" she asked.

I nodded, tucking a piece of hair behind her ear. "It probably is Matrian, but until we know for sure I'll secure the floor and barricade the doors. If anyone is here, we'll know it, and handle it from there. It will be all right, Vi. We'll handle it as it comes, together. I promise."

The look of relief on her face was worth it. She leaned into me, pressing her ear against my chest and wrapping her arms around my waist. I bound my arms around her, and she gave a soft little sigh in response.

I gave us a moment to just hold each other, because we both needed the comfort the other provided. We shared the knowledge that we had both nearly died, multiple times, and we just needed a moment to feel alive and safe.

After the embrace was over, we went back for Ms. Dale. I had managed to drag her through the inner airlock door, but my strength wasn't limitless. Together, Violet and I pulled her onto our shoulders, her legs dragging between us as we took her into the medical suite.

Violet slapped a blood patch on me, which began working immediately. I noticed things were a little brighter, my focus much clearer. I began inspecting Ms. Dale. I had limited medical knowledge, but luckily the medical supplies made it much easier.

I put a blood patch on her, and then began cleaning her up, cutting her outfit off of her so I could assess the damage. Of the three of us, she had the most red fly bites. They were everywhere—the flies had even penetrated the rubber soles of her shoes to get to the bottom of her feet.

"Alejandro told me red fly saliva was an anticoagulant," I told Violet as she helped me undress the woman. "They bite the victims, leaving a puncture hole no bigger than a needle mark, but blood will continue to flow until the chemical in their saliva is neutralized."

Violet nodded, her eyes wide. "So even though we have the blood patches on, it's only a stop gap measure?"

I nodded. "In the cabinet, did you see any packets that look similar to this?" I held out the white packet with the yellow diagonal slash running through it. Violet nodded, and went over to grab a few.

I ripped one open with my teeth, and began pouring the powder over the bites. It immediately foamed when it came into contact with them. Violet stared for a second, then grabbed a packet and began helping me apply it. We started with her back, which was the worst, and then flipped her over to work on her front.

If Violet was uncomfortable with Ms. Dale's nudity, she gave no indication of it. She remained focused and professional in her assistance. Eventually, we got all the bites, and I began working on her shoulder. I cleaned it out, making sure that there was nothing in it, and then applied the same paste that I had used on Violet's thigh. She was going to have a scar, but I didn't think there would be any long-term damage.

After she was patched up, I hooked her up to an IV bag. I pumped in a few milligrams of antibiotics. That was all I could do.

I turned to Violet. "Let me check you over, and then you can get some sleep."

She nodded, smoothing some of Ms. Dale's hair out of her face. "She'll be okay?"

I nodded. "I think she'll pull through, but…" I hesitated, unsure of how Violet would take what I was about to say.

Violet glanced up at me, her face neutral as she studied me. "You want to lock her up," she said simply, looking back down at the older woman. Smoothing a lock of hair from her forehead, Violet stared at the older woman for a long moment. "It's for the best," she whispered. "Even if she's not here for me, she's still dangerous." I watched as she pulled a blanket over Ms. Dale's body.

"Give me the cuffs," she said, holding out her hand. I pulled them out of my pocket, and handed them to Violet. She slipped one onto the hand without an IV, and then secured the other end to the bedframe. The bed was bolted to the floor, so it was unlikely that she could move it.

I looked at Violet. "Just until we know why she's really here," I said, trying to reassure her. She shrugged and I suppressed a sigh. Violet's melancholy was deepening, her exhaustion playing havoc with her emotions. We both knew the reason Ms. Dale was there—for Violet.

"I know. I'm tired. You're tired. Let's get patched up

and find you somewhere to sleep."

She bit her lower lip, and stared over my shoulder out into the hall. "I think we should explore more," she said finally.

I sighed, and shifted my weight from one leg to another. "Violet, you need to rest. You've been pushing yourself too hard, and so have I, for that matter. After we rest, we can explore."

"Aren't you the least bit curious? What is this facility doing out here—why was it built and when and for what reason?"

I shrugged. "All good questions, but not important at this moment. The facility will be here when we wake up."

"Unless whoever is here finds us and arrests us."

"Like I said, I'll stay awake."

"Then we'll have to run again. The red flies are probably still waiting outside. I am wearing clothes covered in blood. If we have to escape, we'll probably just run back into them."

I processed her logic, and in spite of my exhaustion, I found myself agreeing. "Okay," I relented. "But only after we get this bleeding handled. A few bites can kill you from blood loss, if you don't stop it."

I handed Violet a few packets of the powder and took a few for myself. I watched her disappear into the room across the hall.

"Call me if you need help with your back," I said.

She nodded, and offered me a ghost of a smile as she slowly closed the door between us. I returned it, and then moved to the next suite, uncomfortable with the thought of Ms. Dale waking up to a naked male in the room.

Blood was still streaming from them, with no sign of abating, so I began to pour the powder over my bites. It stung, but it was tolerable.

I was able to reach most of the spots, but my back was a problem, and I was guessing Violet's was as well. I slipped my pants over my hips, buttoning them, and moved out into the hallway. Violet was already there, her shirt clutched to her chest.

She shuffled nervously, and then turned around, pulling her hair over her shoulder. I sucked in a sharp breath as I took in the curve and shape of her back. It was wrong of me to feel attracted to her in that moment—she had several bites that were leaking blood—but I did. It took me a moment to jerk out of it.

I grabbed the packet and began pouring it over her wounds. She watched me from the corner of her eye, but I worked quickly, reminding myself she needed medical attention. Then I handed her my packet and turned around.

I tensed as I felt her finger press against each bite,

applying the powder directly. I suddenly recalled the night we had kissed in my cabin, and the bite of her nails and fingers as she dug into my shoulders, our mouths devouring each other.

I was tired—exhausted, really—and incredibly attracted to her right now. It was difficult to maintain control at that moment.

As soon as she was done, I snatched the packet from her hands and retreated to my room, grating out a very insincere thank you as I did so. As I closed the door, I saw her smirk at me, a mischievous twinkle playing in her luminous gray eyes, and I grit my teeth, closing the door.

I got dressed quickly. The clothes were dirty and soaked with blood, but it was all I had. While I dressed, I tried to get Violet's bare skin and the feel of her hands on my back out of my head. It was hard, but I managed.

I opened the door and stepped into the hall, to find Violet waiting. "You ready?" I asked, keeping my voice more clipped than necessary.

She nodded, and pulled her gun out of her pocket, checking the magazine. I did the same.

We stood there for a second, staring at each other. Violet went up on her tip toes and pressed her mouth against mine for a chaste kiss.

"Sorry," she whispered as she lowered herself back down.

I nodded wordlessly, and nodded my head to the door, unable to speak for fear of unleashing all of my pent up passion on her. She nodded, and headed toward the door while I followed from behind, trying to keep my mind on the mission at hand.

CHAPTER 22

VIOLET

I didn't know what I had been doing teasing Viggo like that. It had to be some form of temporary insanity brought on by sleep deprivation. It hadn't been intentional, but when I had heard his breathing change after I turned and presented my back, I felt a flush of pleasure that I could make him respond to me like that.

I had to touch him. He never said that we couldn't apply the powder directly, so I did, taking my time to dab it on each wound. His back was sculpted and muscular, just like his front. The track of his spine was a deep valley that ran from his neck to his tailbone, and framed by two divots in his lower back.

I had been so mesmerized by those divots that I almost forgot that there was a medical need for him to be exposed to me.

I shook my head, trying to clear my thoughts from the intense urges overcoming me. My exhaustion was causing a clear impulse control problem in me. At least, I hoped it was the exhaustion.

The thought that I couldn't control myself around Viggo frightened me. It gave him a power over me, one that would make me vulnerable. I couldn't trust it.

My hands were shaking as I finished applying the medicine. I felt guilty as he moved away from me, his eyes downcast.

It was why I had apologized. We hadn't really talked about *us*. Save for a few kisses that had completely unhinged me, I had no idea where we stood. The dynamic had certainly shifted, but that didn't mean that he necessarily was interested in me like that, right?

Not to mention, I had been part of a plot to set him up. He was struggling with it: I could tell from his actions and reactions. Yet there was something there— some chemistry that kept drawing us together. He had to feel it too, gauging from his reaction in the hallway. I just wasn't sure if it was even possible at this point. I had betrayed his trust in a very intimate way—was there any coming back from that?

I quietly laughed at myself as I pushed open the door. My brooding was useless: I was focusing on the wrong thing. I could deal with my feelings about Viggo later.

Right now, we needed to check out this facility.

The next door led to a stairwell, leading down. Like the previous level of the facility, it had a very industrial feel to it. The steps were corrugated metal but solid. I moved down the stairs, keeping the wall at my back. Looking down the next flight, I saw another door waiting.

Still no sign of people. Come to think of it—I didn't see any cameras either. Frowning, I examined the ceiling closely, looking for anything that loosely resembled a security feature.

"Viggo, do you see any cameras or anything?" I asked.

He looked around, his green eyes searching. After a moment, he frowned. "No. That's weird."

I nodded in wordless agreement. This facility was designed for secrecy—it was built in a place no one could easily survive—so why wouldn't they put up cameras to ensure that no one accidentally stumbled upon it?

That could explain why no one had come up to confront us though.

I moved down the steps to the next door, Viggo following me. We exchanged a glance, and pulled it open. He moved in first, and I followed.

This level had a similar configuration to the first, without the suit chamber at the end. As a result, the hall was longer. Unlike the medical suites, there were no windows on the wall, just door after door. The floor was also covered in a deep navy carpet. Viggo opened the first door on the left, revealing a bedroom. I opened the one on the right, revealing another bedroom.

I stepped inside. There was an inner door, leading to a bathroom, a wardrobe, a desk, and a bookshelf. It was cozy, almost homey, with personal touches here and there to help enforce the feeling of home. It was clearly designed to be lived in long term.

Yet things were messy in both rooms, clothes strewn about. There was no indication of who had stayed there. There were no computers on the desk. I flipped up a picture, featuring a woman and two children—one girl and one boy. The frame was intact, but the glass was broken. It had been knocked over.

"This is kind of spooky," I murmured, giving voice to my thoughts.

Viggo made a grunt of agreement. "It looks like they left in a hurry," he said after a moment.

"So, do you think they abandoned the facility?"

He shrugged. "Maybe they went back to Matrus for Queen Rina's funeral."

"Hm. But to leave it completely empty like this?"

He stared down the hallway, his face pensive. "I don't know," he replied.

"What if they are Patrian, and they abandoned the facility after the bombing? Too much risk for exposure?"

Viggo considered this and nodded. "It's possible. It's a risky gambit though."

"What better place to hide than in someone's backyard," I said blithely.

He looked at me from the corner of his eye, the corner of his lip upturned. "We have no evidence either way."

"Maybe there will be something on a lower level?"

Viggo met my eyes, and I could see the doubt there. "Maybe," he said.

I led the way back to the hallway after casting one long glance at the bathroom. The thought of a shower was a compelling enough reason to work quickly. I promised myself that I would return soon, and then moved down the hall to the next door.

We moved cautiously to the next floor.

"This design is smart," Viggo remarked.

I shot him a look. "How do you mean?"

"Well, each set of stairs is a natural choke point and you have to pass through each level to get down them. If someone enters, they have to follow this path no matter what. It gives the people a better chance of defense. If you can seal them in, or set up a defense in time, you can essentially stop them before they do too much damage."

I contemplated the design while he opened the door. It sounded smart, but to me, it felt like a trap. With no way to quickly move up and down through the levels, any catastrophe happening in the middle would spell death for the inhabitants.

The door opened silently, and immediately, the rich smell of wet dirt filled our nostrils. We exchanged looks, and then I slipped through the door, my gun pointed at the floor.

This room took up the entire length and width of the room above, but had an open floor space. It was brimming with life in the form of trees and plants. I realized a second afterward that all the plants were food, and the trees were producing fruit.

We were probably thirty or forty feet down, which meant it was some sort of hydroponic greenhouse. There were likely ultraviolet lights that acted as sunlight. I had worked on a hydroponic farm once—but the yields from the harvest were nothing like this. The plant life here was flourishing.

"This is amazing. Violet, have you ever seen a farm like this?"

I nodded, my eyes taking in the variety of plant life. "I visited one as part of my re-education program, but it wasn't this successful."

Viggo turned his head to look at me, a questioning look on his face. "What do you think makes it so successful?"

I shook my head. "No idea. I'm not a botanist. I just picked the stuff."

"So does that mean this place might not be a Matrian facility?"

Biting my lip, I shook my head. "If not a Matrian one, then who do you think it belongs to?"

Viggo considered the question and then shrugged. "It seems most likely that it is Matrian, but it is entirely possible it's Patrian. We should keep our eyes peeled for any evidence either way."

I nodded in wordless agreement. Reaching up, I plucked a huge shiny red apple from the tree. When we got produce from Patrus, it was normally the worst parts of the crop. When I'd lived there, I had been pleasantly surprised by the quality of the produce they had.

My stomach growled suddenly and loudly, reminding me that for the past four days, I had eaten nothing but protein gel. Opening my mouth, I bit into the apple, letting the taste and juice explode on my tongue. I moaned in pleasure as I blithely chewed the sweet flesh.

Viggo gaped at me. "Violet, we have no idea if that is safe to eat," he hissed.

I shrugged at him, and took another bite. Viggo sighed, and continued to look around, while I ate my apple.

I ate it down to the core, and when it was finished, I found a composting bin, and dropped the core in, letting out a soft burp.

Viggo gave a surprised chuckle and I looked at him. "What?"

He shook his head.

"No Patrian woman would ever burp in front of a man? Why, is it punishable by death?"

"No, it's just considered rude and unclassy."

I rolled my eyes. "It's gas. Everyone has it."

Viggo chuckled and nodded. "I like that you don't feel the need to hide who you are," he said.

I paused, his words sending a little thrill of pleasure through me. I felt a blush forming on my cheeks.

He held my gaze for a second, his jade eyes bright in spite of the dark shadows that had formed underneath.

I suppressed the urge to go to him, but I wanted to. Now wasn't the time or the place, but my thoughts kept circling around what was between us. I couldn't begin to process it, not with the lack of sleep I was trying to function on. I broke the silence and closed the compost bin.

"This level is clear," I said, sweeping an errant strand of hair from my eyes and tucking it behind my ear.

Viggo exhaled loudly, and then crossed over to the next door. "You ready?" he asked, leaning against the wall next to the door.

I crossed over to him, and twisted the hand wheel, opening the door.

We made our way down yet another identical stairwell, our shoes loud on the steps. Even though we hadn't finished searching the rest of the facility, I was pretty certain that there was no one there. However, it was better to be cautious than wrong.

I was glad Viggo was here: I was sure I would've been too nervous to do this alone. When he was around, I felt more comfortable. I believed that he had my back. I fully believed that he wasn't going to take me back to Patrus. At least, not to turn me in, anyway. Everything I knew about him told me he wouldn't—couldn't— consign another female to hang. It felt strange—like the ghost of his wife was somehow influencing his decisions about me. I wasn't sure how to handle that.

Of course, we hadn't really talked about Patrus or the egg or anything since our fight earlier today, so I had no idea what he was planning, if anything. Had it even been today? It felt like years ago.

Suddenly, a wave of dizziness surged over me, and I sagged against the wall. Viggo was there immediately, his hands on my shoulders.

"Violet?"

I shook my head, waving him off. "Sorry, I just got a little dizzy."

He frowned, a furrow forming between his brows. "I'm worried. Maybe we should stop. I think I can jam the door mechanisms if you want. Then you can get some rest."

I licked my lips, thinking. We had no idea how deep this facility was, and once we were done, we would have to climb back upstairs and through each level. My legs began aching with the thought.

"Let's clear this room. We'll secure the door here, and head back upstairs."

Without waiting for his response, I pulled the door open to the next room. He gave a soft curse behind me as I strode in, but followed behind me.

Like the level above, the floor plan was more open. It was a wide space, filled with book cases, tables, sofas, a kitchen, and a large table.

"This must be the common area," I said, as I took a step down onto the plush white carpet. Everything in here was designed to be comfortable. It had everything a person might need to entertain themselves, and more.

"It's nice," commented Viggo, as his eyes scanned the room. We searched through it, looking at all the things. Most of the books were science-related, but there were a few fictional titles scattered here and there. There were also games, stacked neatly on a shelf.

"They were here for the long haul," I realized, my fingers tracing over the lines of boxes.

"Yeah, they definitely stayed here for a while, whoever they were."

I frowned. "I thought this was some sort of research facility, but it doesn't make any sense."

"How do you mean?"

"Well… if they were researching The Green, they wouldn't have put the living quarters and food toward the top. Too dangerous—you'd want to put yourself as far from danger as possible right."

Viggo considered this, cracking open the door to the refrigerator. "I suppose you're right. Then what do you think they were doing?"

I shook my head. "I don't know." A yawn caught me by surprise, one of those long slow ones that gripped my entire body. I stretched as it happened, well aware of Viggo's eyes on me.

"Okay. I think we need to be done now," I said once it had finished.

I heard Viggo doing something to the door, and looked over to see that he had jammed a long metal rod against the mechanism. He twisted the handle, giving a satisfied nod when it locked, and turned back to me.

"Come on," he said, reaching out his hand. I took it, marveling at how big it was compared to my own.

He led me back through the sitting area and to the door, opening it. Then we made our way back upstairs.

As we climbed, wave after wave of dizziness and exhaustion washed over me, and I felt myself falling, until Viggo's strong arms grabbed me, and he lifted me up, carrying me. With a little sigh, I tucked my head under his chin, and felt the world fade away.

CHAPTER 23

VIGGO

I trudged upstairs with Violet fast asleep in my arms. I wasn't even sure how I was propelling myself forward at this point, but somehow I made it back to the living quarters.

Placing Violet in an empty bed, I tucked her in, smoothing her hair out of her face. She gave a little un-ladylike snore, shifted to one side under the blanket, and settled back down. I smiled down at her.

She looked so peaceful at that moment. The constant torment that she had endured was melting away. I took another moment to soak her in, and then made my way upstairs. There were a few more things I needed to do before sleep claimed me.

I secured the door leading from the decontamination room to the inner hall in a similar fashion to the one downstairs, and then went back to check on Ms. Dale. Color had returned to her skin, so I removed the patches from her. I checked her fingertips and toes to make sure blood was circulating well, and hooked up a second IV bag, so that when the first one drained, the second one would start working.

After that, I headed back downstairs. It was tempting to crawl into bed, but I wanted a shower first. I still somehow had energy to burn. I searched through the rooms, and eventually found one that contained clothes that would fit me.

I staggered into the bathroom, and turned on the shower. The pelting of the water on my back, rinsing me clean, was just what I needed. I could feel the sticky residue from the foam dissolve under the water pressure. Dirt and blood and grime fell from my body, forming a pool at my feet. I compressed the soap dispenser, and scrubbed my skin, determined to remove all of it.

It took washing myself twice to feel clean—I had to wash my hair three times, but finally, when I rinsed off, the water coming off me was clear.

I shut off the water, and grabbed a towel, wrapping it around my waist. The mirror had fogged up, but I used my hands to cut through the water droplets that had collected, wiping it clean.

The face staring back at me was that of a stranger's,

it seemed. The beard that had been growing in the last few days was rough and a little bit wild. The area under my eyes was dark. I looked almost sinister, like an evil villain from a play.

I ran a hand over my face and sighed. I needed to remain awake. The shower had refreshed me slightly, at least.

Toweling off, I shrugged on the black workout pants and white t-shirt I had found. Both were a bit snug, but I wasn't worried about them tearing, and wandered back to the bedroom where Violet was sleeping.

I leaned against the doorframe, resting my head against it, watching her. She was fast asleep, lying on her side. One hand was curled next to her head, the other wrapped around her waist. The rest of the bed was empty, like an open invitation.

I eyed it, wondering how Violet would feel if she woke up next to me.

I decided to deal with it in the morning, and sat down on the bed next to her. I shoved a pillow behind my lower back, and sat with my upper back against the wall. If I stayed in this position, I would be unlikely to sleep.

Violet made a soft sound, and then turned toward me, placing her face on my thigh, using it as a pillow. I stroked her hair softly while she slept.

I wasn't sure if it was the sound of Violet's even breathing or my own state of exhaustion, but I suddenly came awake with a jerk. I wasn't sure how long I had been asleep, but something had woken me in such a way that my body was on full alert.

I focused on my senses, trying to find what had jolted me from sleep, when I heard something upstairs. There was a banging sound echoing down.

Violet was still asleep, her exhaustion more profound than my own. I was loathe to wake her up, but if I didn't, she would be mad at me later for excluding her.

I shook her awake gently.

She woke up, her eyes wild and confused. "Viggo?" she said groggily, her voice thick with sleep.

"Listen," I said, placing a finger on her lips.

She froze for a second, tilting her head. There was a pause, and then the same banging sound, coming from upstairs.

"Ms. Dale?" she asked.

I shrugged. "It might be. Let's just take our guns to be sure."

She flashed me a look, one that told me she would never be caught dead without her gun, and stood up.

I did the same, tucking the gun into the band at the small of my back. Violet was staring at me, her eyes scanning me from top to bottom.

"You took a shower," she said, her tone half-observant, half-accusatory.

"You passed out," I replied with a smirk, pushing past her.

"Viggo?"

I paused, glancing at her from over my shoulder. She was looking back at the bed. She turned back to me, and gave me a nervous smile. "You... weren't... sleeping with me, were you?"

I tossed back my head and laughed. She was too naive at times. "Of course I was, Vi. But for safety reasons." I winked at her, and she gave a deep sigh, then followed behind me.

We headed upstairs quickly. I pushed open the door and heard something clanging from the room where we had left Ms. Dale. I moved up to the door, and glanced into the room quickly. Violet was beside me, her gun out.

"It's Ms. Dale," I whispered. "She woke up."

Violet bit her lip, a thoughtful expression crossing her face. "Wait here," she said, and stepped around me into the room.

"Ms. Dale?"

The banging stopped. "Violet," came the older woman's voice.

"Can you please lie back down? We worked really hard to help you, and I don't want you undermining that while you're still healing."

There was a long pause. "We?"

That was my cue. I stepped into the room, behind Violet.

Ms. Dale's brown eyes raked me over. "You're the idiot who shot me," she said after a moment.

I shrugged. "Guilty as charged."

Scowling at me, she sat down on the bed. "Did you miss, or were you actually trying to wing me?"

"I don't really like to kill women, so…" I trailed off, leaving her to her own implications.

She narrowed her eyes at me. "You're Patrian," she announced.

Violet cut in. "Ms. Dale, this is Viggo Croft. Viggo Croft, this is Melissa Dale. My former defense teacher." Violet took a step closer to the older woman. "Except you're not, are you?"

Ms. Dale stared at Violet, her face unflinching. "You're wanted for your crimes, Violet," she stated simply. "You had to know that Matrus would send agents after you."

"Why you?"

Ms. Dale paused, staring at both of us. "First, answer

my question, Violet—why are you with this Patrian?" The way she said Patrian, like a slur rather than a cultural identity, made me feel a flash of rage.

"My name is Viggo, Melissa," I said.

She did something with her face, a slight tightening in her facial muscles, but I could feel her disdain for me. I almost wanted to laugh in her face.

Violet placed a sharp elbow in my side, not hard enough to hurt, but hard enough to serve as a warning. She wanted to handle this herself.

I sighed, and crossed my arms. Fine, she could handle it herself. I was just going to watch Ms. Dale like a hawk.

"Viggo helped me survive The Green," Violet replied.

"Surely you are aware that—"

"He was sent from Patrus to arrest me for my crimes?" Violet interjected. "Yeah, who in this room hasn't been sent to retrieve me?"

Ms. Dale and I shared a look. I waggled my fingers at her, she gave me a look of disgust.

Violet ignored us both. "Ms. Dale—I did not kill Queen Rina. Nor did I betray Matrus."

"Forensic evidence found your handprint at the scene. You ran away. You killed Lee."

Taking a deep breath, Violet reached into my bag

and I watched her pull out the pieces of paper—Lee's twisted confession and the two pictures. "Lee orchestrated everything," Violet announced, handing the papers to Ms. Dale.

I watched as Ms. Dale looked at the pictures, her face reflecting nothing. Then, she opened the letter. I observed her closely, and I was glad I did. Her lips tightened slightly as she started to read. There was a flash of recognition in her eyes, quickly hidden.

I doubted Violet noticed—she seemed focused on the letter and Ms. Dale's opinion of it. I wanted to warn her that it wouldn't matter—Ms. Dale would still feel compelled to take her in—Matrus needed to catch someone for the crime. Then again, I knew Violet knew that already. She was nurturing a moment of false hope, and I didn't have the heart to remind her that it was false.

The silence stretched out, punctuated only by the sound of paper rustling as Ms. Dale read. Then she handed it back to Violet, along with the pictures.

After taking a moment to collect herself, Ms. Dale started speaking, her voice soft. "Violet, we need to return to Matrus with this, and the egg. We can sort it out when we get back. I'll help you."

Violet hesitated, her eyes searching Ms. Dale's, who offered her a small tight smile.

"You're lying," I announced. Ms. Dale glanced at me, and then turned her gaze to Violet.

"You know you can't trust a Patrian," she said. "They don't care about women. You lived over there with them. You've seen how they treat us. Like we're no better than dogs."

"Hey, Matrians aren't much better," I shot back. She bristled, but I barreled on. "The tests that you run on all the boys, singling them out for aggressive tendencies? You convict them before they have a chance to commit a crime. They're innocent, but you deem them guilty, brand them, and send them away."

"It's to ensure the continuity of our way of—"

"Save it," I said, cutting her off. "Patrians may place women low in social standing, but at least they still have rights. You don't even give those boys that. You just ship them off."

Violet had been standing silent while we argued, but opened her mouth, cutting me off. "I am not going anywhere with either of you," she stated, matter of fact. "Because no matter where I go, I'm dead. Strung up as a villain so that both of your little civilizations can continue to spin and play your petty games."

Ms. Dale opened her mouth to protest, but Violet waved a hand, silencing her. She leaned over Ms. Dale, her face a mask of stone. "Ms. Dale, there is only one thing I want from you," she said, her voice soft and deadly.

Ms. Dale, for her part, looked non-plussed. "You're not in any position to demand—"

"You are restrained, wounded, in a facility where I have a gun and you do not. I am in the position to do whatever I want. And while I don't want another death on my conscience, this is incredibly important to me."

Ms. Dale searched Violet's face for a long moment, and then nodded. "What do you want?"

"Where are the mines?"

Ms. Dale sighed. "I don't know, Violet. To the north?"

Violet absorbed the information for a moment, and then nodded. "Thank you for nothing," she said, before stalking out of the room. I felt torn in that moment. I wanted to question Ms. Dale further, but Violet was clearly upset.

"Do you have any idea what she's been through?" I asked abruptly, the words exploding from my throat.

Ms. Dale didn't bat an eyelid. "That story is just that—a story. I thought maybe… but after hearing all of this… it sounds insane." She paused, giving me a piercing look. "And if you believe it… well, then you're not thinking with your brain."

My jaw clenched, and I whirled on my heel and left,

closing and securing the door behind me. I started to follow after Violet, but I paused, Ms. Dale's words rolling through my head, making me second guess myself.

I wanted to believe Violet so badly at this point. Everything she had done and said… it had been in earnest. Yet, I couldn't get past the fact that she had planned to betray me. That she had spent weeks earning my trust, knowing that I would be indicted for her actions.

I needed to think.

CHAPTER 24

VIOLET

I was livid as I stalked down the stairs back into the living area. My hands were shaking with unspent rage, and I could feel red hot tears threatening to spill from my eyes.

My foot barely touched the carpet before I was running. Down stairs and through the levels, until I reached the common area. Only there could I let out my cry of frustration.

I kicked a sofa, and then snatched a throw pillow off it, screaming into it before I sent it hurtling across the room. I wanted to destroy something—to take my rage out on an inanimate piece of furniture—so that I could just get whatever it was inside of me out.

I felt like I was coming apart at the seams. I tried to sit, to calm my breathing, but it didn't help. The sensation, the urge to fight, was crawling up from a pit in my belly and threatening to force its way out through my mouth.

I had expected… something different from Ms. Dale. At the very least, I had expected her to be honest. The way she had reacted to Viggo after he had called her a liar though… was there anyone in this world I could trust?

My heart told me I could trust Viggo, but even that was uncertain. Almost as uncertain as my feelings toward him, and his toward me.

My eyes darted around the common room. I needed something, anything, to vent my wrath on. My gaze came to rest on a punching bag off in one corner of the room. This corner was clearly designated for fitness, given the weights and machines scattered around. However, I only had eyes for that punching bag.

Without thinking about it, I sprung myself at it, my body tense as a coil ready to be released. I planted a kick against it so hard that it started to swing on the chain that supported it. I landed, and caught it, throwing my arms around it in a bear hug to pull it to a stop.

Once it had settled, I began to punch, kick, and elbow it with a vengeance. My hands were unprotected, but if there was any pain in my knuckles hitting the rough fabric, I didn't notice.

I kept hitting it over and over and over again. There was something satisfying about each thudding strike against the bag. I could feel it resonating through my limbs as I struck it. Each hit was a visceral feeling of release, a promise of freedom, a wealth of control that I had been sorely lacking.

I knew why I was upset—I didn't need to psychoanalyze myself. I was doomed. A dead girl who didn't have enough sense to lie down and accept it. I had fought and struggled and pushed and survived in The Green, only to have the people of this world find me guilty—just so they could have a face to vilify.

And those very same people had sent two out of the three most important people in my life to capture me. I wanted to scream. I wanted to hurt the world like it had hurt me. I had believed, foolishly, that if I just told the truth, I would be believed, but nobody cared about the story of a criminal.

Except for maybe Viggo. Maybe. A nauseating pit in my stomach opened, threatening to swallow me up. If there was just one person in the world who I wanted to believe me the most, it was Viggo. I just wished he would tell me that he did.

I wished for a lot of things. Wishing was pointless, and so were tears, anger, regret, and shame. I needed to move past that.

But I couldn't catch a break either. I had hoped that Ms. Dale would have some knowledge about the mines, but she clearly didn't. Not that I didn't put it past her to lie to me, but then why would she lie about something so small?

I continued to hit, shifting my stance into a purely boxing one. I threw jab after jab at the bag, mixing in hooks and uppercuts when I felt the need to see the bag move from the force of my blows.

How was I going to accomplish anything? Where was my stupid old woman who was going to guide me on this merry old adventure? Why didn't anything ever work like the stories did?

I stopped mid punch, my fist coming to rest on the bag. I took a deep breath, and felt the rage leaving me almost as suddenly as it had appeared. I looked down at my hands—the skin over the knuckles raw and torn, blood welling up from the bigger wounds.

I shook my head, and took a few steps back. There were small blood marks all over the bag, from where I had been punching. I flexed my hands and rotated my shoulders—all habits I had developed from when I was in defense class—and sat down heavily on a couch, pressing my head into my hands and sucking in a deep breath.

This wasn't like the stories—I wasn't some plucky

heroine on a great adventure—I was Violet Bates. A simple nobody who had broken the law, murdered two girls, and then got sent on this mission that had gotten messed up beyond recognition.

I needed to own my part in everything, and realize that my decisions had consequences from here on out. I knew what I wanted—to be free from all this, and to have my brother returned to me. I had a bartering chip—the egg. And more than that—I had a place to hide—this facility.

The first step to moving forward was to finish clearing the facility. From there, I would interrogate Ms. Dale again, and find out if she was interested in making an exchange—my brother and safe passage for the egg.

I wondered how Viggo would react to my plan. I debated not telling him, but the first step to earning back his trust was to be honest in every way that I could. If he didn't go for it… well, too bad. It wasn't his decision to make.

I would have to find a time to tell him. After we finished clearing the facility.

Breathing in, I stood up and began stretching. The nap I had earlier was barely putting a dent in the exhaustion I was feeling. Not to mention, I was still covered in sweat and grime and whatever else had been building up on my skin and in my hair for the past few days.

My skin crawled with the thought of all the dirt on me. A shower would make everything right again.

I turned the hatch and headed upstairs, toward the living quarters.

I reached it in ten minutes—after taking an apple break in the greenhouse—and immediately began inspecting the rooms. I had found a few things that I was reasonably sure I could fit in, and I laid them out on the bed. I had chosen a different room than the one I had slept in—if only because the fact that I had slept dirty in the bed was gross—and stepped in the shower.

It was amazing how a simple thing like a shower went unappreciated. I had missed showers. The water was instantly hot as I turned the dial over, and without a second thought, I stepped under the spray of water, letting the scalding hot water pepper my skin. I was mesmerized by the streams of water—more mud—that came off of me and collected at my feet.

Soaping myself, I exhaled in relief as the water coursed over me, cleansing me of everything. It felt like a weight was being lifted off of me as I scrubbed my skin, turning it red.

Washing my greasy hair—hair that had not been washed in what felt like eternity—was probably one of the best things that had happened to me in that same eternity.

There was a certain amount of civility that came from having a shower for the first time in a long time. It was like I ceased being an animal locked in a constant battle over fight and flight reflexes, and started being a higher functioning human.

As I stepped out of the stall, steam billowing behind me and fogging up the mirror, I felt more whole, like a small part of my dignity had been restored.

As I entered the bedroom, Viggo was sitting on the bed waiting for me. I almost screamed, I was so surprised to see him there. I clutched my towel closer to me, and gaped at him.

He was sitting with his elbows on his knees, his fingers interlaced into a fist that he used to support his chin.

A flash of irritation flowed over me—I just needed a moment of peace!

"Get out," I ordered, stepping around him over to the door. I rested my back against it, and used my free hand to point out the door, further emphasizing my need for him to leave.

He didn't react, save to adjust his seat so that he was facing me. His green eyes twinkled in amusement, and I felt the spark of rage from earlier flare up again.

"Fine," I spat, reaching over to grab the clothes I had collected from the bed. "I'll go."

His hand moved with the speed of a snake, but he was gentle as he caught my arm. I tugged at him, but he pulled me to him, his strength overcoming my own. Although, to be honest, I didn't struggle that hard.

He pulled me into his lap, and I flushed, very aware of how vulnerable I was in this position, wearing nothing but a towel. I pressed my hands against his chest, trying to push away from him, but he held me fast.

Before I could stop him, he had sunk his hands into the wet tendrils of my hair, holding my head in place.

I gave a little gasp, and then his lips were pressing against mine urgently. Something snapped in me, and I pressed against him, my free hand wrapping around the back of his neck. I kissed him back hungrily.

Viggo was careful as he kissed me, holding me only by my hair. Even his kiss was controlled. It was slow and domineering, flooding my senses with electricity that ran from the crown of my head to the tips of my toes. I moaned involuntarily.

We broke the kiss after a long moment.

"What was that for?" I breathed.

His eyes seemed to pierce me. "I wanted your full attention," he replied, the corner of his mouth turning up.

I swallowed, clutching the towel tightly, keenly conscious of its meager protection. "You have it," I replied carefully.

He took a deep breath, closing his eyes for a second, before opening them. "I believe you," he said, his voice somber and sincere.

I studied his face for a long second—both eager and reluctant to trust him—searching for a clue to his true intention.

After a pause, he repeated himself. "I believe you," he breathed across my face, pressing his forehead to mine. He hugged me closer, crushing me into his chest.

"Really?" I whispered. I hated how hopeful I sounded. It felt like a weakness to want and need Viggo's trust.

He nodded, his eyes closed and his face solemn. "Really," he replied, pressing his lips to mine once more.

I hesitated again. "Why?"

Viggo peered down at me, and sighed. "After you stormed out… Ms. Dale said something that was in line with my own suspicions about you." My stomach clenched in uncertainty as I watched him. "But the more I thought about it, the more I felt like it was turning a blind eye to the truth. Ignoring evidence to make the narrative work. That's not who I am or who I want to be. You made mistakes, Violet, but I want to believe that you were in over your head, in an impossible situation. I'm choosing to believe that."

Tears began pouring down my cheeks. I hadn't even been aware that they had been forming. The relief I felt in that moment was palpable, like another stone I could stop carrying.

"Thank you," I sniffled, scrubbing my cheeks with one hand.

Viggo smiled a small smile, and disentangled his hands from my hair in order to wipe my tears away. "You're welcome." He pressed his lips to my forehead.

We held each other for a long moment, just taking comfort in the other's arms. It was exactly what I needed, what I had been searching for. I felt stronger, like I finally didn't have to shoulder everything on my own. I was afraid of the future, but now it felt like I didn't have to face it alone.

CHAPTER 25

VIGGO

Violet had drifted off to sleep again, but I was wide awake. Coming to the decision to believe Violet, believe everything she had told me, had been hard. I'd had to come to terms with things that weren't exactly comfortable for me.

Everything I had told her was true. I had no desire to be another pawn in whatever this game was that our two governments were playing. The easiest way to win this game was to stop playing. But it was more than that—forgiving Violet for her part in the bombing had been hard. It was like I had a bitter peach pit in my stomach, slowly dissolving to acid.

Until I thought about my wife. When she had come to me, covered in blood, she had begged me to believe her. To help her. And while I had done the latter, it had been hard for me to do the former. I blamed her for going out without me. I hadn't put myself in her shoes.

It was my biggest regret, one that still haunted me. I didn't want it to be that way with Violet. For all her faults, and regardless of what the future held, she needed my forgiveness, even if she hadn't forgiven herself. I also needed to forgive her—I did not want to carry this poison pill of anger toward her anymore.

The biggest pill to swallow was that by joining Violet, I was essentially exiling myself. I thought of my future plans to move deeper into the mountains, isolating myself further from Patrian life and politics, and realized that while it wasn't necessarily the way I wanted to do it, I was still doing the same thing, just in a different setting than I originally intended.

For a fraction of a second, I had considered doing the opposite. I could deliver Violet to King Maxen, get my back pay, and go back up to my home and close the world out. I could spend time on my mountain becoming completely self-sufficient, and all it would cost me was a girl. It was akin to selling my soul, and I despised myself for having that moment of doubt. I could never trade Violet's life—any woman's life—for something as selfish as a mountain view and isolation. The price was too high.

While I didn't necessarily agree with the politics

between Matrus and Patrus, I had come to terms with the flaws of both places a long time ago. Cruelty didn't have a gender qualifier behind it—it was an ever unraveling human condition, cast out by pride, power, and indifference—and both nations had their fair share of it.

Yet this small woman curled up against me had reminded me that it was the masses who were cruel, not the individual. I had built a wall up to defend against the cruelties I saw day to day, so that they couldn't affect me. It was self-preservation, pure and simple, one born from the conviction and death of my wife.

I had mourned her. And the tragedy of her loss still ran deep inside me. I had spent so much time wondering what I could have done differently, how I could've helped her adjust, when the reality was that I loved her, just the way she was. But there was no place that could tolerate us both as individuals and a couple. We were doomed from the start.

I stroked Violet's hair before gently extracting myself from her. I hadn't been able to make my wife feel safe—or even comfortable within Patrus—but I could do something for Violet.

It was time to go talk with Ms. Dale.

She was hiding something. As an investigator, I knew that. She was trained to avoid revealing her emotions in any way, but there had been a momentary flash of surprise on her face when she was reading Lee's letter, and I wanted to know what it was.

As I climbed the stairs, I contemplated the interrogation techniques I had learned, and completely dismissed them. Ms. Dale had probably undergone training to be immune to that. It was in what she wouldn't reveal that I would find answers, but it was going to be tricky to do. Odds were that I wouldn't get anything out of her. I still had to try though.

Ms. Dale appeared to be sleeping. I watched her for a few minutes running over the brief outline of a plan I had formulated on the way up. It was the only way to proceed, but I still felt a moment of apprehension as I placed my hand on the door.

I took a moment to accept the possibility that she was all she claimed to be. That she knew nothing, and was only there because of her relationship with Violet in the past.

I opened up the door and let myself inside.

Ms. Dale's eyes were twin slits, and I could see the faintest brown sparkling from them. She opened her eyes fully and sat up, her hands smoothing the thin blanket covering her, before clasping them together.

"Thought about what I said?" she asked carefully, her face a perfect mask.

I leaned against the door, studying her. "Not really," I lied with a little shrug.

"Don't be an idiot, Croft," she said pertly.

I smirked at her. "Not intending to be one," I replied. "You don't know me, Ms. Dale."

There was a small twitch, at the corner of her left eye. I wouldn't have noticed it, if it weren't for the fact I was watching so closely.

It took experience and practice to become a good liar, and even then, there were small tells that could give a person away. A trained liar developed perfect control over their face. Ms. Dale had that mastery over her facial muscles, but I had noticed something in our last interaction, and it was something I was hoping to exploit now.

"Unless you do know me?" I said, sauntering in the room. "Of course, that would be ridiculous. Why would a simple, humble defense teacher know anything about a warden from the other side of the river? There would be no reason for you to know me."

She stared back at me, seemingly waiting. I continued to talk, anticipating silence as a ploy from her. "Then again, you might know if you were more than a simple, humble defense teacher. If you were a spy, you would probably know a lot more."

There it was—that subtle tightness that pulled her

face tight against her skull. Her eyes went flat and hard. I remained calm—her subtle reaction wasn't necessarily an indicator of anything just yet.

"You know, Violet is really talented," I said abruptly, changing the subject.

Brief flashes of emotion passed over Ms. Dale's face—surprise and confusion—before disappearing under that careful mask once more.

"How do you mean?" she asked, her voice devoid of interest. Yet she had asked, meaning she was interested. That was a good sign.

"Well, she was your defense student, right?"

She gave me a tight nod. It was easy enough to give me that information; after all, it was well-known. "I trained with Violet for years," she said curtly.

"Was she one of your more promising students?"

Her face went flat again, but there was a minuscule tightening. "All of my students show promise in a variety of ways. Violet was no different."

"She was able to hold her own against me."

Ms. Dale smirked at me, giving into her apparent pride and disdain for me. That was a good sign—it meant she could be broken. "I trained her well."

I nodded. "It makes me wonder what your plans were for her had she finished her training."

Shrugging, Ms. Dale watched me, her brown eyes

glittering. "It would be up to her, really. You see, in Matrus, we allow women to choose their own path."

"Yeah," I retorted. "While allowing your men limited options in professions."

"At least our men have professions," she replied calmly, picking at some invisible lint on her blanket.

I felt disappointed—I had hoped that going after Matrus would get her irate, or at least irritated, but she was too good for that. It made my belief that she was a spy even more palpable. I decided to call her on it.

"You're a spy," I announced, studying her face.

She rolled her eyes, presumably in exasperation, but it was all behind that careful mask she wore.

"You also know something you aren't saying about that letter."

"What letter?"

I sighed, tapping my fingers on the table next to me. "Don't play stupid with me, Ms. Dale. It's insulting to both of us."

"Oh, that forgery that Violet tried to present as Lee's confession?"

It was my turn to roll my eyes at her. "I think you and I both know that it wasn't a forgery." Ms. Dale fell silent. I studied her face, and nodded. "Yeah, that's what I thought."

I turned on my heel, prepared to walk away, when

she bit on my bait. "What makes you think it's not a forgery?"

I half turned, and shot her a disbelieving look. "You really think that Violet forged it?"

She paused, and then inclined her head a fraction of an inch. I started laughing, letting the sound fill up the room for several long seconds, before letting it die in heaving gasps.

I held up my hands. "I'm so sorry, Ms. Dale. Clearly, I was wrong. I mean—if you can't figure out why it's the real deal, then I was clearly mistaken. You go back to sleep."

"Of course I know why it's real, you idiot, I—" She paused, her mouth agape, and I felt a supreme sense of satisfaction roll over me. I was going to be smug for the next few days, but I'd earned it.

I crossed over to the foot of her bed, letting the smile play across my lips. "You recognized something in that letter. Something important." I pulled it out of my pocket. "It was toward the beginning." I scanned the first paragraph nonchalantly, while she watched, her face pulled back in that mask. Yet her eyes were glistening, probably in anger for what I had gotten her to confess.

"I bet it's one of these names here," I drawled as I watched her. Again, there was that tightening, like she was barely keeping her skull from leaping out and snapping at me. "One of his accomplices, maybe? Chris Patton? Duncan Friedman? Seb Morrissey? Jacob Venn?" Her face remained blank as I listed the names, and I felt an instant irritation. I scanned the rest of the letter. She had reacted to the names jab, but none of them had inspired anything.

I froze as I started scanning the letter again. "It's Desmond, isn't it?"

This time, Ms. Dale's eyes flicked away, starting at a fixed spot on the wall. I paused as I pondered that. Desmond was Lee's middle name, according to Violet. So why had Ms. Dale reacted to that?

I stared at her, the question on the tip of my tongue, my mind trying to understand what Ms. Dale was telling me with her silence. I stalled myself, my mind not willing to reveal my ignorance, but it was puzzling. There was no reason for her to react to her own spy's name. None whatsoever.

Unless the Desmond in the letter was the name of another person, and it was coincidental that they shared the same name.

The realization hit me like a ton of bricks, and for a second I felt a rush of elation, until I realized that I still had no idea who the Desmond in the letter was.

But Ms. Dale did. I studied the older woman while I

ran through everything in my head. That meant that Lee wasn't necessarily crazy, he just happened to be working with someone else whose name was Desmond. It was a coincidence, nothing more, but it had thrown Violet and me completely down the wrong path.

I wanted to hit myself for being so quick to jump to assumptions. Desmond, whoever he was, was a player in this, and I was betting Ms. Dale knew who he was and what he wanted. I could work with that.

Placing my hand on the foot board of the bed, I leaned over. I started to say something, when a sound down the hall stopped me.

Ms. Dale and I exchanged looks as a loud clanging sound came from the room with the airlock. There was a banging sound, and then silence. I backed out into the hallway, pulling my gun and feeling like an idiot for not barricading the airlock door.

The hand wheel on the hall began to turn but stopped with a clang. Then it moved in the opposite direction, and there was a slight thud as something impacted with the door. I saw the rod I had shoved in the mechanism start to fall.

Violet flashed in my mind, and without waiting to see who opened the door, I turned and ran, the sound of the rod clattering to the ground masking the sounds of my footsteps.

CHAPTER 26

VIOLET

A hand over my mouth tore me away from the deep sleep I had been enjoying. I opened my eyes, fists clenching to lash out, when I saw Viggo's face inches from my own. He looked grim, and pressed a finger to his lips. I nodded and he removed his hand.

I sat up on my elbow, clutching the sheet to me, while he went around the room. He tossed my borrowed pair of pants at me, and began packing up my bag in a hurry. I pulled the pants on under the sheets, then hurried to put my shoes on.

Standing up, I looked at him. "What is it?" I mouthed.

He shook his head, his eyes staring at the door that led to the upper level. "We need to move," he whispered back. He held out the bag to me.

I took it, and almost fell over at the unexpected weight in there. Pausing to open it, I saw the gleaming silver case of the egg.

Looking up at Viggo, he shook his head again, and then nodded to the door leading down. "Move," he commanded.

I hefted the backpack over my shoulder, and began to move as quickly as possible down the hall. I heard a clang upstairs just as I reached the door. Spinning the hand wheel, I pushed open the door, and stepped through. Viggo followed quickly, closing the door.

"I can't barricade the door from this side," he whispered.

Nodding, I headed down the stairs, trying to make my footsteps as quiet as possible on the corrugated metal of the stairwell. I could hear something banging from upstairs, and I looked over at Viggo, who shot me a smug grin.

"I barricaded it. It'll buy us a little—"

He cut off as the sound of something screaming filled the air. It took me a second to realize that the sound was the straining of metal on metal.

"Go," Viggo urged, gently pushing me back to the door to the next level.

I went. The door practically flew open under my hand and I stepped through, making my way across the orchard to the next door. Viggo closed the door behind us, tightening the hand wheel. I heard him fiddling with something, but I was too preoccupied with making it to the opposite door and opening it to pay attention.

The door swung open to the stairs, and I looked back. "Viggo," I hissed. "Leave it. We're wasting time."

Viggo took a few steps back to check his work, when something on the other side of the door slammed into it so hard the door frame shuddered.

He began running toward me, waving me forward. I ran, leaping down the first flight of stairs and landing on the first landing. Viggo had already caught up, his legs tearing down the stairs two or three steps at a time.

My heart was pounding in my throat. "What did that?" I whispered, flinching. My whisper felt too loud in this small concrete space.

Viggo shook his head, his hands spinning the next hand wheel. "No idea. I think it's best not to find out."

The door swung open and we both stepped in. Viggo closed the door, and I raced to the couch. Grabbing one of the massive arms, I began to pull it toward the door, straining with effort.

"Leave it, Violet," Viggo whispered.

"It'll slow whatever it is down," I insisted, digging my heels into the carpet and dragging it a few feet closer.

"We should keep moving," he hissed, heading to the next door.

"Who do you think it is?" I asked, giving up on the couch and moving next to him.

He bent over to fiddle with his barricade. He had jammed a piece of iron pipe through the locking mechanism, and was now trying to pull it back out. I twisted the wheel, trying to give him slack, but it was already turned as far as it could go. His fingers were white, and I could see the cords of his muscles flexing as he pulled.

Gritting his teeth, he planted his feet on the door and began to pull using his whole body. Behind us, I could hear someone struggling with the hand wheel.

"I did too good a job on the door," Viggo snarled, gripping the iron pipe tighter.

I quickly slid my arms around his waist and began to help him pull. Suddenly, there was a bang on the door, similar to the one from the level above.

Viggo and I froze. I released Viggo, and moved on all fours to the second couch, pushing it from the wall.

"C'mon," I hissed at Viggo.

He shook his head, still straining against the bar. "They'll know we're still here if this door is still barricaded."

I watched him pull, realizing he was right. The banging on the door was growing louder now. I looked at it, stunned to see that the metal was beginning to flex under the force of the hits.

"They have some sort of battering ram," I breathed.

Viggo looked over his shoulder and gave a curse. He relinquished his grip on the bar and crawled over to me.

"We don't have a lot of time. There's got to be another way out of here."

I shook my head, my eyes darting around. "There's nothing. Only the two doors."

Viggo was breathing heavily as he fitted his large form next to mine. We pressed in behind the couch, listening as the banging continued.

He pulled his gun out. "We can shoot it out," he said, his green eyes studying mine.

I hesitated, my mind racing over the possibility. I shook my head. "No, we don't know how many there are. They could be wearing tactical gear, and who knows what kind of weapons they have. It's not smart."

Viggo exhaled sharply. "Do you want to surrender to them?"

I thought about it for a second. It would guarantee temporary stay of execution, nothing more.

Frustrated by the lack of options, I kicked the wall, hard enough to make the vent to my left rattle. The rattle caught my attention, and I focused my gaze on the vent.

"Viggo," I hissed, pointing at the vent.

He exchanged a glance with me, and then nodded. We crawled over to it.

Viggo slid his fingers through the grate, and began to pull. It didn't want to come out, no matter how much Viggo pulled.

I ran my fingers over the edges, and found the holes for four screws, bolting it in place. Without hesitating, I pulled off my bag, positioning it between me and the wall, and fumbled around for my knife.

Pulling it out, I opened it up, and began attacking the screws. The banging had seemingly stopped, but I wasn't going to waste time investigating why.

Viggo had noticed what I was doing, and reached in his pocket, pulling out his knife. We worked in tandem, sliding the tips of our knives into the slots of the screws, and turning.

"Lefty loosey, righty tighty," I reminded myself, remembering my mother saying that one time when I had asked to help her hang some shelves.

Viggo frowned at me, and I shrugged. I caught the flash of a smile from him, and it almost made me forget my fear and smile with him. Almost.

The first screw I was working on slid out of the hole and fell to the floor. I blew a lock of hair out of my face, and started working on the other.

There was another bang, and I heard the sound of metal bending. The loud metal groan that filled the room made me want to cover my ears.

Viggo and I exchanged worried glances. My hands were shaking as I moved to the next screw, but I kept focus. I could barely hear the sound of voices coming from the hall, my heart was beating so loudly in my chest.

Viggo's second screw fell to the floor, and he scooped them up and slipped them into his pocket. His eyes were now on me, urging me on voicelessly. I managed to catch the screw head with the tip of my knife, in spite of my shaking hands, and began twisting the knife to the left.

There were sounds coming from the door now, but I was too anxious to try and make sense of them. The screw slipped free finally, after what seemed like an eternity, and I exhaled in relief.

Viggo pried the grate from the wall, and grabbed my bag, sliding it in first. He then grabbed me by the shirt collar and started to shove me into the hole. The thin aluminum groaned under my weight and we both froze for a second, waiting to see if we had been noticed.

When nothing presented itself, Viggo's hand pressed on my shoulders, urging me forward. Using my elbows, I wiggled into the pitch black hole. I came to a three-way intersection about four feet in, and wiggled around it to give Viggo enough room.

I waited for a second, but when Viggo didn't follow,

I pushed myself backward. It took some doing, but I managed to shift back far enough just in time to see Viggo placing the grate back over the hole.

"Viggo," I hissed.

I couldn't make out his face through the grate from that distance, but I heard his voice clear as day.

"Can't fit. Besides, they know someone is in here, they just don't know who."

"Viggo!" I wheezed, a sudden panic overtaking me. There was no telling what they would do if they caught him.

"Calm down, Violet," he whispered, his strong voice floating down the vent. I heard the scrape of the screws on the grate as he fit them in, finger tightening. "How many times have I rescued you?"

"What?" I gasped back, confused at the abrupt change of topic.

"They're coming. The door is opening. How many times?"

I wriggled in the vent, maneuvering myself back toward the grate. "I don't know! Why?"

I heard him slide the final screw in, twisting it with a grunt. Once it was done, he dipped his head down, so I could see his face. I reached for the grate, trying to grab it.

"It's your turn to rescue me now, Vi," he whispered, a small sad smile playing on his lips.

I bit back my cry, but tears were dripping down my face. I couldn't lose Viggo—not now. We'd been through too much.

"They're coming," he whispered. "Move away from the grate."

I watched as he disappeared from sight, his fingers coming through the grate. He heaved at it, like he was trying to pull it out, but I realized it was an act. I slowly backed away from the grate, obscuring myself in the darkness of the vent.

I had bitten back my tears and all sounds, when I heard someone speak.

"Well, well. Looks like we found a rat," came a feminine voice caked with amusement and menace.

"Oh. Hello… ladies," Viggo said, his fingers sliding back through the holes slowly. I could imagine him holding up his hands, trying to act cool and calm.

"Where is Violet Bates?" a second voice asked, her tone flat and even.

"Beats me. I'm just looking for my dog. Have you seen him? Brown fur, answers to the name—"

There was a wet cracking sound, one I recognized as flesh striking flesh, followed by a boneless sound of someone's body hitting the floor. I covered my mouth with both hands to keep my cries from escaping.

CHAPTER 27

VIOLET

I waited for them to hear me, to find me, but there was no indication that they had noticed me yet.

"Was that really necessary, sister?" came the first speaker. That was interesting—the two were related. I wondered who they were. Matrian, from the sound of it.

"Probably not, but it was fun," came the first voice.

There was a pregnant pause, and I held my breath, afraid to move. One panel flexing under my body weight, and they would know where I was. Viggo's sacrifice would have been in vain.

"Check the vent," commanded the toneless voice of the second woman.

A shadow passed over the vent, and I pressed back deeper into the darkness.

There was a long pause as I felt, rather than saw, the eyes probing the hole I was sheltered in.

"Nothing there. Wherever this Violet is… she wasn't with him. They must have separated on one of the upper levels. Maybe she hid, and then took off while we pursued him."

The shadow disappeared.

"Very well. Let's take this man to one of the interrogation rooms, and find out where she would go."

"We should kill him," responded the first voice, disdain thick in her voice. I sucked in my breath at the way she casually suggested it.

"Interesting. Why?"

"Because even if he does know where she is, he won't tell us. It's a waste of time."

"I see." I heard one of them walking around. Viggo gave a groan, and I bit back my protest. It would do no good to say anything. But if they agreed to kill him, I would tear out of this vent and kill them both before they got a chance.

Risking the noise, I reached for my bag and found my gun. The heavy press of the cold metal and grip calmed me and made me feel more in control, knowing it was there.

"Sister," came the same voice. "I think killing him is extremely unwise."

"Oh," came the snide response. "Taken in by his pretty face?"

"Hardly. But he could have other information that could be helpful to us."

"Like?"

"Well, really. How would I know? But killing him now means we'll never have the chance to figure it out. And that would not make Elena happy, knowing that we had a Patrian agent in our grasp and killed him before we could extract anything of interest."

"Is that our job now? Making sweet Elena happy?"

The sound of a slap echoed through the room, followed by a few staggered steps landing heavily on the carpeted floor.

"You dare hit me," shouted the second voice, an indignant rage thundering through it.

"You are being disrespectful to our new queen," came the toneless response.

There was a pause. "Of course. You're right. I apologize."

"Accepted. Now, shall we get this huge specimen of a Patrian into an interrogation room? I still want to question Ms. Dale and see what she knows."

There was a wordless sound of assent, and then a shuffling around. I held very still as I heard them pick up Viggo's unconscious form and carry him out of the room, leaving me alone in the darkness.

In my head, I counted to one hundred, just to feel sure they were gone. As I lay there, I ran my mind back over their conversation, trying to figure out who they were.

They were clearly agents of the new queen, Elena. Elena was Rina's eldest daughter, and first in line of succession. She had been training her entire life to assume the role of Queen, and had served in various cabinet roles in the government. I was surprised to hear that she had already been crowned, given that her mother had been murdered less than a week ago. When Queen Rina's mother had died, the nation had grieved for a month before the coronation of her daughter.

Yet they spoke about her in such a casual way, implying a more informal relationship. Were they just disenfranchised agents, or did they know the queen personally? Why would they be here? Ms. Dale had already been sent, so there was no need for further agents. It really didn't make any sense.

I rolled those thoughts through my head while I counted. After one hundred, I pressed my foot against one of the walls, until the metal popped loudly. Then I waited.

No sounds of activity. I exhaled slowly, and then scooted my way back up to the grate. The metal I was lying on groaned as I moved, and I froze each time, waiting to be discovered, anticipated it even, scenarios playing out in my head. But nobody came.

Once at the grate, I began pushing against it, using my feet for leverage. It turned out to be fruitless. Viggo had secured it to the wall too tightly.

After ten minutes of pushing, I finally gave up. Wiping my face, I pushed myself back into the tunnel, and started to think.

The first goal was finding Viggo, wherever he was. To do that, I needed to find a way out of these ventilation ducts.

Reaching for the bag, I exchanged the gun I was holding for a flashlight and clicked it on. The light illuminated everything, and I breathed a sigh of relief. I didn't think I would have lasted long without a flashlight.

The light cut through the darkness, ending about ten feet away, where I could see the vent making a sharp left. Thinking about the layout of each level, I began to wiggle my way through it. The space was tight, and as I moved, I realized that there would have been no way for Viggo to fit.

He probably knew it earlier than I did. I was so focused on the situation that I had completely overlooked the environment.

I pushed the bag in front of me, making my way

down. It was awkward, holding the flashlight and pushing the backpack, but I managed. The duct groaned and banged with each movement I made, but I eventually figured out where to put my weight on each section, keeping the noise to a minimum.

I slid the bag around the corner, and followed it through. About three feet in front of me, the vent slanted down at an angle. I considered going back, but there was nowhere to turn around, and I didn't feel like doing this in reverse. I wrapped my hand around the strap of the bag, and pushed forward.

I saw a dim yellow light coming from ahead as I carefully descended. I pushed toward it. The slant leveled out about three feet before the source of the light, which I could see was another grate. I approached it cautiously, making a concentrated effort to move as silently as possible.

Once there, I sneaked a glance through the grate. It was the stairwell, and it was empty. Taking a chance, I placed my hand on the grate, and pushed. It was fixed in place.

I didn't waste any time trying to bust it open. The stairs were too exposed anyway. I would be trapped if anyone came through. It was better to proceed downward.

I moved forward and reached another downward

slope. My arms were beginning to ache with the strain of using them to control my descent, but I had no room to turn around, so I made do.

Once the slope evened out again, I came to a fork—left or right. Ultimately it didn't matter, but if this level was situated like one of the upper levels, with individual rooms divided by a hallway, I would need to search both sides for Viggo, and that would take time.

I moved left, pushing the bag in front of me. I turned the corner, and paused. There was a vent a foot away from me. Hurriedly, I clicked off the flashlight, so the light wouldn't attract attention. Darkness flooded in, leaving me completely blind for several seconds.

I focused on my breathing, and not the creepy-crawly sensation that tickled the back of my neck. I did my best to block my mind from associating that sensation to the centipedes that I had been covered with a short time ago, but it was hard. My hand twitched with the urge to slap the area. I clenched my fists and forced by breath in and out evenly and slowly.

It took several seconds, but the sensation disappeared. Licking my lips, I slowly moved down the darkened tunnel. I paused at each vent, listening intently. The darkness was making my hearing more intense, and it was hard blocking out the sound of my own breathing and heartbeat, but I took my time, and moved slowly.

The rooms on this side appeared empty. I checked each grate after I was certain the room was vacant, but they were just as firmly bolted as the others. I left my bag at the junction that led to the next stairwell, and proceeded to the other side. As I came around the corner, I noticed that a light was streaming from one of the vents.

I carefully made my way over, taking extra care not to shift any of the panels. As I neared, I could hear the sound of breathing coming from the room. I paused just inches from the light, and listened, counting in my head. The breathing was even and deep, meaning the person in the room was either sleeping or unconscious.

I risked a glance inside. I couldn't see much beyond floor level, but someone was tied to the chair. I recognized Viggo's shoes and pants.

"Viggo," I whispered.

The breathing continued uninterrupted. I reached out and grabbed the grate, giving it a little push. Like all the others, it didn't budge.

I gave a sharp exhale of frustration, and released the grate. I was beginning to think that there was no way for me to get out of the ducts, and that while Viggo had saved my life, he had unknowingly condemned me to die of dehydration and starvation in my new hiding place.

I debated waiting until Viggo woke up so I could talk to him, but I had no idea how long that would be, and I risked exposing myself if they came in to check up on him.

"I'll be back," I whispered through the grate, pushing myself backward.

I headed back to the junction, and maneuvered my way down the next slope. The stairwell was empty again. I was guessing the two mystery women had headed back upstairs to check on Ms. Dale, so I headed down.

The next level was an open area, much like the greenhouse room and the common room, but it was cleaner, more pristine. I could make out some lab equipment from my position on the ground. There was also what appeared to be an office tucked into a corner, but I couldn't see much—just a book case and a desk. The level was empty as well.

I tested grates as I went, moving along toward the next stairwell. I was going to find a way out of here, rescue Viggo, and get us both out of there.

CHAPTER 28

VIGGO

I came to consciousness slowly. I could taste the coppery tang of blood in my mouth, and the left side of my face felt like someone had gone at it with a shovel. I cracked open my eyes, or eye, rather. The left one was swollen over. I had been in enough fights to know that it would be a couple days before I would be able to open it fully.

The light in the room was blinding. It took several seconds and a lot of squinting before I began to make things out. This room was different than the others. That meant I was on one of the lower levels.

It was also sparse—there was only a table and some chairs, but they had been pushed off to the corner. The walls were all bare, except for the one I was facing, which had a massive mirror built into the wall. I squinted at the mirror, and realized it was probably two-way.

Which was impressive, given the size of it. Two way mirrors weren't easy to make—it cost more to make them than it was worth—so the fact that there was one adorning the wall showed certain disregard for the cost. Then again, I was sitting in an underground facility miles away from civilization, surrounded by some of the most dangerous environment known to man… or woman. Whoever had built it had spent a lot of resources to do so.

I caught a glimpse of myself in the mirror. Blood had dried all along the left side of my face, from the wound in my eyebrow. The flesh along my jaw and cheek was purple and brown, bruises already forming. My lip was split open and swollen as well.

I tried to remember other blows, but I could only recall that woman punching me once. Yet that one punch had come close to fracturing my jaw, if the bruising was any indication.

How could she hit that hard?

Better yet, how had only two women broken down the door? When I had turned around to confront them, the corner of the door had been pulled back, and there were only two women there. There could have been more people in the stairwell, but I didn't hear or see anything to indicate that.

The women had also been identical. It wasn't strange in itself, but the way they had carried themselves—they were important somehow. They were definitely operatives for Matrus, that much was sure. I wondered if Ms. Dale knew that another team had been sent out after her.

I hoped Violet was okay. I remembered my quip about her coming to my rescue, but suddenly I wanted her to do anything but that. I was in trouble here, and if she came after me, then she would likely get caught too.

I shifted in my seat, and I could hear the clinking of metal on metal. It took me a minute, but I realized I was cuffed to the chair by my hands and feet—one pair of cuffs around my wrists, one around my ankles, and even one extendable pair around my knees. I leaned my head back, so that I was staring at the ceiling, and sighed, running through my options.

Escape. That was what I needed to do. Before Violet had a chance to get herself caught. It was the only way to keep her from harm. They would likely be aware that I was awake now, which meant interrogation was coming.

So, first order of business was to get out of this chair. I straightened up, and flexed my arms from where they were bound behind my back. They had slipped the cuffs through the rungs in the back of the chair, but the chair was metal, and likely weaker than the cuffs were. If I could get enough leverage, I could be able to bend or even break the chair.

Taking a deep breath, I began to pull my hands back, the chain between the cuffs growing tight. This angle was terrible for it—I couldn't get leverage—but I pulled anyway, bringing my shoulder blades together to pull. After about a minute, my arms began to shake from the strain, and I had to relax them.

Just then, the door began to open. I rotated my shoulders and placed a bored look on my face. The door swung open, and Ms. Dale stepped in.

She was fully clothed—likely in borrowed clothes, like Violet and me—and her arm was in a sling. There were dark shadows under her eyes, like she hadn't slept in a while, and her face was in that same neutral position that I had come to expect from her.

We stared at each other for a few seconds, and then I chuckled. She arched an eyebrow at me.

"Sorry," I said. "I just feel like you should be saying something like 'the tables are turned now,' or something sinister like that."

Her face remained neutral. "Are you thirsty?"

I pondered the question for a moment. I was thirsty, but this was a power play—if I said yes, I was acknowledging that I was under her control. If I said no, I was stubborn. Remaining silent was no better either.

"Maybe," I hedged, shifting in my seat. "What did you bring?"

She looked down her nose at me condescendingly. "Water, of course."

I made a face. "Water? No, thank you."

Shrugging, she moved over to the table, setting down the cup and water pitcher that she had been holding. Leaning her hip on the table, she studied me.

"How's your face?" she asked.

It was my turn to shrug. "It'll heal."

"It doesn't look good."

I laughed. I didn't mean to, but I did. "Ms. Dale, I appreciate your concern, but this is nothing. You should've seen me after my fight with Langston Humphreys. The man had fists like brick walls. Granted, I knocked him out after a minute, but he got in a few good punches."

"Yes. I've read all about your extracurricular activities," Ms. Dale said, settling back on the table. "You are quite an aggressive specimen of a Patrian male."

I exhaled, a flash of irritation coming over me. She made me sound like a dog when she spoke like that. "What do you want, Melissa?" I said, using her first name intentionally.

"Violet."

"Well, that's too bad. I don't know where she is."

Ms. Dale looked over at the mirrored glass for a second and then back to me. "You're really quite impressive, you know that?"

I leaned back in my chair, recognizing what she was doing. I clenched my jaw, determined to remain silent. I was not going to rise to her bait like she did with mine.

"I mean it. I'm not talking about your physical prowess, but rather your intellect. You're observant and have keen deductive reasoning skills. You picked up cues from me that even the most talented interrogator would have overlooked."

I shrugged, waiting for the other shoe to drop. She studied me for a long moment, her brown eyes flicking over me as if I were some puzzle she was trying to solve.

"They're going to kill you, Viggo," she said softly.

"Who?" I asked.

"The twins. Please believe me when I say that I didn't know that they were going to be sent out to retrieve Violet."

"What does it matter if they sent out another team?"

Ms. Dale's face tightened in a way that was uniquely her, and I straightened up, my mind filtering through the possibilities.

"You're afraid of them," I said, my eyes widening.

She didn't respond, but I could see the truth there.

A long silence stretched out between us. She sat on the table, staring at her hands. Her face and eyes revealed nothing, but I could sense a struggle within her. I remained quiet, waiting to see what decision she arrived at.

"I taught them everything they know," she said eventually.

I frowned at that bit of information. Who were these twins and why would Ms. Dale be teaching them? I felt that pushing this woman on that subject would get her to close down on me, so I decided to go a different way.

"How can you do this to Violet?" I demanded.

Her head swiveled sharply as she looked over at me. "I don't know what you're talking about," she said.

I rolled my eyes. "Yes, you do. You may not have said it, but you do. Violet is innocent, and you're willing to let these two women tear her apart. And for what? For a country that claims that they are pacifistic and peaceful?"

Her face hardened and she stood up. "Matrus is –"

"Just as messed up as Patrus. Believe me, I know."

She let out a sharp breath, and I realized I had made her angry. Angry was good—it meant less control over the information she revealed.

"You really can't be that naive," she hissed. "Our

queen was murdered. Murdered. And her murderer? Dead. If there is no one to hold responsible for this crime, if we can't make an example out of someone for what they did…"

I gaped at her. "Are you insane?" She stared at me, her mouth still open to speak, but I barreled over her. "You are talking about condemning an innocent woman to death for regicide, all to maintain face. For what reason? To show that you are in control?"

"People need–"

"People need to be treated like adults. What you're talking about is tyrannical and cruel. Which… I've come to expect from Patrus, but from Matrus?"

She exhaled again sharply, her body vibrating from tension. Her jaw clenched and she stood up.

"Where is Violet?"

I shook my head, clamping my own jaw down. "I don't know," I grated out.

"We need to find her."

"She wasn't downstairs when I went to look for her."

"They are going to kill you if you don't give them what they want."

I bared my teeth at her in the semblance of a grin. "At least I'll finally be able to protect a woman I care about," I said grimly.

A pause filled the room, and she took a step closer,

placing a hand on her hip. "I take it you are referring to your wife?"

I scoffed over the flare of rage and pain. "How deep does your file on me go?" I asked bitterly.

"Deep enough," she replied, arching a brow.

Arrogant Matrian. I ground my teeth together and clenched my fists. "Clearly," was all I could respond.

"Where is Violet?" she repeated. "Where is the egg?"

I shrugged, suddenly tired of the questions. "I honestly couldn't tell you."

She nodded, her face flat. "All right, let me ask you this. After you're dead, who will be left to protect her?"

I froze, stunned by her words. It hadn't occurred to me that once I was dead, Violet would be alone and unprotected. It was a devastating thought, one that made me sick to my stomach.

"If you help us find her, I promise you, Viggo, I will do everything in my power to help her get through this alive."

I stared at her, allowing my disbelief and disdain to show. "I don't know if you've just been doing this too long, or if you're just a cruel human being, but you and I both know that it's not true. I'm not even sure if you believe the lies that you're saying, or if you've just bought in to them as well. All I know is this—Violet is capable of taking care of herself. And if you're smart, you'll walk away from all this."

A slow sound of applause filled the air, and the twins sauntered in from the hallway. "What a lovely speech," one of them said. "Too bad that it'll be the last one you'll ever make."

Ms. Dale shot me a look of deep pity, and turned to the twins.

"Ladies, I was just—"

"We know, Melissa," said the other one, her face twisted in a sinister grin. "You did your best, but now it's our turn."

Dismissed, Ms. Dale stepped over the threshold into the hallway. She took one last look back at me before she disappeared, leaving me and my fate to the two women standing before me.

CHAPTER 29

VIOLET

I felt as if I had been crawling around these ducts for hours, which was actually probably true. Luckily, all of the ducts ran the same way, laid out perfectly and repetitiously. Unluckily, every single grate I tried would not open, no matter how hard I strained.

What was worse was that in his hurry to collect my things, Viggo had forgotten to pack a canteen, leaving me without water. I had been crawling and sliding around for hours, sweating profusely, and I was thirsty. Not to mention, I still wasn't at my best. The bits and pieces of sleep I had managed to slip in had only helped steady me, not revitalize my strength.

That I was already feeling thirsty wasn't a good sign—it meant dehydration was setting in. I needed to move fast, and get out of these ducts.

After the interrogation level and lab, I had continued to crawl downward. I hadn't found any of the machinery responsible for pumping the oxygen throughout the facility, but I figured they had to be at the very bottom level. I hadn't noticed any machinery on the top of the building when we had come in, and it made the most sense: It would be easier to maintain from inside.

My logic was sound, but I still felt apprehensive. Especially after seeing the level after the lab. I had been stalling for a few minutes now, trying to come up with a reason to head back upstairs that made sense, but I couldn't come up with one.

I peeked back through the grate I was next to, and bit my lip. This level I could make out clearly from the floor. It was designed like a child's playground. There was a sand box, swings, a see-saw… everything you could find at a park.

But it was pristine—unused. Like no children had ever played on it before. My mind kept mulling over reasons to explain its presence, but none of them felt right. I had considered the possibility of the researchers who had lived here having children, and this was a designated day care area.

Except that there were mirrors everywhere. At first, I had thought it was just a design thing, until I found an abnormal bit of ventilation, which led to a small room. As I strained on the grate, trying to open it, I realized that I could see the glass. It was a two-way mirror.

I realized then that the room was used to observe and study. Which made my theory moot, as no one would be comfortable with their children being studied like lab rats.

Then why did this room exist? What was the point of it?

Yet more and more questions to add to my ever-growing list. I sighed, and leaned back, resting my head on the duct, rubbing my thumb against my other fingers.

Suddenly, I wished Viggo was here. He likely wouldn't be able to offer up any explanation for the room, but at least his presence would be comforting. I tilted my gaze upward, trying to imagine what was happening with him right now. My heart clenched in my chest as dozens of images ripped from the darkest part of my imagination.

"Get it together, Violet," I said softly, jerking myself out of my grim thoughts. I sighed, rolling my eyes at my need to talk myself through my current dilemma. I was being ridiculous and wasting time.

And yet…

"Okay, Violet," I began. "You know the vents

upstairs are all sealed. You could use your gun, but that would attract attention. So… if you want to save Viggo and get out of these vents, you're going to have to head down to the next level."

Saying the words out loud helped, but not a lot. I ran my hand over my face and grimaced as I realized I had likely wiped all the grime and dirt I had been acquiring all over myself. So much for my miraculous shower from earlier.

I rotated myself in the vent, until I was back on my belly. Pushing the bag toward the next downturn that delineated a staircase, I used my hands and elbows to drag myself behind it. I had secured the flashlight to the bag using one of the straps, which gave me some freedom, but not much.

I approached the juncture for the next stairwell, and heaved the bag into it, before sliding down after it. I was well aware that I was making a lot of noise, but truthfully, I hadn't seen or heard anyone since I had left Viggo's level above. It was like they hadn't bothered searching the lower levels.

Then again—why would they? The door had been secured. For all they knew, I was just hidden somewhere above.

Actually, that reasoning didn't really fly. They'd had more than enough time to search the upper levels.

There weren't many places to hide. So why hadn't they come down yet, looking for me?

I rounded the corner and slid down the next vent. I wasn't sliding fast, so when the vent came to an abrupt stop at solid wall, I had enough time to slow myself down.

The bag continued to slide downward, the light from the flashlight illuminating a hole in the vent where it met the wall. A hole that the bag was sliding toward without any sign of stopping.

Cursing, I shot after the bag, sliding down quickly. I reached out with my left hand, managing to snag the loop at the top. Quickly, I spread my arms and legs, slowing myself down to a halt. The bag teetered at the edge, rocking back and forth for a few seconds, before slowly going over.

I braced for the weight, and managed to keep it from dragging me over, but I heard something clatter below. Pulling the bag back up, I realized the flashlight had fallen. I shifted the bag to my side, grabbed the edge of the hole, and looked down.

The flashlight was still on, somehow, and had fallen about fifty feet straight down. It was illuminating the wall, and I could make out something jutting from it. The light wasn't powerful enough to reach up here, leaving me in darkness.

I felt the edges of the hole carefully. They weren't sharp, which indicated this hole was intentional. I reached along the sides of the vent, feeling my way around. Like the rest of the vent, it was made of the same thin and flexible metal. I couldn't reach the wall in the back, not without moving forward.

Taking a deep breath, I grabbed the edge, and moved more of my torso over the empty space. I used my legs as a brace, spreading them wide and pushing against the sides of the duct. Slowly, I let go with one hand, using my other hand and muscles in the small of my back to keep me straight.

I tried not to look down as I reached across the remaining gap. One wrong move here and I would fall to my death. I took a deep breath, steeling myself against that thought. Besides, it was just another death filled situation. I should be used to those by now.

I felt for the wall, my fingers searching. The concrete was cold under my hand. I slid my hand around, keeping my breathing heavy and my muscles tight. My hand hit something cool and metallic over my third pass. I followed it from the wall, to where it curved around to be parallel to the wall, and then curved around again to intersect with the wall again.

It was a ladder.

I pulled back from the edge and sucked in a few deep

breaths of air. My arms and legs were aching from the exertion, and I was sweating again. I needed to get out of this place, and I guessed I was going to go down to do it.

I managed to slip the backpack on my back, but it took a lot of bending and straining, as well as a few choice words, before I did so.

The next part was even trickier—grabbing the ladder and maneuvering my body over there wasn't going to be easy, especially since I had no room to turn around in the vent. I was going to have to grab on with both hands, and then drag my legs over. I also had to hope that I wouldn't lose my grip and fall.

Taking one last breath, I grabbed the edge of the vent and slid myself over the void. I braced my legs again and reached out with one hand. I was already straining, thanks to the added weight of the backpack.

It only took me a few seconds to find the rung of the ladder again. I gripped it with my hand, and then released the edge of the vent with the other. A moment of weightlessness came over me, reminding me of falling through the air and into The Green, and I panicked, reaching out blindly with my other hand.

There was a second where I was certain I was going to fall, and images of me impacting the unyielding concrete below ran through my imagination. Then my hand found the bar, and I gripped it with all my might. I took a moment to calm myself, sucking air in and out, until I realized I wasn't going to be calm unless I was fully on the ladder.

With that in mind, I pulled myself over. My hips and stomach were completely over the hole now, and that roiling sensation in my stomach intensified. I wrapped my arm around the rung, hooking it with my elbow. I grabbed my wrist with my other hand, locking myself into place, before I let my legs come out and fall.

There was a brief moment of discomfort as my legs swung over the edge, but as soon as my body impacted the rungs, I planted my feet firmly on one with minimal scrambling. Afterward, I rested my head against the bar I was clinging on to, and took a deep breath.

After a few moments, I began to descend.

The darkness made climbing difficult. I had to go slowly, reaching with each foot and hand, making sure they were firmly settled before I trusted my weight to them.

It came as no surprise to me that I had started talking to myself. It was strange, but the sound of my own voice helped me focus.

"All right, just reach down with your foot until you hit the rung… good, good. Make sure you really wedge it on there—no toes here—the shoes aren't that good.

Great, good job Vi—just keep going and you'll be down in no time."

With my little pep talk, I made it down easily. The relief of solid floor beneath my feet poured through me, and I slid down the wall to sit down, wiping the sweat off my forehead.

I rested against the wall for several moments, breathing heavily. As I sat there, my mind once again returned to Viggo. He needed me right now, and I wasn't moving fast enough. It was enough to spur myself back on my feet. I scooped up the flashlight and looked around. There was an archway to my left, and it led to a cat walk. I had found the maintenance area, which was great, but I needed to make sure I could get back to the other levels.

Stepping through the archway, I walked out on the catwalk, shining my flashlight around. The catwalk ran along the wall, while the other side widened into open space. I pressed my free hand against the wall, resolved to stay as far away from the space as possible.

I moved the flashlight up, and I could see dim lights coming from the area above, but I couldn't make anything out.

Frowning, I moved slowly, ever cautious of the floor below. After several hundred feet, it ended at a door. Suddenly apprehensive, I pushed it open slowly.

The room was some sort of station, with buttons and panels lit up everywhere. I looked around for a few seconds, and found a water cooler in the back. Grabbing a mug from one of the desks, I filled it up and drank the first and second cups of water, pausing only long enough to fill the mug back up.

Once I had downed as much as I could handle, I went to the opposite door and opened it, finding a hallway with stairs heading up. My legs started to ache just from the sight of it.

Sighing, I gripped the shoulder of my bag tightly and began climbing up. At least I was out of the vent.

CHAPTER 30

VIOLET

Sweat was dripping from me as I reached the top of the staircase. My shoulders ached from the strain of carrying the weight of the egg and the supplies in my bag, and my lower back was no better. I took a small break at the top, setting the bag down and stretching to help relieve the tension.

Truthfully, I was a little apprehensive about opening the door. This level was already different from the other ones, and I wasn't sure what was waiting on the other side.

Yet Viggo was at the forefront of my mind. I had to be strong enough for him. I couldn't let him down a second time.

After I had finished stretching, I pulled my gun out of the bag and slipped it in my pocket, taking care to ensure the safety was on, then checked to make sure my flashlight was in the other pocket.

Once I had all of my tools ready and accessible, I slipped the backpack on again, and slowly turned the hand wheel on the hatch.

It swung open after a few turns, and I paused at the threshold, waiting for any signs of life. Silence and a sickly yellow light poured through the opening. I stepped through slowly, my shoes scraping on the metal flooring.

I closed the door behind me, watching as the hand wheel turned itself. Then I turned to behold the room itself.

The space was massive, stretching out further than I could see. Great concrete boxes hung from the ceiling by massive cables. Catwalks formed pathways between each cube, with small sections jutting out toward each box. Handrails ran the lengths of the walkways, and as I approached one, I realized that everything was hanging over empty space.

Immediately, I was struck by vertigo, my vision blurring and contorting as I gazed down into the bottomless cavern beneath me. My stomach started doing backflips, and my breathing became ragged. I reached out blindly, gripping on to the handrails.

Looking up, I focused on the concrete cube that

hung five feet away. I took deep even breaths and eventually the sensation passed. When I finally could focus again, I realized I was covered in a cold sweat.

Shuddering, I debated turning back. I clearly wasn't dealing well with heights, and this room was having a very visceral effect on me.

I shut the thought down. I needed to keep moving, and get to Viggo before he was hurt. My heart trembled and I felt the cold press of determination—anyone who hurt Viggo would suffer.

It was that thought that helped me flip the switch between panic and calm. I had to keep going. Looking down was what caused the problem, so I decided to keep my eyes level.

I focused on the cubes. They were massive, probably ten feet by ten feet. Looking left, I could see rows and rows of them stretching out before me. The right was the same.

Biting my lip, I moved left to the first intersection, my feet clanging on the floor, filling the eerily silent space with noise. A few times, I paused at the sound of echoing footsteps, sending a spike of fear through me that I wasn't alone. I listened intently as they faded back into the silence, and exhaled sharply.

I turned down the first row, shining my flashlight on the cubes. They were labeled with a combination of letters and numbers. The letters were the same, the numbers in order. Once in the catwalk cutting between them, I realized that there were windows on this side, similar to the windows in the observation rooms and surgical suites.

I walked over to one of the jutting platforms. There was a five-foot space between the end of the ramp and the concrete block. Studying the block, I could see clamps on the side, where the block would attach to the cube.

Examining the ramp, I realized that there was a keypad on the handrail. I took a tentative step closer, trying to ignore the empty space that was immediately in front of me, and focused on the remote. There were a series of buttons on it—two with two arrows pointing opposite directions, one massive red one, and one green one.

I ignored the red and green ones, and concentrated on the arrows. I picked it up. There was a slight whine as I stretched the wire out from a spool somewhere inside the post, and I almost dropped it. I took a step back and pointed the device at the cube.

The arrows went forward and backward from that angle. Biting my lip, I braced myself, and pressed the back button. I heard something clunk, and the catwalk shook almost imperceptibly under my feet.

Frowning, I pressed the forward button. There was a whirring sound, and suddenly the catwalk began to move slowly toward the cube. I remained still, much to my relief.

I held down the button and watched as it made contact with the cube. There was a loud grating sound, and the gears whirled to a stop.

The green button was flashing now, and after hesitating a second, I pressed it. The clamps closed down on the ramp with a bang.

I placed the remote back on the handrail, and studied the five feet of catwalk before me. I was intensely curious about the contents of the cube, but at the same time, readily aware that Viggo was in serious danger. I felt the press of time warring against my own curiosity.

Eventually, I reasoned that whatever was in there might be able to help us. There could be weapons or who knows what—maybe creatures from The Green. I knew how to survive them if it was, but it might be able to provide a distraction. I had no ideas on how to rescue Viggo—maybe whatever was in those boxes could help.

Taking a deep breath, I crossed quickly, trying to ignore the fact that there weren't any hand rails on the extension.

I kept my eyes on the window, and moved. I felt a

moment of panic, but before I knew it, I was on the other side, my hands pressing against the concrete structure.

Between my hands were several other buttons, glowing softly. There were several more here than on the remote control on the platform, and there were no labels on them. Frowning, I moved my hands away from them, worried about what one accidental press would do.

Instead, I focused my attention on the window. The room was dark, and I couldn't make much out. I squinted my eyes, trying to pick up on any sign of movement, when something banged so hard on the glass that it flexed, and I jumped back in alarm.

Luckily, I landed on the catwalk. The window banged again, and a third time.

Biting my lower lip, I pulled out my flashlight and approached the window cautiously. Another bang and I realized that whatever material it was, it wasn't glass, but it was strong enough to withstand the blows of whatever was inside.

Clicking the flashlight on, I shined it through the window. The light cut through the darkness, revealing a room that was barren. There was no furniture, only four concrete walls, a corrugated floor, and a concrete ceiling.

As I examined the floor, I realized that whatever was in there could see the void beneath, and I felt the blood drain from my face. Being stuck in that room would be my worst nightmare come to life.

I panned the flashlight around, looking for whatever was in there. For a second, it seemed like the room was completely empty, when suddenly something leapt up from the floor, slamming against the window.

I jerked back and angled the flashlight down. Going on my tip toes, I saw a pale form crouched on the ground just under the window.

It stiffened, and straightened slowly, and my free hand came up to cover my mouth as I realized what it was.

It was a human boy. His brown hair matted and unclean. His skin was abnormally pale, and his brown eyes watched me warily. He was wearing some sort of gray overalls, but they were torn and ragged. Judging from his height and size, he appeared to be around eight years old.

"Hello?" I said, pressing my hand on the window.

The boy stared at my hand for a second, cocking his head to one side. He reached up with one hand, and I smiled encouragingly.

The boy froze, and then his face contorted. He lifted his lips in a snarl, and without warning, he launched himself at the window, his head slamming into it with such force that his eyebrow split open.

He staggered back, clutching his head, and I realized the box was soundproof. I watched him shake his head a few times, and then turn around to face me. He opened his mouth and seemed to be screaming in rage at me.

I watched as he reached up to touch the wound on his eyebrow, his fingers coming away wet with blood. With a sickening smile, he began smearing the blood around on his face, painting his face in such a way that it gave him a savage appearance.

He moved back over to the window, and placed his hand against it, leaving a bloody handprint.

Then he smiled—an eerily innocent smile that made my stomach churn and my heart beat faster—and began to spin around the room.

As he spun, I noticed a dark mark on his hand. It took a few seconds for me to realize that it was a black crescent moon tattooed on his flesh.

I felt the pit of my stomach drop out from under me and I staggered back a few steps from the cube.

My hands were shaking as I angled the flashlight to the rows of cubes stretching out next to me.

These were the lost boys of Matrus. The boys who failed the test.

My heart was palpitating as I moved back to the main catwalk. Licking my lips, I shone my flashlight from one cube to another. I had no idea what they were doing to the boys, but I did know my brother could be in one of those cubes.

I moved across the catwalk to the cube opposite, using the remote controls to extend the catwalk. It might not be likely that my brother was in this one, or the next one, but he was down here, in one of these cells.

"Tim!" I shouted before I could stop myself, my voice reverberating through the empty room. My voice lingered in the precipice, Tim's name fading slowly in the void.

I knew what it was to be caged and imprisoned. But these boys were completely isolated—something I'd not had to endure. The thought of my brother enduring it for eight years made my vision cloud up with tears.

I was determined to find him, and I would not leave this facility until I did. *Let anyone try to stop me.*

So I moved from cube to cube, seeking the first person in the world whom I had ever failed, determined to make it up to him.

CHAPTER 31

VIGGO

The wet cracking sound that punctuated the explosion of pain was so loud, my eardrums throbbed. There was a dim moment of blackness, and when I came to again, I was bent over, my face toward the floor. I could taste the blood as it welled into my mouth from my re-split lip, and I spat it out on the floor.

Coughing, I sat back up and glared at my attacker. "Who taught you how to hit?" I said, baring my teeth at her.

She just grinned in that calm, eerie way and raised her hand for another blow.

I braced myself, but kept my eyes on hers, trying not to convey my fear as her hand came down.

She hit harder than anyone I had ever come up against, and that was with an open hand. There was something going on with her—she was insanely strong, but slim. Lithe even. There was nowhere for her to hide muscle, so then how was she hitting me so hard?

As I came to from her latest blow, I rocked my jaw back and forth, making sure it wasn't broken. Whoever she was, she was good at controlling her blows.

She also liked to change up the location of her hits. My entire body throbbed from her attention, and I was pretty certain she had broken a few of my ribs. I spat more blood on the floor, and slowly sat up.

Instantly a wave of dizziness overcame me, and I doubled over as my stomach heaved. I definitely had a concussion.

I rotated my head and looked at the second twin, who was calmly sitting on the table, her legs crossed, her head angled up at the ceiling.

"Don't you want a turn?" I asked, and her head swiveled, her blue eyes coming to rest on me. She gave me a small, tight smile.

"No," she replied. "I don't think that I would."

The first twin grabbed me by the collar of my shirt and hauled me back up. I hissed with pain and glared at her.

"You're mine, pretty Patrian boy," she declared, running a finger down my cheek. I flinched away, shooting her a disgusted look.

"You can feel free to hit me all you want, but please don't do that again," I stated.

The twins exchanged a look, and the one hovering at me let out a choked laugh. "This one is feisty," she declared.

I grimaced, and spat more blood on the floor. Just what I needed—a psychopathic fan with a mean left hook.

"Listen, ladies," I coughed, drawing their attention back to me. "We haven't been properly introduced. My name is Viggo Croft."

"We know," chimed in the one from the table, and I felt annoyance radiate off me.

"Yes. I know that you know," I replied. "But I would very much like to know your names."

The two exchanged looks and fell silent for a moment. I took the opportunity to breathe, trying to calm my stomach and keep from vomiting all over the twins of terror.

"Why should we tell you?" asked the one over me.

I shrugged. "Why not? I'm chained to a chair, completely at your mercy. Odds are, you're going to get bored, or tired of me soon, and then I'll be dead."

There was another silent moment, another reprieve from the blows that kept coming, and it was a welcome one. I knew that trying to draw them into conversation was a risky move, but I didn't have any other options available at that moment. Maybe if I kept them talking, an opportunity would present itself.

"That is illogical," said the one perched on the table.

I squinted at her. "How do you mean?"

She gave a little shrug, her face neutral. "You have no need for our names because you're right, we are going to kill you soon."

I gave a little sigh. "Yet, what harm will it do?"

"You could escape."

Her sister's head whipped around to regard her. "Excuse me? You think this little Patrian male could escape us?"

The twin shrugged again. "It's not outside the realm of possibility. It is likelier, however, that he will die here, but it is best to remain cautious."

The first twin laughed outright. "Who's going to stop us, sister mine? Ms. Dale is completely loyal, and if this Violet girl shows her face, I'll crush it."

The second twin *tsked*, and smoothed the front of her uniform. "We have no idea where Violet is or what tricks she has up her sleeves."

"But you can't seriously think that anything she has can contend with us."

"We're not exactly immune to bullets, sister."

The first twin scoffed and turned on her heel to face me.

I offered her a bloody grin. "So you and your sister fight a lot?"

She paused, drawing her brows up in confusion at my change in topic. "We disagree from time to time."

I nodded. "That happens with family."

The second twin smiled. "You have no idea."

The first twin lifted her hand for another blow.

"Hey, before you hit me, I was just wondering about something."

She lowered her hand, huffing in irritation. "What?" she snapped, folding her arms across her chest.

"What would you do if I could prove Violet was innocent?"

The twins exchanged mirrored looks. "What do you mean," asked the one on the table.

"Well, I'm fairly confident that Violet did not kill Queen Rina."

The one in front of me seized my shirt and picked me and the chair off the floor, hauling me up to eye level. I squirmed, my hands gripping the sides of the chair and looked over at the floor that I was dangling over.

She held me up, her face red and eyes bulging with rage. "Don't you dare utter her name, you filthy arrogant Patrian," she shouted, spittle flying.

She shook me for good measure, before flinging me

away. I impacted with the wall hard, sliding down it into a heap on the floor. It took me a few seconds to clear the shock and stars from my eyes.

When I did, I realized I was lying face down, blood trickling from a fresh cut on my forehead and with my ribs on fire.

I tried to get on my feet, but the chair I was still secured to was limiting my movements. I gave a low groan, and rotated my head back over to the twins.

The one who had thrown me was shouting at me. I couldn't make it out—it felt like cotton had been stuffed in my ears—but the second twin was blocking her from me, holding her back.

I watched as the second twin pushed the first back, making soothing motions with her hands. The second twin slammed her fist into the table, and I gaped as the metal bent and buckled under her fist. I couldn't even do that.

Nor could I throw a grown man tied to a chair into a wall. Whatever I was dealing with—it was like it wasn't human, not anymore.

I groaned again, and the second twin walked over. I tried to look up at her, but I could only angle myself to see the tops of her knees. She knelt down, and I experienced a moment of weightlessness as she righted my chair.

It took me a moment to calm my nausea and focus. I was hurt and my vision was graying out. I could now hear snippets of their conversation as they talked over me.

"—your temper is going to—"

"He had no right—"

"—our sister's orders—"

"—a liar, we should just—"

"—where she is—"

"—cares? I want to—"

"No!"

My mind drifted in and out of consciousness, but I clung to what I had seen and heard, piecing together the information. When it finally dawned at me, I started laughing.

The two stopped their bickering and turned toward me.

"You two…" I heaved, my breathing labored. "You're the twins."

The two stared at me, mirrored looks of confusion reflecting off their faces.

"The twins. The *twins!*" I emphasized. They exchanged looks and I sighed. "You're the daughters of the queen. Her twin daughters. What… Third and fourth in line of succession?"

"How could you know that?" one of them hissed,

and I recognized her as the one who had been hitting me.

I chuckled, my ribs aching. "You told me in everything you did," I heaved, a smile playing on my lips. "In how mad you got when I mentioned the queen's name. In your argument. In how you comport yourself."

The first twin's face watched me passively. "That's a lot to assume, with just pieces of information," she stated calmly.

I nodded my head toward her sister. "She just confirmed it," I replied dryly.

The second sister's head swiveled around and she shot her sister a look of warning. She then turned her gaze back to me. "It doesn't matter that you know who we are. You're going to be dead soon."

I shrugged. "What are your names again? I had them memorized, but I've forgotten them. It's like… Elena, Tabitha, Sarah and Mara?"

"Selina and Marina," hissed the second twin, her eyes flaring.

I gave her a smile. "Sorry. You have a lot of sisters. Are all of them as freakishly strong as you are? Also, which is which?" The twins remained silent, and I shrugged. "I guess I'll just pick one. You, calm one— you're Marina, and the angry one is Selina."

The angry one rolled her eyes. "I'm Marina, *you do it*."

I shrugged again. The edges of my vision were going dark—I was going to be unconscious again soon. "I don't think it really matters at this point," I slurred. "All that matters is you hear me out about Violet before you kill me."

Selina squatted down in front of me, her eyes flicking all over my face. "Your left pupil is blown," she observed. "You're losing consciousness."

"You think," I snapped back sarcastically. "I was thrown into a wall, and Marina did a pretty good number with her super strength."

I yawned then, suddenly feeling very tired.

"Should we repair the damage, Marina?"

"Why? He's not going to tell us where the girl is. He's also too smart—look how he figured out who we were."

"I warned you he was observant," came a voice from the door.

I angled my head toward the door to see Ms. Dale leaning against it, her arms across her chest.

"Melissa," chided Selina, stepping over to the older woman. "You need your rest. I told you we would handle this."

"Don't speak to me as if I were a child, Selina," said Ms. Dale, her eyes widening. "I trained you both for years. Just because you aren't in my class anymore, doesn't mean you get to act like you are superior."

Marina huffed. "We are superior," she declared, flopping down heavily on the table.

Ms. Dale smile. "Oh really?"

Without any warning, she pulled a gun out and shot Selina square in the chest. Marina roared, and rose to her feet, but Ms. Dale calmly angled the gun toward her, and pulled the trigger twice.

I flinched, expecting a loud bang, but the gun only emitted a hissing pop.

"What was that?!" I wheezed, my voice thick and heavy.

Ms. Dale crossed over, and pressed something against my neck. Instantly my heart beat increased, and I felt a surge of energy. I sat up, instantly aware.

"What was that?"

She held up a patch with a red cross through it. "Adrenaline," she replied, taking a step back.

I frowned deeply at her. "What are you doing?"

"Look, I don't know how long those tranquilizers will last, and I need to talk to you, Patrian."

"My name is Viggo, Melissa," I grated out. "And fine, you want to talk? Release me from my cuffs, and let's go."

"No. I'm going to talk first, and then you're going to dart me."

"Won't they remember?"

She shrugged. "Unlikely. The tranquilizer has an effect on short term memory. I'm not sure how long it will keep them out though."

"What are they?"

She shook her head. "That's not what I'm here to talk about. Are you willing to listen?"

I looked at the two women lying unconscious on the floor. "Okay. Talk."

CHAPTER 32

VIOLET

It was hopeless. I had checked dozens of cells, but had found no sign of Tim. Of course, it didn't help that the room was massive. I kept searching for an end to the rows—a wall where I could finally see an end to all of the madness, but I still hadn't encountered one.

Each row had twenty-six cells—thirteen on each side, with a corresponding letter of the alphabet. The rows were differentiated by numbers. I had entered in the twenties. I had assumed that meant there were forty rows from start to finish. I quickly realized there were far more than that once I reached forty, with no end in sight.

Every cell I had seen had a boy in it. Every one. Some were older, some were younger, and all of them seemed to be suffering.

Much like the first boy I encountered, many of them attacked the window when I peered in. Others sat in corners, crying and hyperventilating. Some just stared at me, their faces slack, their eyes out of focus. They had been standing in that same spot for a very long time as evidenced by the defecation on the floor.

It broke my heart seeing all of Matrus' young boys there. A part of me wanted to release them. However, I had taken a closer look at the mechanism holding the cells over the void, and it seemed that it was designed to detach from the ceiling above, dropping however many feet below. Fiddling around with the control panels on the cells could kill them.

So, I just kept on checking, thinking that somehow, if I found Tim, I could find a way.

But time was running out on me. I felt its press on the back of my neck. Viggo was in very real danger, and I had just wasted time down here. I was torn, yet again, between the two people I cared about most.

My foot swung out, kicking one of the metal posts with a resounding clang. I gripped the handrail in frustration and I longed to scream out my rage. In the stories, it was never this hard, but choosing between Viggo and Tim was an impossible task.

I needed to think logically. I had wasted a lot of time already checking cubes, and there were countless others. If I kept looking, chances were that by the time I found Tim, Viggo would be dead.

Tim could wait—Viggo was in more immediate danger. I swiped the tear rolling down my cheek angrily, a flash of rage coursing through me. It wasn't fair, and it wasn't right, but I had to be the one to make the decision. No matter how much it tore at my heart.

I swallowed, staring at the cubes in front of me. "I'll be back," I promised them in a whisper. I knew they couldn't hear me, but I needed to say it.

I shouldered the bag with the egg, and began running back the way I came. It didn't take me long to reach the twenties, but I passed them, ticking the numbers down as I ran.

As I had guessed, there were steps leading up to a hatch door next to Row One. I raced over to it, spinning the wheel and stepping through to the stairwell.

Blowing a lock of hair out of my face, I headed upstairs, taking the steps two or three at a time. At the top, I opened the door to the play area.

I could see much more from here than through the vent, but it still felt eerie seeing all of the toys and playsets. It was intensified now that I knew who it was designed for—not that those poor boys actually could have fun here.

I felt sick to my stomach at the injustice of it—these

boys were human beings, capable of anything, but because of some stupid test, they were cast out and made to do who knows what.

I felt defiant in that moment, a burning desire racing through me to tear away the establishment that put them there.

Latching on to that fire, I let it propel me through this level and up to the next one.

I paused as I entered. Everything gleamed under the lights here. It seemed so pure and clean compared to the levels below. I wanted to break everything in the room, but I refrained.

My footsteps echoed through the laboratory as I walked. There were various stations set up throughout the level, each one with a name plate assigned to it. I didn't recognize any names, but I made a vow to write them all down.

As I made my way to the next hatch, I paused when I saw a room by it. It was the only closed room on the level. The walls were glass, and I could see a desk and computer within. I was prepared to walk by it when the name plate on the door caught my attention.

Prof. Alastair Jenks.

I sucked in a sharp breath, my fist clenching as I remembered the scientist who had sent me for the egg. This was his laboratory.

No wonder the place was abandoned. All of the scientists had likely returned to Matrus in order to attend his and Queen Rina's funeral.

A surge of anger coursed through me, a bitter taste growing in my mouth. These were supposed to be *my* people—the good guys, when compared to Patrians. But they weren't good guys. They had used me and Tim both to accomplish their plans, without a second thought to the fact that we were both human beings.

I became aware of my emotion. It was hate. I hated Matrus for what they had done to me and my family. It burned deep and low in my belly, like a fire that could never be quenched. I wanted to make them pay for what they had done.

At the same time, I was repulsed by my hatred. Sure, I had given in to rage a few times, but I had never really hated anything in my life. It scared me so much, that I had to push it all aside, to deal with it later.

I frowned, my mind churning. The Matrians had left everything here, including the boys. Who knew how long it would be before they came back?

How were the boys being fed? How were they being cared for?

I felt the fire in my belly burn hotter as I contemplated the questions, and again, I had to swallow them down and bury them. Before I could stop myself, however, I had already crossed over and checked the door to Mr. Jenks' office. To my surprise, it swung open. I hesitated for a second, and then crossed over to the computer. Clicking it on, I waited for it to boot up while I began searching through the drawers. There were several file folders in the bottom left drawer, but they were requisition forms, not information about the boys.

The computer beeped, and I turned, half expecting it to be unlocked. It wasn't. I began looking around, and then paused when I saw something glittering from a cabinet tucked back in the corner of the room.

Standing up, I crossed over to it.

It was another egg—sitting on the top shelf of the cabinet.

Testing the doors, I found them locked, but I remembered a set of keys in the desk. I grabbed them, and started testing each one in the lock. Eventually, one turned, and the cabinet door swung open.

Grabbing the egg, I looked it over. It looked identical to the one in my backpack, except for two things. The first was a tiny label taped to the bottom. It read: *Trial One, Failure.* The second difference came in the form of a slight crack through the keyhole at the base.

I held the egg in my hands, thinking. I knew that I needed to come back here—Mr. Jenks would likely have files on each boy, which meant I could find my brother. Viggo could help me. He'd gotten into Lee's computer to find the tracker map Lee had used to watch me, so he had to have a way of getting into computers.

More importantly, I needed to clear my head and focus on the task at hand. Finding Tim and learning about what had been done to him was important to me, but I was too focused on it, and I hadn't thought about what I was going to do to rescue Viggo.

I knew there were three people for certain—the two nameless women and Ms. Dale. That was a lot for me to try and take on by myself. I needed leverage, something they wanted and would bargain for. I looked down to the gleaming silver case I held, a slow smile playing on my lips.

I could both give them what they wanted, and not at the same time.

Without hesitating, I carefully placed the broken egg on the desk. Pulling my backpack off my shoulders, I pulled the real egg out.

The label designating the failed test came away freely under my fingers. I applied it to my egg and then replaced it on the shelf. I closed the cabinet doors and locked them. I took the 'fake' egg and placed it in my bag. Then I grabbed the key that hung around my neck. I untied the fabric it hung on, and took the key off.

There was a small key on the key ring. It wasn't exactly the same, but maybe they wouldn't notice. I took it off the keychain and slipped it onto the fabric, retying it around my neck.

I slipped the real key in my pocket. It made me nervous to do so, but I didn't want to leave both the real egg and real key in the same room together.

Satisfied and with the beginning ideas of a plan forming in my mind, I put on my backpack.

I gave one last look at the office as I swung the door shut behind me. It was the best I could do under the circumstances. With a little luck, I could bargain with the women upstairs, save Viggo, and then rescue my brother.

I looked up at the ceiling. Viggo was up there, waiting for me. I wasn't going to let him down. Besides, I needed to catch up with him on the whole saving each other's life thing.

I headed to the hatch. It swung open easily under my hands, and I entered the stairwell cautiously. When I didn't immediately encounter anyone, I let out the breath I had been holding, and stepped further out into the landing, keeping my footsteps as silent as possible.

I anticipated a guard in the stairwell, yet there were no sounds coming from the landing above. Still, I moved slowly and cautiously.

Each second weighed on me heavily. My heart was beating loudly in my ears. It took me twice as long as I wanted to go up the first flight of stairs. When I reached the top, I ducked down, and peered up to the next landing.

It was completely devoid of anything. Straightening, I moved up the stairs and to the hatch that separated me from Viggo.

Slowly, I placed my hands on the wheel and began to turn. Everything in the facility was well maintained, and the wheel turned silently under my hands. As long as I didn't turn it too far, no one would hear me open the door. However, if they were looking at it, they would see it spinning. I hoped that luck would find me again, but just in case, I pulled the gun out of my pocket and clicked the safety off.

Taking a deep breath, I pushed the door. I kept my body pressed against the side of the door, just in case anyone inside opened fire. As the door swung open, I peeked through the widening gap down the hallway.

Nobody.

I was beginning to doubt the proficiency of this team. It seemed like they didn't care if I took them unaware.

Still, I had doubts. It could be a trap—maybe they were hiding inside the rooms themselves, waiting for me.

Viggo had been in the third room to my left. Taking a deep breath, I crouched low and entered the hallway.

I peeked through the observation windows in each room as I passed, but they were empty. Except for Viggo's.

I glanced in quickly, and saw Ms. Dale standing over Viggo.

He looked terrible, his face bloody and raw. Viggo and Ms. Dale were talking, but I couldn't make out what they were saying.

I started to go for the door, when I saw Ms. Dale reach to the small of her back. I noticed the pistol there. My heart leapt in my throat. She was going to kill him! I felt the icy hand of determination clawing at my spine, whispering to me that I had to stop her. My hand tightened on my gun and I moved over to the door and swung it open, leveling my gun at Ms. Dale.

"Don't do it," I ordered as the cold rage raced through my veins.

CHAPTER 33

VIGGO

I gaped at Violet as she barreled through the door, her gun drawn. She looked amazing, in spite of the streaks of dirt caking her from top to bottom.

Her gray eyes were focused solely on Ms. Dale, her stance spread, her hands steady. She was ready to kill.

"Violet," I said softly, and I saw her eyes flick to me and then back to Ms. Dale.

"Release him," Violet commanded.

Ms. Dale looked from Violet to me. Bending over, she started rummaging through the twins' pockets. Violet watched her steadily, her focus unwavering. A part of me wanted to tell her to stop, that Ms. Dale was helping me, but after what Ms. Dale had revealed to me, I wasn't sure what to do. I needed to sit on the information, until I could process it. Now was not that time.

I heard the jingle of keys as Ms. Dale pulled them out, and slowly stood up, her hands raised. She backed up over to me, carefully stepping over the two unconscious women on the floor, and reached over to unlock my hands.

I flexed them as soon as I could, ignoring the twinges of pain coming from other places as I did so. Snatching the keys from her hands, I released my legs quickly, and then stood up.

"Pass him your gun," Violet ordered, her focus never wavering. Ms. Dale slowly reached behind her back, and pulled out the gun. She pinched it between two fingers, and passed it over to me.

Once the gun was in my hand, I aimed it at her, and took a few steps back. It was more a stagger then a walk, but it was better than I could ever hope for, given my current state.

"What took you so long?" I asked Violet as I stared at Ms. Dale.

I caught a shadow of a smile cut across her lips. "I had to make you wait so you would appreciate it more," she replied.

"Consider me appreciative."

"Are you two quite done flirting?" Ms. Dale asked, her voice frosty.

"You do not get to speak to me," Violet hissed, her

grip tightening on the gun. "Not after what I've seen."

I heard the rage behind Violet's voice, and I looked at her, concerned.

She shook her head, her hands starting to tremble. "I ought to shoot you right now. Did you know?"

"What?" Ms. Dale asked.

Violet's jaw clenched, her face hard and unrelenting. I had never seen her like this before. The joking Violet was gone, replaced by a creature of rage. I could practically feel the room heating up from her fury.

"Violet," I said, keeping my tone even. Her gray eyes flitted to me and I raised my eyebrows at her. "What did you see?"

Violet took a shaky breath. "I found them," she grated out. "I found the boys who failed the test."

I blinked as I absorbed the information, quickly analyzing the implications of it. For her to be this angry meant that how she had found them was less than pleasant.

Ms. Dale shifted, and I glanced over at her. Her face looked pale and her mouth was pinched in a small frown. I catalogued her reaction, but turned my focus on Violet. Ms. Dale could wait, for the time being.

"How bad?"

Tears were glittering in her eyes as she stared down the barrel at Ms. Dale. "Bad," she whispered.

I nodded, hesitating over the next question. "Are they dead?"

She shook her head, unable to articulate. "Worse."

I took a step toward her, and she flinched away. For a second, I thought she was going to point the gun at me, but she just looked at me, her face promising violence.

"Violet," I said softly.

"What?" she snapped.

I let out a slow breath. "Where is your brother?"

Tears finally spilled onto her cheeks, and she lowered the gun a little. "I don't know," she admitted in a croak.

"Okay. Let's go find him," I urged her.

She was wavering, her instincts warring within her. I knew what she was feeling in that moment—I felt it myself after my wife had been hung. It was a deep resentment, a need to punish those responsible for the pain and injustice that had been suffered. She was teetering on the brink of darkness. I had faced that same evil from within, and I hadn't given in.

I knew Violet would win. It never crossed my mind that she would pull that trigger. She was capable—we all were—but at her core, Violet didn't want vengeance, she wanted her brother back. She wanted peace.

My relief was almost palpable when she finally

lowered the gun. "Cuff her. She's coming with us."

I nodded, and aimed my gun at Ms. Dale. The older woman gave an irritated sigh, and then grabbed one set of cuffs.

"Is this really necessary?" she asked, indicating her shoulder.

"In front of you, so you can keep the sling on," I suggested with a smile.

Her mouth pinched in disdain and annoyance. I kept my eyes and gun on her while I moved to Violet, taking her in my arm.

She pressed her face against my shoulder. "Are you okay?" she whispered.

"Of course," I lied.

"Who are they, and why are they unconscious?" she asked, indicating the two women.

"Oh, yeah. Violet, meet Selina and Marina, third and fourth in line of succession."

Violet's eyes took in the two women at the floor. "Did they faint at the sight of your face?"

I chuckled, and then gave a grunt of pain as my ribs protested. I was relieved, however, to see a spark of the old Violet.

"Actually, they decided they wanted to improve upon my good looks."

Ms. Dale watched our exchange as she slipped the

handcuffs over her wrists, her face contemplative. I didn't like the look there, but now wasn't the time.

"What's the plan?" I asked.

"Cuff these two and head downstairs," Violet replied as she stepped over Selina's legs. She stooped and quickly snapped cuffs over the twin's wrists.

"Violet—" I said, intending on warning her about their super strength.

She flashed me a look so cold and dangerous, I half expected to start bleeding from a cut. "What?" she snapped.

I grimaced. She had every right to be upset, but I wasn't going to allow her to take it out on me. I walked over to her and gripped her hard by the shoulders.

"First of all, you need to calm down—you are getting angry with me, and I'm on your side."

Ms. Dale scoffed, but I ignored her, focusing my attention on Violet. Her eyes were wide and wet, and her bottom lip was quivering.

"What's the second thing?" she asked, her voice barely a whisper.

I sighed. I wanted to tell her that it wouldn't do any good, but she had too much on her plate at the moment. I could see the strain in her, and the urgency in which she wanted to head back downstairs was palpable.

So instead, I pulled her tight to my chest and hugged

her. It took her a few seconds, but then she returned the hug, wrapping her arms around me gently. It still hurt—but I held it back from her. She was hurting more than both of us—my wounds were physical and would heal. Hers were emotional and would scar heavily. She had enough on her plate—I couldn't add to it at that moment by telling her about the twins.

Especially given her state of mind. She might kill them, something I knew my Violet wouldn't ultimately want. But she was upset right now—I had no idea what she was capable of.

So, I held my tongue and waited. I gave Ms. Dale a hard look when she opened her mouth, and she shut it too, although not without shooting me another look of annoyance. I had to admire the spine in that woman, if nothing else.

Violet released me after the hug was finished, and then headed downstairs. I flicked the gun at Ms. Dale, who gave another exasperated sigh before following her. I took up the rear.

I wasn't in good shape. The adrenaline patch that Ms. Dale's had given me would last another forty-five minutes, and then it was going to be lights out for me. I knew I should mention it to Violet, but it felt selfish and wrong, especially when she was on the crux of finding her brother.

Violet, being Violet, surprised me again. "There's a laboratory down there," she said. "There should be a first-aid kit. We can patch you up."

I smiled and my heart swelled. Even on the cusp of finding her long lost brother, she was still capable of thinking of others. She was remarkable.

I followed her—albeit slowly—downstairs. As the door swung open, I whistled at the size of the laboratory before me.

"Whatever they were doing down here was important."

"I think it's related to the egg," Violet said as she pushed open the door to Mr. Jenks' office. "And the boys. He…" She paused, and I could see that whatever she had seen of the boys was haunting her. I wanted to get her to talk about it, but I knew better than to push her.

"You don't have to tell me anything right now. Let's just focus on finding your brother."

Violet swallowed and nodded, her face a mixture of apprehension and fear. "Okay," she whispered.

As I entered the room, I looked around. Immediately, my eyes lit on the cabinet in the back as a familiar object caught my eye.

"Violet, did you see this?"

She looked over at me and shook her head. "No. I didn't even come in here. What is it?"

"It's an egg."

"Really?" She hurried over to stand beside me. "It is."

Reaching out, she grabbed the cabinet doors and pulled. The cabinet shook, but the doors stayed fast.

"Maybe there are some keys in the desk," she said.

"Worry about it later," I replied. I guided her over to the desk, and sat down heavily in it. Handing her my handheld from my pocket, I watched as she plugged it in to the tower.

Immediately, the loading screen popped up. I looked over to where Ms. Dale was leaning casually on one of the windows. "Why don't you sit down," I suggested.

She immediately plopped down, looking relaxed and calm, like she wanted to be there. It was a power play, but a good one. It definitely irritated me. I stared at her for a moment until it passed.

I turned to Violet who was glaring daggers at Ms. Dale. "Violet—it's going to take a minute to load," I explained patiently. "Why don't you go find that first-aid kit?"

Violet bit her lip and nodded, heading off to the lab. I could hear her opening cabinets and rummaging through drawers.

My handheld beeped softly, and I looked at the computer as it unlocked. It only took a second for me to locate a folder labeled subjects—Mr. Jenks was clearly organized. My eyes bulged as I saw the hundreds of files listed there.

Clicking the search, I typed in Timothy Bates and hit enter. The search finished just as Violet entered, carrying a little white box in her hands.

"This was all I could find," she said, setting the box down on the desk.

"Forget that," I said. "I'll take care of me. I found your brother."

"You did?!" She quickly moved behind me, peering over my head at the screen. "Fifty-five B," she exclaimed excitedly.

I nodded at her. "Go. I'll watch Ms. Dale. If something goes wrong, I'll fire my pistol."

She nodded and turned on her heel, running out of the room.

I let out a long breath, my ribs and body aching. I should start patching myself up, but to be honest, I was curious.

Clicking on the file, I began to read.

Ms. Dale coughed and I swiveled my head toward her. "What?"

"You know what you have to do," she replied, her gaze and voice steady.

I smirked at her. "I know what you think I should do. But since your opinion isn't really relevant at the moment, I'll make my own decisions."

I turned my attention back to the computer. I attempted to set up a file transfer from the computer to my handheld, but the handheld couldn't handle the data size.

Just then, Violet peeked her head back in. "Viggo," she said insistently.

I blinked at her. "Why are you back?"

"I don't know how to open the cube. There's a panel, with a lot of buttons on it. Is it in the computer?"

Frowning, I began looking at the files, looking for anything under security or cells. Violet fidgeted impatiently while I searched. After a few long minutes, I looked up at her. "I can't find anything."

She frowned, running a nervous hand through her hair. "What do you think I should—"

"Get him out," I said. "By any means necessary."

"I could hurt him," she whispered, her eyes wide.

I stood up and crossed the room to her, placing my hand on her shoulders. I winced as I lowered my face down to hers. "They already have. Do what it takes, Violet. Get him out."

She nodded wordlessly, and went up on her tip toes to press her lips on my cheek. "Thank you," she whispered.

Then she whirled and took off, running toward the

door at the end of the room. I watched her go, and then turned back to the computer.

Ms. Dale stood up and I twisted my head toward hers. "Let me go with her."

I hesitated, studying the older woman. "Why?"

"Because I might be able to get her brother out."

I moved back over to the chair and sat down heavily, my body aching. "If you hurt her…" I warned.

She narrowed her eyes at me. "I won't," she replied, moving toward the door.

I watched her leave, heading after Violet. Pinching the bridge of my nose, I sighed, hoping that Ms. Dale would come through and help Violet. After everything she had put her through, it was the least she could do.

I turned back to the computer and began scanning files, pulling out what I thought would be the most relevant and transferring them over. While they worked, I clicked open the file labeled personal correspondence, and began reading, hoping it would shed light on what the purpose and goal of the facility was, as well as give me some names to work with.

I wasn't sure how I could use the information just yet, but it gave me something to do, while I waited. A part of me felt that I should accompany both of them down, but my injuries were too bad. I was already feeling dizzy again, in spite of the adrenaline patch. If anything, I would only slow them down.

Besides, waiting down here meant I could intercept Marina and Selina if they came looking for Violet. I could provide a distraction if they did, and buy Violet a little time, if nothing else.

CHAPTER 34

VIOLET

I raced down through the levels, repeating the letters to Tim's cell like a prayer. I had no idea how I was going to get him out, but I was going to figure it out.

I couldn't believe how close I was to finally seeing him again. It had been eight years - he would be sixteen now.

While I had been in the re-education centers, I'd often fantasized about being reunited with him. They were silly, but I'd found myself wondering how tall he was now. Would he be taller than me? What had happened to him after he fell in the river? Was he all right? Did he remember me?

That last one worried me a lot. That, and if he did remember me, did he forgive me for that night that he was captured?

Of course, that had been when I believed as everyone else did—that he had been sent to the mines. Now that I knew he was being used as some scientists' lab rat, I only cared that he was okay. If he wasn't, I wasn't sure what I would do.

I entered the lower level, impatiently shoving the door open so hard that it clanged loudly as it impacted the wall. The sound reverberated in the room, the echo of it coming from several directions.

I ignored it and ran down the catwalk. It took me a matter of minutes to reach Row Fifty-five. I bypassed all of the other cubes, shining my flashlight at each one, even though I knew "B" was the first one on the right side.

Once there, I deftly grabbed the remote, and input the commands. I tapped my foot impatiently as the ramp extended. As soon as the ramp connected with the cube, I hit the button locking the clamps in place, and crossed over.

Shining my flashlights in the window, I saw him.

He was sitting in the corner, his arms around his knees, staring blankly ahead. His black hair was longer, curling down around his shoulders. He was bigger, more muscular, but pale. I could make out the slightest bit of a beard growing in along his jaw and upper lip. His face was gaunt, cheeks sunken in, bags under his eyes.

It was like looking at a stranger. Gone was the baby-faced boy who had held my hand as he marveled at the stars and the beauty of the world around him. In his place was a young man who had clearly suffered. I didn't know him, and I didn't know what he had been through.

My arms ached to hug him. To wrap him in them and shelter him from the horrors that plagued him. Guilt wracked me as I looked at him. I pressed my hand on the window, trying to will him to look at me. Would he even remember me? Did he hate me?

Doubts danced through my head, but I tamped them down. It didn't matter how he felt about me. I loved him, and I was going to do everything in my power to get him out of that box.

I looked down at the buttons in front of me and bit my lip. All of my earlier concerns about not messing with the buttons were quickly evaporating in the face of seeing Tim again. But in spite of what Viggo said, I wasn't sure I could justify pressing those buttons in the hopes that they would let him out. Not if it meant him suffering more.

I rubbed my fingers together and examined the buttons on the panel. They were all the same size and color—gray—with a soft glowing blue light to illuminate them.

I looked over to where my brother was sitting in the

corner. "I hope this works," I croaked, knowing he couldn't hear me.

Hands reached out and snagged my wrist before I could touch the panel. Turning, I gaped at Ms. Dale.

"What are you doing here," I hissed, jerking my hand from her grip.

She turned and looked through the window, a small frown playing on her face.

"I had no idea…" she whispered, her brown eyes studying my brother.

I frowned, clenching my fist. The rage was back, looking for someone to turn on. I bit it back, bitter taste and all.

"Why are you here?" I replied, taking a deep breath.

She was examining the panel now, her eyes probing. "I told Viggo I might be able to help you. Her fingers stroked lightly at the keys and my heart jumped.

"Don't," I said sharply, and she froze. Her eyes turned back to me and she frowned.

"Violet, I don't want to hurt your brother," she said patiently, her voice soft. "I'm trying to determine where the control box is on this."

I fidgeted, torn between my distrust of Ms. Dale and my desire to see Tim freed. "You really think you can get him out?" I asked.

Ms. Dale hesitated and turned back to me. "I'm not

an electrician, Violet. I've had some experience, but this is a bit beyond me. However, I will do everything I can to help you get him out. But I need you to understand— I might trigger some things while I am doing this. He might get hurt. I just figure… it's better if I hurt him, than you."

My stomach clenched, and I resisted the urge to punch her. The rational part of my mind recognized that Ms. Dale was telling me the truth so that I would be prepared. And I was grateful for that. I had no idea what I was doing, and I knew that I wouldn't be able to live with the guilt if he died while I was trying to free him. But the emotional side of me wanted to keep hitting her until she stopped moving if anything happened to Tim.

I sucked in a deep breath, and then nodded. I took a step back and crossed my arms, watching.

Ms. Dale examined the panel for several minutes, stroking the concrete walls around it and under it. I crossed my arms, my patience beginning to wear thin, when I heard an audible click.

A piece of the wall disappeared under her fingers, revealing a lit area, filled with wires. She examined the wires closely.

"There are a lot of wires. I'm not sure what all of them lead to. I think one of these green ones might be to a door mechanism, but I'm not sure. May I pull one?"

I hesitated, and then nodded. "Do it," I whispered, flinching at the harshness of my own voice.

She nodded and then pulled a wire.

Immediately, something flashed yellow, and letters began scrolling from left to right across the glass.

Stress Test—Level 1—Initiating Test.

Immediately, a blinding white light came on in the box. I looked at Tim, whose eyes had gone wide. I watched as he immediately slapped both hands over his eyes. Ms. Dale straightened up, reading the screen.

With a curse, she squatted back down, her fingers sifting through the multitude of wires.

The lights started flickering rapidly, the colors shifting and throbbing. Just looking at it from this side made me nauseas.

"Ms. Dale?"

"I'm sorry, Violet. It was the wrong wire. I'm trying to follow it to see if there's a kill switch. Watch him and let me know if he's in any danger."

Even with his eyes covered, it was clearly still having an effect on Tim. He was shaking his head, his mouth open and locked in a silent scream. My stomach churned as I watched him. Whatever he was experiencing in there was clearly hurting him. I looked at the keypad, but the panel had gone black. On the screen, more rolling test appeared—*Test in Progress—two minutes remaining.*

I slammed my hands on the window, trying to get Tim's attention, to give him something to focus on, but he didn't seem to hear or notice.

I watched him rock back and forth, screaming, until he stood up. He began banging on the walls, keeping his eyes closed.

I kept one eye on the timer and one on him, my hands pressed on the glass.

"Hurry up," I screamed toward Ms. Dale. His pain was breaking me, in a multitude of ways. She didn't respond, but I could feel her moving next to where I was sitting.

The lights were increasing their strobes, and my eyes started to hurt from it, but I kept my gaze on Tim. Eventually, he bent over at the waist and began retching, expelling the contents of his stomach on the corrugated floor.

Then he collapsed, curling up into a ball, trying to shield himself from the lights. A few seconds later they shut off, bathing him in darkness again.

I was aware of tears streaking down my cheek. I was sick to my stomach at what I had witnessed. "I'm sorry Violet—I couldn't find the mechanism to stop it," Ms. Dale said quietly from where she was positioned.

I closed my eyes and fought for control. A dark part

of me blamed Ms. Dale, but in my heart, I knew she was doing what she could to help me. And yet…

Wrapping my arms around my stomach, I looked at Tim, conflict tearing through me. Maybe it would be better to leave him in there for now. At least until we could find some sort of guide to tell us how to open the door.

As soon as I thought that though, I realized it couldn't wait. Not with the two unconscious princesses upstairs. They would eventually be missed or escape, and if they managed that, and figured out who Tim was to me, they would use him against me to get what they wanted.

Not to mention, when the scientists who lived in the facility returned—if they returned—they would subjugate him to these tests over and over again. Better to hurt him now to free him, I wasn't going to leave him here a moment longer.

Gritting my teeth, I looked down at Ms. Dale. "Keep trying," I whispered to her.

"Maybe you should go," she suggested. "I'll keep working here but… maybe it would be better if you didn't see."

I frowned and then shook my head. "I'm not leaving him again," I declared. I was determined to stay right here until the door opened.

Ms. Dale nodded, her face an impassive mask. She turned back to the wires. "I'm going to pull another wire," she announced, and my fist clenched.

"Do it."

I heard her grunt and the sound of a spark filled the air. The panel went dark again, and the window screen lit up, text rolling across the surface.

Endurance Test—Level 1—Initiating Test.

I bit back a cry at the words, slamming my fist against the glass.

"Close your eyes, Violet," said Ms. Dale, from where she was busy trying to find the wire to stop the test.

I ignored her, pressing my face close to the glass. I needed to know, even if I didn't want to know.

Water began to pour down from the ceiling, the force of it splashing water everywhere.

Tim's head lolled under the torrential waterfall in the middle of the room, his hair already wet. The room was filling up fast.

He picked himself up, his movements relaying the state of exhaustion he was in.

I watched as he leapt up and grabbed on to a pipe on the ceiling. He hung there, looking down and waiting. He looked so resigned, like he had been through this thousands of times before.

It bothered me that he never looked out the window. It was like he knew it wouldn't do any good to try and plead with whoever was on the other side. I could imagine him trying many times, only to be met with blank stares of indifference.

The water was now at his ankles. Tim didn't panic—he didn't waste any energy fighting what was happening. He merely hung there, watching the water patiently as it rapidly rose. It reached his neck in a minute. I watched him expel a long breath and then suck in a lungful of air just before the water reached the ceiling.

He didn't move after that. His eyes were closed, his black hair floating all around his face. I watched a timer click on, counting up from zero.

I held my breath as I watched the numbers climb. First a minute, then two. At two and half, my nervousness increased. How long was this going to last?

When it hit three and a half minutes, I began to pound on the glass, determined to break it. "Help me," I said to Ms. Dale.

She looked up at me from the wires, her face reflecting her own frustration. "I can't," she said, helplessly.

"He's *dying!*"

She stood up and placed a hand on my shoulder. "He won't die," she insisted. "There will be safe guards to prevent it."

I jerked out of her grasp, tears dripping down my cheeks. "You don't know that."

Ms. Dale nodded, her face melting back into the

impassive mask. "Yes, I do. Whatever they were doing down here, they wouldn't let him die so easily. Test subjects aren't that easily replaced."

I flinched at the harshness of her words, but in a strange way, they comforted me. She was right, but it didn't make what was happening okay. My gaze flicked over to Tim and the timer, holding my breath as the numbers climbed up to the four-minute mark.

At four minutes, I saw Tim open his eyes. He slowly pushed air from his lungs, little bubbles running past his face.

He seemed so calm. I, however, started screaming, tears running down my face as I began beating against the window in earnest. Ms. Dale tried to hold me back, but I shrugged her off, my hand fumbling for the gun in my pants.

A bio-monitor came online. I watched as his heart beat slowed, and then stopped.

My brother was dead.

"No," I shouted, pulling the gun free of my pants, and unloading it into the glass.

Ms. Dale's fists swept up and knocked the gun out of my hands. I stared at her in disbelief.

"How could you?" I hissed, stooping to retrieve the gun.

She took a careful step back, lifting her cuffed hands up, palms out.

"You could compromise the cube, Violet, which might make it disconnect from the beam above."

I glanced up at the beam, anger writhing in my stomach. I opened my mouth, intent on shouting that it didn't matter, when there was a whirring sound coming from the box. I turned, and watched as the water immediately drained from the room. Tim's body landed heavily on the floor, his eyes wide and vacant. My hands were shaking as I covered my mouth.

There was a zapping sound, and Tim's body gave a little jerk. Then, he blinked. Immediately, he began expelling the water from his lungs onto the floor, sucking in deep breaths of air.

That was enough for me. I staggered back a few steps and vomited, bracing myself on the handrail.

I was disgusted beyond rational thought. And I wasn't letting Ms. Dale pull any more wires. I was going to rip that cube apart rather than subject my brother through one more of those hideous test.

Looking over at the wires, I felt the white hot rage from earlier filling me. Before Ms. Dale could stop me, I reached over and grabbed a handful of the wires and yanked, pulling as many of them out as I could.

Sparks flew and I jumped back. The key pad went dark, and there was a humming sound coming from the box. Heart in my throat, I looked up to make sure Tim was okay, and I noticed more words flashing on the screen.

System malfunction—Test Subject 55 B in danger from faulty equipment—Initiate relocation protocol? Y/N?

My eyes grew wide. Whatever I had done had triggered something, but the panel was broken. How was I going to initiate the relocation protocol?

Ms. Dale came up from behind me and reached out to touch the 'Y' button on the screen. It went green under her finger, and there was a hissing sound.

I took a step back, and watched, wide-eyed, as the glass pane got sucked up into the concrete. There was a grating sound, of stone on stone, and a small gap appeared just under the window, creating a narrow door.

Without hesitating, I stepped through.

"Tim?" I gasped, looking at where my brother was still laying on the floor, water still streaming off him.

He didn't react, not even a flicker of movement from his eyes or body.

I bit my lower lip and moved closer to him. "Timothy? It's me. It's Violet."

Nothing. Licking my lips, I settled myself on the floor in front of him. "I'm your sister. We've been apart for a long time, but I'm here now."

Still nothing. I fought the urge to cry, but tears still slipped from my eyes as I looked down at my brother.

"It's my fault you're here," I whispered. "If I had just planned everything better, you would be safe in Patrus. You wouldn't have had to go through this nightmare. But I promise you, baby brother, I am going to get you out of here, and I will never let anything bad happen to you ever again."

I watched him for a long time, looking for any trace of movement. He remained perfectly still, his eyes focused on a spot somewhere behind me, his chest rising and falling in deep even breaths.

My lower jaw convulsed as my guilt mounted. Eventually, I began to sob in earnest, burying my face in my hands.

"Please," I begged him, wanting him just to look at me. To show me somewhere, deep inside, he was still there.

I didn't know how long I sat there crying, when I felt something touch my hand.

Lifting my head, I gazed into my brother's eyes.

His eyes were cloudy and confused. "Violet," he whispered, his voice raw and deep.

I threw my arms around him and held him tightly. He was stiff under my arms, tension radiating out from him. I didn't care—I hugged him anyway. I never wanted to let him go.

I heard Ms. Dale cough and I turned my gaze toward her. She was looking through the door opening at us. "I'll… I'll go back up to Mr. Croft," she said quietly.

Wordlessly, I nodded, tears still streaming from my eyes. She hesitated for another moment. "I'm glad you found your brother," she added, as she turned to leave.

I was too, but I was also worried for him—whatever had been done to him while he was here… he would carry the scars forever. I cried harder, trying to feel strong for him, but feeling helpless myself.

CHAPTER 35

VIGGO

I sat back in the chair, my mind trying to process everything I had read on Mr. Jenks' computer. Ms. Dale strode in and sat in the chair. I looked at her inquisitively.

"She's fine. She's comforting her brother."

A dark thread of suspicion cut through my thoughts, but as I studied her face, I saw sincerity behind that carefully constructed mask. She also looked tired—like whatever she had seen had an effect on her. I resisted taking a jab at her, it would be counter-productive, and I had too much on my plate.

"How much of this were you aware of?" I asked, indicating the computer.

She said nothing, just stared at me with that blank face. I sighed, and folded my hands on the desk.

"You've realized that you can't really hide anything from me, right?"

Shrugging with one shoulder, the corners of her mouth quirked up. "That remains to be seen," she replied arrogantly.

I felt a dull throb in my skull—a reminder of my concussion—and I shook my head at her. "You are something else, lady."

"How do you mean?"

I leaned back into the chair, it squeaked under my weight but held fast. "I mean that you are going to pick a side very soon."

"I have a side," she replied curtly.

"Matrus? The people who want you to catch an innocent woman as a public relations prop?"

Her mouth pinched and she looked away. It was progress. Minimal, but progress none-the-less.

I leaned forward, pinching the bridge of my nose to try and relieve the growing headache. I was starting to feel tired, a sign that the adrenaline patch was beginning to wear off. I still hadn't done anything to patch my wounds—I had been too curious to stop reading for long enough.

Turning back to the computer screen, I re-read a few of the conversations between Queen Rina and Mr. Jenks.

It seemed that the two of them had been conspiring on this project for the better part of thirty years. I couldn't understand the science aspects of it—they were far too technical for a layman like myself—but luckily for me, neither could Queen Rina.

Mr. Jenks had diluted the science enough that I could understand his and the queen's ultimate goal. Apparently, they had stumbled on to a way of enhancing humans. I had gathered that Mr. Jenks had been studying the insemination program, focusing on the unborn embryo.

I didn't understand his theory, but he believed that exposing the unborn child at a certain stage of development with radiation or chemicals would trigger a mutation. And for some reason, Queen Rina had allowed him to experiment on her own unborn children.

It had apparently been a success, but it was limited, and there were some larger problems that developed in association with the experiments. Yet the queen's children had survived and were considered enhanced. There weren't many specific details about her offspring beyond that, but Mr. Jenks' research carried on.

In studying the princesses' genetic code, he had found the areas which triggered these physical enhancements. Strength, speed, intelligence, agility... he had unlocked the key to advancing the human race. The next evolutionary step forward.

But it was an artificially forced evolution, and with that came consequences. In this case, psychological ones. He found that the children born often manifested intense psychological issues.

It put a stop to his in vitro experimentation, but he didn't stop. He believed that there was a way he could awaken these mutations on fully formed humans and, given enough time and study, he could create a single human with all the enhanced abilities he had catalogued.

The queen had funded him, helping him create a laboratory and giving him test subjects in the form of the boys deemed too aggressive for Matrian society.

He had limited success in waking the dormant genes in the boys, using pills. Yet the same psychological issues persisted in each individual. It varied, from hyper-phobia to bipolar manifestations. There were even several cases of schizophrenia.

Mr. Jenks didn't let that stop him. He'd pressed forward with his research, determined to create the ultimate enhanced human.

And he eventually thought he had. I stared at the picture of the egg, its shell open, the small embryo resting inside. It seemed that Queen Rina had been scheduled for implantation (by some specialized process I didn't understand), but had it been a successful test, more would be created and implanted into the women of Matrus.

He had even managed to prevent the embryo from dropping a chromosome and becoming male, ensuring that every implantation would result in an enhanced female.

No wonder King Maxen had wanted it. It represented a very real threat to the continued existence of Patrus.

Of course, the selfish king had then tried to duplicate the technology, probably planning on having his best scientists reverse engineer the process. He had to have had a spy on the inside, someone close to the project, feeding him data. It didn't matter, though, Violet and Lee had stolen it back.

I could now understand why Lee wanted to keep it out of both nation's hands. It was too dangerous for any one nation to control exclusively. Of course, why he had determined to steal it as opposed to destroying it was still a mystery to me.

Looking over at Ms. Dale, I felt a wave of rage wash through me.

"So. Selina and Marina. How were they enhanced?"

She gave me that blank face again, and I resisted the urge to shout at her. I took a deep breath and shook my head, pulling myself up to a standing position. A rush of dizziness came over me, and I swayed back and forth for a moment before it passed.

"You are going to collapse soon," she replied dryly.

I shook my head, holding up a hand to her. "That may be true," I grunted. "And then you'll be able to kill me. But until I do, you are going to answer my questions."

"No. I won't. I've told you more than I intended to. You've just learned a great deal of information, much of it I don't want, nor need, to know. Take that, and run."

I shook my head. "Not until you tell me about Lee's contact."

Her face tightened again, the mask coming down like a massive gate.

Frustrated, I slammed my hand against the desk, satisfied when she jumped in surprise.

"You are, by far, the most infuriating Patrian male I have ever met," she said icily.

I opened my arms. "And you, Melissa, are the most irritating Matrian woman I have ever met. You play these games like somehow you can play both sides at once, never seeing that you are toying with human lives. What you did… I don't know how you live with yourself. I don't even know why you told me what you told me. All I know is that you are going to get Violet killed."

She stared at me disdainfully, and gave a little sniff. "I've helped you more than I should," she hissed, standing up. "I've put everything I believe in aside to help Violet. But you can't ask me to turn my back on my own civilization. I already feel sick enough revealing what I have to you, Patrian."

I gaped at her for a moment. "I really don't understand you. It doesn't matter. It doesn't matter if I'm Patrian and you're Matrian. Not when both sides are wrong."

"What do you suggest we do? Flee to The Outlands? No one has ever returned, and I don't know about you, but I like being alive. I like what I do. If Patrus gets its hands on the egg—"

"It would be just as bad if Matrus did. We need to destroy it."

"You can't!"

"Try to stop me," I replied.

We stood glaring at each other for a moment, neither of us backing off, nor willing to admit that the other had some points.

I had to imagine that this was how it had been at the birth of our two civilizations. One man and one woman in a room, arguing about who was right, both too proud to admit that the other did have a point.

Of course, Ms. Dale was deep into propaganda territory, as far as I was concerned. She truly believed that women would have a better handle on enhanced abilities than men did. I, on the other hand, knew enough about the nature of people to know that if they had any type of power, they would inevitably abuse it, regardless of their gender.

Just then, a loud clang sounded from the staircase upstairs. Ms. Dale and I exchanged looks for a split second.

I rushed out of the office, looking for something to jam the door mechanism. Ms. Dale was hot on my heels.

"The cuffs," she cried, holding her wrists out to me. I fumbled in my pocket, pulling the key out. I unlocked them quickly, and she rushed over to the door, using the cuffs to stop the mechanism mid-turn. I heard a screech of outrage on the other side.

"So sorry, Marina," I said through the door. "We aren't ready to have guests yet. Come back in a few days, and we'll have dinner."

The door thudded from Marina's reply, shuddering in the frame.

"Why must you always antagonize others?" Ms. Dale muttered.

I shrugged, and then grabbed on to the counter as another wave of dizziness struck me.

Ms. Dale studied me for a few seconds, her mouth

pinched, and her brown eyes flitting over me. "You can't stand against them," she stated. "We need to run. I'll help you reunite with Violet. You take her out of here."

"No," I replied with a cough.

"No? What is your plan, Patrian? Stand here and distract them with your corpse?"

I shook my head, and hobbled over to the first-aid kit, opening it up. Spotting what I wanted, I peeled the adrenaline patch off my neck. Pulling out three more, I began opening the foil packets with my teeth. Ms. Dale's brown eyes widened.

"That much adrenaline will kill you," she said.

"Doesn't matter. I won't be able to keep up anyway." I rested my hands on the table, and glared at Ms. Dale. "You need to get Violet out of here."

She scoffed. The thudding had increased, and I could hear the groaning of the bolts in the door. Time was running out. "You would trust me with that?"

I shook my head. "Not even remotely. But Violet is down there getting her brother right now." I locked eyes with her, and leaned back slightly under the ferocity of it. "Violet will not let any harm come to her brother. If you want the egg returned, you get her out to a safe place. She'll barter with you, and I know that you'll keep your word, given what you've told me."

I felt guilty about leaving Violet in the hands of Ms. Dale, but I could buy Violet time. I hated that I wasn't going to be there for her. It felt like I was abandoning her. I needed to fulfill my vow to her. But I needed to keep her safe.

I pulled the handheld out of the tower and held it out to her. "Give this to her. Take your stupid egg, and get her safe."

Ms. Dale reached out for the handheld slowly, hesitation breaking through the tight mask on her face.

She was taking too long. I tossed it at her, and she caught it with her good hand.

"Go," I ordered, slapping the first adrenaline patch on.

Turning on her heel, she strode from the room. I followed behind her, the other two patches ready to be placed. It was a lot of adrenaline, and it would make my heart explode, but if I could slow Marina and Selina down long enough, it would be worth it.

Just then, the door gave a harsh groan and broke open. I ducked, but I heard Ms. Dale's cry of pain as the door clipped her shoulder.

The twins stepped in through the gaping hole, sinister smiles on their face.

"Hello ladies," I said, applying the two patches to the back of my hands under the guise of cracking my knuckles. "I've been waiting for you."

CHAPTER 36

VIOLET

I helped Tim up the stairs slowly, coaxing him upward one step at a time. His arms were wrapped around his waist, and he kept fidgeting at every sound, his eyes wide and scared. I kept a steady hand on his back, and whispered soothingly to him.

He hadn't said a word since uttering my name back in the cell, but he looked at me like he understood what I was saying. Occasionally, he would reach out with a shaking hand and touch me, like he still didn't believe I was real.

I hid my hurt from him. It wasn't a pain he had caused and I didn't want him thinking it was. I had claimed ownership over his abuse, guilt eating me up. I should've found a way to get to him sooner, to free him before he was even subjected to this place. Later, when we got out of here and found somewhere to sleep, I would cry my eyes out, but for now, I needed to be strong for him.

I told him about my adventure while we walked. I wanted to distract him from the levels leading up to the laboratory. I left out a lot of details, but I told him about Viggo, Samuel, Lee, and the egg. I probably talked about Viggo the most.

I was nervous about the two of them meeting. I had no idea how Tim would react to Viggo, or vice versa. They were both important to me, and I wanted it to go well.

I told Tim that. He looked over at me from out of the corner of his eye in such a way, that a laugh escaped me.

"I'm being ridiculous, aren't I?"

There was a hint of movement from his shoulders, and I felt a slim ray of hope enter me. He had shrugged. He could understand me, and he was listening. Before I could stop myself, I wrapped my arms around him in a hug.

It was different, now that he was older. He had definitely grown up from the small eight-year old boy I had lost. He was taller than me, and he had lost the baby fat that had clung to him when he was younger. Still, it felt good having him in my arms.

I was very aware that he didn't hug me back. It hurt,

but it wasn't his fault. I doubted that in the eight years he'd been imprisoned anyone had offered him a hug. I squeezed him tighter, as if afraid he'd disappear on me.

He twitched under my arms, and I reluctantly released him from my hold. It was his way of telling me he was done with the hugs—something I had learned on the climb up after I had kept hugging him. When it got to be too much for him, he found a way to tell me.

I reached out and took his hand in mine. "C'mon," I said, guiding him up. "Let's go meet Viggo."

We were near the top landing leading to the laboratory and I relinquished his hand for a moment as I spun the hand wheel and opened the door. I propelled myself and Tim through it, but a sudden crashing noise made me freeze.

There were sounds of a fight coming from the area around Mr. Jenks' office. My heart in my throat, I grabbed Tim's hand and dragged him down to the floor, crawling on my hands and knees to take cover behind a counter.

Tim followed me, his expression tense. He looked at me quizzically, but I shook my head and put a finger to my lips. His gray eyes studied me while mine surveyed the area, my mind cycling through what I should do. It took three seconds for me to decide to hide Tim, and then go help Viggo.

I scanned the area, looking for a place for Tim to hide. To the right, across the aisle, there was a cabinet under a sink.

I crawled over to it, keeping low behind the counter. There were several similar counters filled with lab equipment blocking the view to us, but there were clear paths on either side where he and I could easily be exposed.

I peered around the edge of the counter, checking to see if anyone was down there. I didn't see anyone.

There was a loud crash, and I heard Viggo's grunt of pain. I winced in sympathy, an icy chill settled under my skin. I was moving too slowly.

Waving Tim over, I quietly opened the cabinet, positioning the door to hopefully shield us from being seen. Bottles of cleaners were inside, but I pulled them out quickly, and gestured for Tim to get in.

He shot me a panicked look, shaking his head. He started to back away, but I grabbed his head with both my hands.

"It'll be okay," I whispered. "I won't leave you. I promise. But I can't help Viggo and worry about you at the same time, okay?"

We stared at each other for a long moment. I tried to convey how sincere I was with my eyes and face, and eventually, Tim nodded.

It was an awkward fit for him, but we managed. I handed him my backpack, and he wrapped his arms around it and nodded at me. I could see the stress and anxiety in him, and I hated it, but I didn't have time to comfort him.

From the sounds coming from up front, Viggo was putting up a good fight, but he was injured. He needed my help. I carefully closed the cabinet doors, sealing Tim in, and turned toward the commotion, making my way slowly toward the sounds of fighting.

As I approached the last few rows of counters, I pulled the gun from my pocket and clicked off the safety. I kept checking between each row, making sure that no one was hiding there. That was how I discovered Ms. Dale.

She was lying in the other aisle adjacent to the one I was on. One of the twins was on top of her, a hand on the back of her neck and a knee planted in the small of her back. She was struggling, trying to unseat the twin, but it was clearly not having any affect.

The twin was looking toward the sound of fighting and not in my direction. I used the opportunity to quietly move through the gap between counters.

Ms. Dale looked at me, but I didn't stop long enough to see if she gave my position away. I just cleared the space and pressed my back to the end of the counter.

When no immediate cry went up alarming them to

my presence, I peeked around the corner to see the commotion.

Viggo and the other twin had locked arms in a wrestling move. I watched Viggo straining against her, pushing her, but she didn't move.

He was hurting. I could tell by how he was breathing—it was labored and intense. Sweat was pouring down him, and his arms and legs were shaking from the strain. His jaw was clenched and his teeth bared.

"Come on, Marina," he coughed. "Give it up."

She gave a cold laugh. "You can't beat me, you idiot. Although I'm impressed by how you are holding up."

He gave a shuddering gasp. "Yeah, what can I say? I'm not willing to roll over for a sadistic thing like you."

I watched as he suddenly dropped his hip, and rotated, using Marina's strength and redirecting it past him, rolling her over his back into the air.

She slammed into the glass wall of the office and slid down to the floor, shaking her head as if to clear a punch. Viggo stood over her, his fists clenched. He drew his hand back, about to strike, when there was a loud sound of a gunshot, echoing through the room.

My heart stopped for a moment. Viggo paused and looked down at his body. I couldn't see what he was looking at, but I didn't need to.

Blood was already staining the back of his shirt, pouring from the exit wound that the bullet had made. He gave a staggering step toward Selina, who came around the corner, one hand on the gun, the other on Ms. Dale's hair, dragging her forward.

Then he crumpled, like a marionette tumbling to the floor after all the strings had been cut.

My brain refused to process what I was seeing, but my body was already acting. I was up on my feet, my finger squeezing the trigger before I could stop myself.

Everything moved in slow motion. Selina's face had barely started changing to one of surprise as she saw me when the first bullet entered her neck. The second bullet entered just below her left eye, while the third perfectly between her eyebrows.

She fell to the floor, the gun skittering from her hand. I didn't even look at her.

I was vaguely aware of Marina struggling to get to her feet, but I ignored her, my focus entirely on Viggo. I crossed the floor, sliding to my knees at his side as I did. I pulled him on to his back. His eyes were closed, his body pale.

I was hearing a high-pitched sound in my ears, and it took me a moment to realize it was me—I was screaming. I clamped my teeth together, cutting my scream off. I pressed my hands to the hole in his chest, trying to create a seal to keep his blood in. It kept pushing past my fingers, staining my skin.

Pushing down as hard as I could, I felt the slow burn of tears as they poured out of my eyes.

"Don't die," I begged him.

Aware of movement behind me, and I tilted my head.

Ms. Dale hobbled over to me, a purple bruise growing on the right side of her face and neck.

"Violet," she said, placing a hand on my shoulder. "We have to go."

I shrugged off her hand, looking down at Viggo. "I can't leave him," I cried. "I won't."

She grabbed my shoulder again, and shook me, but I just started screaming at her, cursing at her to leave me alone.

Kneeling down next to me, she grabbed my face with her hands, making me look at her. "Violet, think about your brother. You need to be strong for him now. Viggo would not want you to die down here."

"He's not dead," I screamed in her face, jerking away from her hands.

She grabbed my shoulders and began to shake me. "Not yet, but he will be. We need to *go*."

I just shook my head, a deep numbness setting in under my skin. I kept pressing my hands to his wounds, ignoring her.

"You aren't going anywhere, you bitch," came a snarl from the other side of the room.

I turned my head, and saw Marina on the floor, cradling the body of her sister to her. Her eyes were glittering with a mixture of rage and tears, and it was directed at me. I stared blankly at her as she gently set down her sister's body and made her way to her feet.

"I'm going to kill you," she said as she stalked over to me, her fists clenched.

CHAPTER 37

VIOLET

I stared at Marina, numb and suddenly extremely tired. "Okay," I responded simply.

She sneered, shaking her head at me. "You don't care, do you? You really are a sociopath."

I just shook my head at her. I had no words. It was like my voice had been stolen from me. I couldn't cope with the fact that Viggo was fading, each beat of his heart pushing him closer to death.

Pain exploded on my face as she reached out and slapped me. "You killed my sister and my mother," she snarled.

I felt her hands on my shirt, clutching it tightly and using it to lift me up off Viggo. I tilted my head to look at her, still unable to speak.

"Don't you care?!" she screamed in my face, spittle

hitting my cheek. "You're a traitor and a murderer, Violet Bates."

"I'm a pawn," I whispered, my voice finally returning to me. "Nothing more, nothing less."

She lifted me higher, and I looked down. I should have been stunned or surprised to see my feet dangling almost a foot off the ground, but I couldn't seem to manifest any feeling. Not with Viggo's blood staining my hands.

"You can't even take responsibility for what you've done, can you?" she screamed, shaking me. "Well, I'm going to make sure you pay for this! And I'm going to make your death is as painful as possible."

The look she shot me was one of disgust, disdain, confusion, and rage. She screamed again, and then suddenly I was flying through the air.

I barely registered it, but my body drew from years of muscle memory and braced for impact as I slammed into a cabinet. A line of pain across my back cut through the numbness that had enveloped my body.

As I lifted my head off the floor from where I had slid, I was aware of Marina's footsteps growing closer. I started crawling away from the sound, my hands seeking a hold on the concrete floor.

I felt her hand grab my hair, yanking it hard enough to bring me to my knees, and force me backward. I grabbed at her hands, clawing at them in a desperate attempt to get her off.

Suddenly a flash of color darted past me, and I felt something impact Marina, causing her to let go of my hair. Looking over my shoulder, I saw Ms. Dale locking her good arm around Marina's neck, hauling her back and away from me.

Shakily, I rose to my feet and turned toward the two. Marina had already peeled Ms. Dale's arm away, and was twisting it around in her hand. Ms. Dale grunted in pain as Marina twisted her arm. She took a step into Marina's hold, and then twisted her body and neatly flipped Marina over her back and onto the floor.

"You were never a good student, Marina," Ms. Dale said as she placed her boot to Marina's neck and pulled on the arm she was still holding.

I heard an audible pop, and Marina screamed as Ms. Dale neatly dislocated her shoulder. I took a step past them, spotting my gun on the floor near Viggo's prone form.

Then Marina grabbed Ms. Dale's foot with her good hand and heaved, sending Ms. Dale crashing over a counter through some lab equipment and landing heavily on the other floor. I reacted, racing toward the gun.

Marina kicked out her leg and tripped me. I caught

myself as I fell, twisting to my side. I landed heavily, my back and hip protesting the impact.

I set it aside and began sliding myself toward the gun. It didn't matter—Marina was on me in seconds. She straddled my body, and pushed me over on my back, holding me firm with a hand on my sternum.

I struggled, my legs kicking out to find leverage, my hands on her arm trying to push her off. I just needed her to move a fraction of an inch, and I could repel her.

Except she was so strong. It was like a mouse trying to fight off a cat. She began pressing her hand deeper into my sternum, and I felt it in my lungs. She cut off their ability to expand, making it impossible for me to breathe.

I reached up, going for her eyes, but she swatted them away with her free hand, and began pressing harder. I felt the weight against the bone. I tried to suck in air, but the pressure was too tight.

I began gagging, dark spots dancing before my eyes. I reached over my head blindly, my hand seeking the cold metal of the gun. Marina's eyes followed the line, and she smirked.

I kept trying to suck in air. The dark spots were growing, and I could feel the fight leave me as I struggled to breathe. My vision darkened, and I felt my limbs going limp.

Suddenly, Marina's weight vanished, and I was able to suck in a cool breath of air, my vision clearing. There was a deep ache as my lungs expanded. It felt like I couldn't breathe fast enough. I was light-headed and dizzy, but I pushed past it as another burst of adrenaline hit my system.

Looking over, I saw Tim, his arms wrapped around Marina, hauling her back off me. She was screaming, struggling against him, but he held her fast.

I frowned, baffled at how he was holding his own against her. I watched Marina's feet kicking out, scrambling for purchase, but Tim kept a firm grip on her. She planted an elbow into his ribs, and he grunted, but maintained his stance.

The gun. Turning, I began crawling toward the other side of the room. Viggo's pool of blood caught my eye and as I looked over at him, his face had become even paler, his breathing shallower. The sight caused a surge of energy to propel me, but then Tim gave another grunt, and I whirled.

Marina had her hand around his throat.

His legs were dangling.

I forced myself to my feet and took a step toward them, intent on clawing her eyes out if I had to, when he planted a foot against her chest.

I gaped as he grabbed her forearm with his hands

and pushed hard with his leg. Marina's grip on his throat slipped, and she stumbled back. Tim landed lightly on his feet, his breathing heavy. The two sized each other up for a long second, taking careful steps in a semi-circle around each other.

Heart in my throat, I took a step forward intent on intervening, but Tim threw his hand up behind him, stopping me.

The tension between the two of them stretched out, like a rubber band being pulled too tightly, and then they snapped into motion, the two of them slugging it out with fists and knees.

Marina's damaged arm dangled uselessly at her side while she fought my brother one-handed. However, Tim was clearly not schooled in martial arts—his punches were poorly timed and aimed.

The sound of their fists on each other's flesh filled the room. I turned toward the gun, intent on retrieving it so I'd be ready to fire in case Marina got the upper hand… but as my eyes darted across the room, it had vanished.

Panic rose in my chest, and before my brain could even make sense of its absence, a loud crack sounded behind me. I twisted to see that Tim had landed a punch on Marina's face. She staggered backward, blood spilling from her mouth. She spat it out, wiping her mouth with the back of her hand.

"So, you're one of Mr. Jenks' little toys," she smirked. She rotated her good shoulder as she stalked around Tim. He watched her warily, his face bruised. Marina paused in her march, sizing him up. "I'm one of the originals," she announced, a sadistic glow lighting in her eyes.

With that, she launched herself at Tim, catching him by surprise and tackling him at the waist. She landed on top of him and began punching him in the face.

A rush of rage clouding my mind, raw instinct took over and I leapt onto her back with a shriek, wrapping my legs around her waist. I bound my arm around her neck, locking my other hand around my wrist, and began to squeeze.

She pushed up on her feet and began shifting me from side to side, like a dog shedding water from its fur, but I held on tight, applying more pressure to her windpipe. I felt a stab of satisfaction as she gasped in response to me cutting off her air.

She staggered back a few steps and I held on fast.

I hadn't been paying attention to my surroundings, however, and she slammed me into a wall, hard enough that I lost my grip.

I reacted, but not fast enough, and the back of my head impacted the concrete. Blinding pain rushed in. I couldn't catch my breath, and was instantly nauseas as wave after wave of pain surged through me.

When I could finally open my eyes, I looked around. Marina was standing over my brother, hauling him up on his knees. She grabbed his chin, studying his face.

He gave a groan, and I stretched out my hand. "Don't," I gasped, as I tried to move toward them. Dizziness assaulted me, and I couldn't seem to find the strength in my limbs to make them do what I wanted.

Marina looked over at me, and grinned sinisterly. "Is this your brother?" she asked, her voice laced with wonder and excitement.

I clenched my jaw. "Don't hurt him. I killed your sister. Me. Not him. Leave him alone."

She chuckled as she caressed the side of his face. He flinched away, but she grabbed him by the back of the neck, holding him tight. "Oh no, no, no," she tsked. "This is just too perfect."

I groaned, and managed to make it to my side. "Please," I begged.

Her laughter rang out, bitter and filled with the promise of pain. "You took my sister," she hissed. "It's only fitting that I take your brother."

I cried out in protest and watched in horror as she sauntered around Tim, until she was behind him. Lazily, she placed her hands on his head, one on the back of his neck, the other snaking around under his jaw, gripping the other side. I knew the hold—it was for breaking necks, and felt a scream building up in my throat.

"Say goodbye, Violet," she taunted, her eyes burning deeply into mine.

I looked at Tim, who was staring at me, tears in his eyes. I reached for him, trying to find the power to move, to stop her, when a gunshot rang out.

Marina's eyes widened, and she slumped onto her knees, blood trickling out from the still smoking bullet hole in her forehead.

Looking toward where the noise had emanated, I gaped at Ms. Dale who was braced against the counter, the still smoking gun in her good hand. Blood was trickling from a gash on the side of her head, matting her brown hair to her forehead.

She relaxed her arm and tossed the gun on the counter, leaning heavily against it.

Tim crawled over to me, and curled up against me, his body trembling. I sat there, stroking his hair, too numb to even feel relieved.

CHAPTER 38

VIOLET

I wasn't sure how much time had passed before I broke through the shock that had settled over me. It couldn't have been long—none of us had moved since Ms. Dale had shot Marina—but it was still too long, considering.

I launched myself over to Viggo, cursing myself for not getting back to him sooner.

Blood was pooled around him, and he was pale—paler than I'd ever seen him. I dropped to my knees, blood soaking through my pants. My hands were shaking as I reached for the hole in his chest. Less blood was trickling from it than before, and I didn't see Viggo's chest moving.

Shuddering, I reached to his throat to see if I could feel a pulse. I pressed against the vein and waited to feel anything—a reassuring bump under my fingertips that told me there was still a chance—but there was nothing.

I was breathing in sharp gasps, hyperventilating as I checked his wrist for a pulse.

"No," I whispered. I grabbed his shoulders and shook him. His head lolled side to side, but he didn't move.

"No," I said more insistently, shaking him harder.

"No!" I screamed, slapping him across the face hard.

I covered my mouth with my hands, trying to contain the scream that was building in my chest, wrapping around my heart like a heavy chain, tearing it apart.

I heard Tim moving up behind me. I felt his hand press down on my shoulder.

Looking up at him, I removed my hand from my mouth. "He's dead," I whispered, not trusting myself to speak a decibel louder for fear of releasing that horrible scream.

Tim's grey eyes flitted over Viggo's body. Licking his lips, he knelt down next to me, and placed his hand on Viggo's chest. I watched as he cocked his head, seemingly listening to something.

His eyes met mine, and he grabbed my hand, replacing his hand with my own.

"Tim," I protested, not wanting to feel the emptiness

where Viggo's heart once beat strong and true.

Pressing one hand over my mouth, he placed another hand over mine. I looked at him, a mixture of confusion and anger rolling through me. Then I felt it. A small little thump under the palm of my hand.

Eyes wide, I looked up at Tim. He reached up and pointed to himself, and then pointed upstairs. I stared at him blankly.

"I don't understand," I whispered.

"He wants to go upstairs to get medical supplies," Ms. Dale said in a tired voice behind me.

Whipping my head around, I looked at her. She was still leaning heavily on the counter, her face weary. I opened my mouth, prepared to tear her apart for even daring to speak to me after everything, when her words hit me.

Medical supplies.

I was an idiot. I should've been halfway upstairs by now, and instead here I was, wasting time mourning someone who wasn't dead yet.

I suddenly felt alive with purpose. Rising to my feet, I started barking orders.

"Tim, you press down on that wound. If you can, there's an exit wound on his back—get something on it to help slow down the bleeding. He doesn't have much blood left. Ms. Dale, see if there are any of those blood patch things in the first aid kit, and then apply as many as you can."

"Violet…" Ms. Dale started to say, her voice filled with doubt.

"Don't," I said, cutting her off. "You will do this, right now, or I will kill you myself."

Her brown eyes examined me closely for a second, and then she nodded. "All right."

I watched as she moved into the office, grabbing the first aid kit from the desk. While she was gone, I knelt next to Tim.

"Tim, where's the bag?" I whispered. He was already following my orders, his hands stained red with Viggo's blood. He looked up at me, and then his eyes flicked back toward the opposite side of the room and then back to me. "All right. Don't show Ms. Dale, okay?"

His head bobbed up and down. I straightened up just as Ms. Dale came out of the office. I crossed over to the counter while she knelt next to Viggo. Picking up the gun she had discarded, I turned.

"Ms. Dale—you know more about first aid than I do. What do I need from upstairs?"

Ms. Dale was applying a patch to Viggo's neck. She paused and looked at me, her brown eyes studying me. "A lot," she replied blithely.

I grit my teeth—this was already taking too long. "Be

more specific," I said in an icy tone that promised pain.

She sighed and rested back on her heels. "Violet, he is close to death. I'm not sure there is anything in that room that *can* save him."

A huff of air escaped my lungs as I eyed her. "Melissa," I said, using her first name. "Give me a list, and get out of my way or I will kill you. You are wasting my time."

"He's a Patrian," she hissed, straightening. "You can't ask me to help the enemy."

I let out a sharp bitter laugh and she stepped back in surprise, her brown eyes wide. "You are so full of it, Melissa," I hissed. "You just killed an heir to the throne of Matrus." I let out a laugh as her gaze drifted toward Marina. "You're one of us now, whether you like it or not. Matrus won't take you back, and you'd die in Patrus. So either get on my team, or get the hell out."

Ms. Dale stared at me for a long moment, her face an impassive mask. "He means that much to you?" she asked.

I met her gaze without flinching. "Yes."

"Why?" she demanded, holding her ground.

I thought about it for a second, a thousand reasons racing through my mind at once. "Because he's ahead in the whole saving lives department, and I can't let him die while I'm still in his debt."

It was a glib reply, and didn't even begin to touch what I was feeling. I owed Viggo so much more than I could possibly give. He had saved my life, multiple times. I had betrayed him, and he had chosen to forgive me. He had given me his trust and his compassion. I might not be ready to admit it yet, but I was in love with Viggo Croft. I couldn't let him die.

A flash of irritation danced across her face. "This isn't a game, Violet," she said.

"I know that, Melissa," I replied. "We all owe him our lives, even you. He carried you for miles with red flies chasing us. So get to work."

She hesitated for a split second, and then nodded, sinking back to her knees. "You'll need more blood patches, a bandage, portable scanner, cauterizer…"

I listened as she listed off items, making a mental check list. As she wound down, I was already heading toward the door.

"Don't let him die before I get back," I called as I left.

I ran. It was five flights of stairs and four levels up and down. I was exhausted, bruised, likely had a concussion, broken ribs, and emotionally damaged.

None of it mattered though—not with Viggo's life on the line. I made good time up the stairs, in spite of my lungs burning and sweat pouring from me with exertion. It was pain and pain was good at the moment—it was helping to keep me on my feet, in spite of my exhaustion.

I reached the last landing and stepped through the open door, my mind intent on finding what I needed.

Rushing to the cabinets, I threw them open and began tossing item after item on to the bed. I ran through the list Ms. Dale gave me, taking extra care to make sure that I got everything she asked for, and then some.

I wiped sweat off my face with the back of my hand. Carefully, I arranged the items on the bed, listing them off to double check that they were there. After a moment's pause, I carefully gathered the corners of the bedsheet, making a makeshift bag.

I tied the corners together tight, to ensure that they didn't bounce around when I ran. A few of the more delicate items I held, not wanting them to break. After making sure one more time I had grabbed everything I needed, I carefully heaved the bag over my shoulder.

It was heavy, but not too heavy that I couldn't handle it. Running wasn't going to be a problem, hopefully.

Once again, I was feeling the clock ticking down, pressure mounting in me to do something. I stepped out into the hall and moved toward the door leading to the stairs. I stepped over the threshold, and took a deep breath.

Then I began to run. I began slowly at a light jog. My makeshift bag bounced against my back, but nothing inside it shifted out of place. I took the stairs two or three at a time, my heart already pounding in my chest.

Something was nagging me at the back of my mind—something I had overlooked—but I couldn't put my finger on it.

I raced through the living quarters and through the door to the next staircase, my mind whirling. The nagging sensation intensified, and I felt a spike of fear and anxiety.

I tried to push it away, but the hair on the back of my neck was standing on end as I entered the common greenhouse. I slowed down and came to a stop in the middle of the room.

Looking around, I couldn't see anything out of place. Yet I couldn't shake the feeling that something was wrong. I turned around, staring back at the way I'd come. The door was open, and I couldn't see anything lurking on the stairwell.

Frowning, I half turned back to resume running when I paused. Looking back, I stared at the door, suddenly confused.

The door leading to the stairwell down was *open*. I blinked, trying to process the implications of that. The door automatically closed after a few seconds, sealing itself—likely to keep each level secure in case of a breach. It took me a second to remember that the door from the stairs to the first level had been open as well. So had the one from the second level into the stairs. The door at the bottom of the stairs had been torn off, but the one on the opposite side was standing wide open.

The only way to keep the door open was to prop it that way. But from where I was standing, I couldn't see anything keeping it from closing. I could examine it closer, but my instincts were telling me that was a bad idea.

In fact, my instincts were telling me that I was in great danger. I looked to the door on the other side of the room, surprised to find it open as well.

I hesitated. I remembered opening them on my way up. Maybe the system was broken somehow? The fight between Viggo and Marina had caused damage in the lab—maybe something had been damaged, and now the doors weren't self-closing.

That didn't explain the door I hadn't opened on the top level though. Licking my lips, I decided the best course of action was to head downstairs and get back to the others, quickly and quietly.

I took a step toward the door. A small sound behind me of another footstep hitting the ground seconds after mine spurred me into motion.

I ran, grasping the bag bouncing on my back with a sweaty hand. I didn't even look back—whether it was paranoia or there was something else in here with us—I knew I had to get to the others fast.

I leapt through the threshold, grabbing the handrail and using it to make a quick course change. I heard the footsteps behind me now, racing after me, and my heart picked up speed. I cleared the first landing, practically leaping down the next.

The door in front of me was closed, and I grabbed the hand wheel, spinning it hard, panic giving me adrenaline and speed.

Then something struck me hard from behind, and I collapsed on the floor, my vision blurring and going gray. I blinked, trying to clear my vision, when I felt something press over my mouth and nose. A strange chemical smell filled my nostrils as I inhaled.

Viggo's pale face, spattered with blood, filled my mind, and I struggled to fight off the drowsiness that was overwhelming me.

And then the darkness was dragging me down.

CHAPTER 39

VIOLET

I woke up with a start, my mind suddenly aware. Adrenaline spiked my system and I sat up, looking around.

I was in one of the bedrooms on the second level. The room was dark, but there was a yellow light coming in from the light under the door.

Ripping off the blanket, I stood up. I was wearing a light white dress that came to my knees. It was too big in the shoulders and a bit snug on the hips, but it wasn't uncomfortable.

Something shifted on the bed, and I jumped back. There was a gentle whine, and a thumping sound. I backed up slowly, and pushed on the bathroom door, swinging it open and letting the light illuminate the room.

Samuel whined again from where he was laying on the bedspread. His tail was thumping as he looked at me. I stared at him, wondering how the hell he had gotten here.

It took me nearly a minute to remember how I had gotten here. Once I did, I raced over to the door, my hand twisting the knob. I needed to find Viggo and Tim.

Samuel barked and leapt off the bed. I pulled at the door, but it was locked. Beating my fists on it, I shouted, hoping that whoever had attacked me hadn't locked me in the room and left me to die.

I tried to think about who it could be as I attempted to force the door open. I realized that whoever it was wanted me alive, not dead. They had locked me in the room, but they hadn't chained me up. In fact, gauging from the bandages I was now feeling wrapped around my ribs, they had patched me up.

It didn't matter—I needed to find Viggo and Tim. I hit my fist on the door for several minutes, shouting for someone to open it, but no one came. After a while, I tried using things I found in the room to hit the lock with, to no avail.

Eventually, I gave up, and began examining the door closely. The hinges of the door were on this side. If I could find something slim enough, I might be able to unscrew them from the door.

I tore the room apart looking. Samuel watched me, whining softly for attention. I emptied drawers onto the bed, tossing aside clothes and pens and notebooks, growing more and more frustrated as I did.

I tested every surface in the room, seeing if I could peel something off to use on the screws. Eventually, I tried going after them with my nails. The only progress I made from that was a few hangnails.

Defeated, I sat down heavily on the floor, resting my back against the door.

Samuel peeked out from under the bed, staring at me with his warm brown eyes.

"Hey buddy," I murmured, patting my thigh. He crawled over on his belly, his ears lowered. I held out my hand to him and, after a moment of hesitation, he licked it. He then proceeded to try and crawl into my lap.

I patted him on the head, and sighed.

"It's always one thing after another," I told him. His tail picked up speed, thumping on the floor. "Why, just once, can't things go my way?"

He stared at me in response, and I leaned my head back, resting it on the door. Samuel rested his head on my thigh. I felt the cold press of the metal from the buckle of his collar digging in uncomfortably, and I took a moment to twist it around his neck.

Then I froze. Looking at his collar, I clenched my fist in frustration over how I had overlooked it. It took me a second to unhook it and rising to my feet, I started at the top screw. I had to fiddle with it for a few moments, trying to find the best way to fit the buckle into the slot, but after a few trials, I managed to position it just right.

I began twisting the buckle. It was painstakingly slow, and more often than not it slipped out of the screw. However, finally the screw began to loosen under my efforts. I twisted until I could get my fingers on it, and then used them to unscrew it.

I had just pried the second one out, when I heard the doorknob rattle. Surprised, I took quick step back, just missing the door as it swung open.

A young man was on the other side. He was just a few inches taller than me, with blond hair and bright blue eyes. He was wearing a black uniform with no insignia anywhere on it. The uniform was skin-tight, clinging to the bulging muscles of his arms and legs. His expression was carefully neutral.

"Violet," he greeted me.

"How do you… Where are Tim and Viggo?"

The man stared at me. "I'm not at liberty to discuss that at this time."

I grated my teeth together, my fists clenched. "You better get liberated real soon," I threatened.

Smirking as if I amused him, he crossed his arms. "I can tell you that your brother and boyfriend are alive."

Relief washed through me, but I ignored it. "Who are you and what do you want?"

"Forgive me. I should have introduced myself. My name is Owen Barns, and I want to escort you down to the laboratory so that you can be debriefed."

I absorbed his information quietly. "Are you with Matrus or Patrus?" I demanded, crossing my arms.

He quirked a blond eyebrow. "Neither," he replied, offering his arm.

I gaped at him, staring at his arm like it was a snake about to bite me. How could he be from neither nation? Who was he, and why was he lying to me? Instantly, I distrusted him. "I think I'll walk myself," I said.

Owen shrugged. "Suit yourself. After you." He stepped back out of the doorframe and held out an arm toward the hallway.

I moved into the hallway, heading for the door at the end. The doors to all of the rooms were closed, and I wondered if Viggo and Tim were in one of them. I started to reach for one of the doorknobs, when Owen's hand grabbed my wrist with a firm but strong grasp.

"You will be permitted to see your companions after your debriefing," he said. "Until then, please keep your hands to yourself."

Grimacing, I snatched my hand out of his grip and stalked to the door. I wanted to get to the bottom of this.

We moved downstairs quickly. There was sign of activity everywhere, but I couldn't see anyone anywhere. I commented on it, but Owen just smirked at me and urged me to continue down.

I really wanted to punch him, and hopefully I would get the chance to. However, regardless of how empty the levels were, I needed more information before I planned my escape. Like where Viggo, Tim, and Ms. Dale were, and how many other people were with Owen.

He opened the door to the lab, and I stepped through. The area had been cleaned up, but I saw the two bodies lying in the middle of the floor covered with a tarp, and I paused.

"The twins," Owen said behind me.

I shot him a contemptuous look. "I figured that out," I said dryly.

A soft sound coming from Dr. Jenks' office caught my attention, and I turned toward it. An older woman was sitting behind the desk, staring at the computer from behind a pair of spectacles. Her hair was dark, with white streaks running from the temples. It was casually styled. She was wearing the same uniform as Owen.

Owen held out his arm with a flourish, pointing me into the room.

I ignored his antics and strode inside.

"Who the hell are you?" I demanded.

The older woman turned her head toward me, her blue eyes flicking over me.

"Violet Bates," she said, settling back in the chair.

She watched me for a long moment in contemplative silence. I could feel her gaze like a weight. Whoever this woman was, she had a commanding presence. I felt uncomfortable under her scrutiny.

"Owen, you are dismissed," she said.

Owen said nothing, but closed the door behind me, sealing me in with this woman.

"Sit down, Ms. Bates," the woman said, her tone brooking no disobedience. I contemplated standing in open defiance of her, but I realized it was a childish ploy. I sat down in the chair.

"Who are you?" I asked.

She arched an eyebrow at me, tapping her fingers on the table. Taking off her glasses, she studied me.

"Who do you think I am?" she asked, interlacing her fingers.

I paused. "I don't know. The guy—Owen—he said you weren't with Matrus or Patrus. Are you a rebel faction?"

She inclined her head a fraction of an inch. "There are some that would say that, although we have taken great care to remain on the periphery of both societies."

"Why?"

"Why do you think?" she asked.

"Because you don't agree with either society's position?"

"Is that a question, or are you certain?"

I sighed in frustration. "Look, to be honest, I don't care. All I want is my people returned. If you have no allegiance to either side, then that should be easy enough."

She nodded at me. "That's true. But let me ask you this: Where would you go?"

Hesitating for a moment, I shrugged. "I haven't really gotten that far ahead," I admitted.

A small smile played at her lips. "I figured. What if I were to offer you a solution?"

I stared at the older woman across from me warily. "At what price?"

The smile on her lips grew. "I knew I would like you, Violet," she said. "You don't ask what the solution is— you skip to the price. That's practical, and very clever."

"You didn't answer my question."

"To be fair, I haven't answered any of them," she replied. "But I will, eventually. First—tell me what you know of this place."

I frowned. "You've already read the computers. I'm assuming you've seen downstairs."

"I have. I'm more interested in your observations at the moment."

Sighing, I ran a hand through my hair in frustration. "It's a laboratory." She gave me a look of impatience, but I ignored her. "A Matrian facility for experimenting on humans."

"Go on."

"They're... trying to do something. Enhance people."

"How?"

I shrugged, but as I did so, I realized I knew the answer. "Make them stronger. Faster. Smarter."

"Why?"

I paused, thinking about it. "I... I don't know." Rubbing my hands on the front of my dress, I contemplated the question. "Because, if they can make people stronger—better—they can have an advantage."

"What do you think they would use that advantage for?"

I looked at her. "Defeating their enemies," I replied, a hard knot forming in my stomach.

The woman leaned back, an extremely satisfied look on her face. "Exactly."

I had been reaching, trying to come up with answers regarding the why of things, and I finally had an answer. My eyes flicked over to the egg sitting in the case.

She followed my gaze, shifting in her seat. "Mr. Jenks' perfect human," she said, pinching the bridge of her nose between two fingers. Abruptly, she stood up and walked over to the door. "Come with me," she ordered as she strode out of the office.

After another look at the egg—the real egg—sitting behind the glass panel, I obeyed, quickening my stride to follow her.

CHAPTER 40

VIOLET

She led me downstairs to the lowest level before stopping, resting her hands on the handrails and staring out at the rows of cubes hanging suspended over darkness.

"Mr. Jenks' test subjects," she said without looking at me. "I dedicated a huge part of my life to trying to find them, but I never thought I would find them like this."

I studied her. "Who are you?" I asked again.

She gave a long sigh, and then turned around, resting a hip against the rail and folding her arms across her chest. "I'm going to tell you Violet, but you have to promise not to react until after I say what I have to say."

I nodded in wordless agreement and she sighed again, looking out over her shoulder before replying: "My name is Desmond Bertrand."

I stared, dumbstruck, as she pulled a familiar piece of paper from her pocket and held it up. "I believe you knew my son," she said.

"*D-Desmond?* Lee's *mother?*" I blurted, shock rolling over me. "But, that's a male name—and Lee said that his mother was dead!"

"A lot of people think I'm dead. I went to great lengths to make it look like I died. As for my name—all the women in my family have been given male names. It's a silly tradition, but one I probably would have followed if I had ever had a daughter." She gave a smirk, her eyes meeting mine. "Just something to break the gender lines for women and proclaim our equality, I suppose."

"But—"

She held up a hand, and my protest died on my lips. "Let me finish, Violet."

I closed my mouth and waited.

"When I escaped Patrus and gave birth to Lee on the river, I knew there was an advantage to be claimed there. I ensured that Lee was given the freedom to choose which nation he wanted, and advocated that he become a spy of Matrus.

"He began training at a young age. He wasn't very good at the physical aspect of spy craft, but mentally, my son was quite adept. He excelled at lying and convincing others to do what he wanted. A few years later, I wanted another child—without the hassle of marrying or finding a male to help—so I signed up for artificial insemination.

"Around the same time, the testing of Matrian males changed. More boys started being flagged for violent and aggressive tendencies. Before, it had been maybe one in twenty that were taken. Now, it was closer to one in ten. Like so many others, I believed it was a good thing. Lee passed the test with flying colors, which didn't surprise me. But my second son, Jay, did not, and he was carted off.

"I was beside myself with grief. My son, my sweet baby boy, had been taken by his own country and shipped off to the mines, and I was never going to get to hold him again. Suffice it to say, I was not pleased.

"Neither was Lee. We faked my death together and I headed north, hoping to find and rescue him. I spent one year looking for these mines, and you know what I found? Nothing. It was then that I realized that our government was lying to us.

"I contacted Lee, and he managed to intercept some information about a facility where the boys were sent to. I found sympathizers who had been affected by the changed policy, and I organized them. Together, we broke into the facility. It was an exact replica of this place, but somehow, someone had tipped them off that we were coming.

"At the time, I had no idea what their goal was. I spent years trying to find out. It wasn't until Lee received orders to retrieve this egg that we got a break. Lee managed to use one of the phone calls between you and Mr. Jenks to infiltrate his system. He couldn't get much, but what he did get indicated the egg was the final stage of Mr. Jenks' research.

"Which is why I told my son to steal it. And to leave no witnesses."

I stared at her, my body tensing. "I see."

"Violet. Did you kill my son?"

I hesitated under her point blank question. I thought about lying for a second, but then Marina's grief stricken face crossed my mind. Her words rolled through me like thunder. I couldn't hide from the things I had done, and I couldn't lie about them either. Lies were increasingly common, I had learned, which made the truth worth more. I wanted to be worth more too, regardless of how she reacted. I figured it was better knowing than not. "Yes," I said softly.

Desmond sucked in a deep breath of air and turned around, clutching the handrails tightly. I took a half step back, expecting an attack from her at any moment.

She stayed in that position for a long time, and then

slowly turned back around. "Thank you for your honesty," she said hoarsely.

I froze, unprepared for her response. My brows furrowed in confusion. "Don't you want revenge? To punish me somehow?"

She gave a bitter laugh and shook her head. "When society believes that an eye for an eye is acceptable, eventually everyone will go blind." At my expression, she sighed. "It's not your fault. Not really. I gave Lee the order to terminate everyone involved with the mission."

"But I—"

"You defended yourself, Violet," she said with a heavy sigh. "You had no idea what the big picture was. If I had known how resourceful you were, I would've had Lee bring you to me. But to me, you were just another pawn, and I was ready to sacrifice you. It's not your fault my son is dead—it's mine." She held up the letter. "I never knew he felt like a pawn as well, though," she said wistfully, her fingers stroking over the letter. "I thought he wanted to help me. But it seemed he had other plans."

It took me a second to understand her cryptic statement. Then I remembered the letter, and how it had described his plan to continue northward.

"He wrote the letter to leave to you," I said softly, and

she nodded, a tear escaping the corner of her eye.

I bit my lip, taking a step back. I couldn't begin to process everything that was happening. A part of me wanted to retreat back to my room, pull the covers over my head, and forget everything that had happened.

Yet curiosity won out. I took a step forward. "What do you want from me, Ms. Bertrand?"

Desmond looked up at me, her blue eyes tired. "I'm not going to lie, Violet. I'm not a good person—I've never pretended to be—but what Matrus is doing is wrong. And I want to stop them. For good."

"How do you mean?"

"I'm talking about a rebellion. A real one. And I want your help."

I scoffed, taking a step back again. "You can't! They're too strong. You have how many people?"

"More than you think," she replied.

"Well they have more. They have weapons. They have supplies."

She held out her hand toward the cubes, her voice dangerously low. "We have the very boys that they cast out."

I stared at the cubes. "They're broken," I whispered, thinking of my brother. "Traumatized."

"Then we'll help them," she replied simply.

"What do you expect me to do?"

She gave a great sigh, and grabbed my shoulders, forcing me to look her in the eyes. "Let me ask you this question. What are you willing to do? Go through the options, and you tell me which one is your best one."

I hesitated, suddenly feeling lost. On the one hand, I hated Matrus. I wanted to see them pay for what they had done to my brother. To Viggo. On the other hand... the cost of waging a war would be high. Innocent civilians would suffer in any conflict. I wasn't sure I could shoulder that burden.

"Can I... Can I think about it?" I asked.

Desmond nodded, releasing my shoulders. "Of course. You must be hungry. And I assume that you will want to check on your people. Owen?"

I nearly jumped three feet as Owen appeared out of nowhere, light dancing across the fabric of his suit until it faded to black.

"I'll take her," he said in a chipper voice, offering me an arm.

I gaped at him. "What the... How did you do that?"

He gave me a little smirk. "One of the tricks of the trade," he said.

My mind suddenly made an intuitive leap. "You're the thing that grabbed me in the forest," I said.

Owen exchanged a look with Desmond. "I'll explain everything, if you decide to join us," said Desmond.

I looked at both of them, too overwhelmed to respond. "Just take me upstairs," I replied, pivoting on my heel and heading back to the door as fast as possible. The room felt tight, like it was closing in. I needed to escape from there, and make sure Viggo and Tim were all right. Ms. Dale as well, although she was a dim after thought, at this point.

Owen jogged up behind me, slowing down to a walk as he caught up. "That was a lot, huh?"

I glanced over at him, and shook my head. "I really don't know what to make of all this."

"Yeah. I, uh… read your file and kind of pieced together what happened in here. You've been having a pretty rough time, huh?"

I paused mid-step, my head whipping around to look at him. "Rough time?" I hissed, spearing him with a look. "You have no idea what I have been through. So don't offer me your false sincerity or pity. Just shut up, and take me where I need to go."

Owen's face became neutral, but I detected a small flash of pain before it disappeared. "All right," he said in a clipped tone.

We remained silent as we made our way upstairs. I grabbed an apple off the tree as we passed through the greenhouse. Once in the living quarters, Owen opened the immediate door to my right, revealing Tim.

He was sleeping on the floor, blankets and pillows piled up around him in a makeshift nest. I started to say something, but Owen shook his head and closed the door softly.

"Don't try to stop me from talking to my brother," I whispered angrily, trying to push past him. He placed a heavy hand on my shoulder.

"The last time someone accidentally woke your brother up, he broke their jaw. I just didn't want him reacting strongly and accidentally hurting you."

I stared at him for a long moment, the anger draining out of me. He looked so peaceful in his sleep, but I remembered how animalistic he had seemed fighting Marina. I didn't know the extent of his problems, which meant I had no idea what it would take for him to get better. "Is he okay?"

Owen hesitated and shook his head. "Not exactly. Desmond will have to explain more later, but for now, you can see he's safe and sound. We haven't hurt him."

"Then show me Viggo."

Owen hesitated again. "He's upstairs," he said softly.

I pushed past him toward the next staircase. Owen padded along beside me silently as I pushed through the door.

Once upstairs, he pointed me to a room and I went in.

Viggo was lying in the bed, hooked up to machines. They were beeping softly, monitoring his vitals.

He was unconscious, but he looked better—there was more pink in his skin than when I last saw him. I let out the breath I was holding and moved closer, taking his hand in mine.

I expected him to wake up when I touched him, but he didn't. My heart sank into my stomach as I stroked my thumb over his hand. I wanted to cry to see him like this. He was strong—how could a simple gunshot bring him down like this?

"What's wrong with him?" I asked Owen without looking at him.

He cleared his throat. "He's not so good, actually," he replied, and I shot him a look.

"What do you mean?" I demanded.

Licking his lips, Owen fidgeted. "He... um... well, according to the Matrian spy, he used an excess of adrenaline to fight. It um... it damaged his heart."

I blinked absorbing the information. I reached out, smoothing a lock of hair on his forehead. "C-Can you fix it?"

Owen sighed. "Not with the equipment we have here," he said tiredly. "We need access to a surgical laser to repair the tear in his heart. Without it..." he trailed off, and I stared at him.

"Without it, what?"

"He'll die."

I sat down heavily in the chair sitting right next to the bed, a hard rock forming in my stomach.

"Violet?"

"Go away," I said, shutting my eyes. I heard him hesitate for a second, but after a moment, he left, leaving me alone with Viggo.

I sat there for a long time, holding Viggo's hand, silently willing him to wake up and tell me that Owen was wrong. Yet he never did.

I hated seeing him like this, so helpless and vulnerable. How was I going to get him out of here if I didn't accept Desmond's offer? I was in no position to carry him and Tim out of here. Where could we even go?

My mind drifted to Desmond, and I sighed, leaning back in the chair. She seemed so in control. Everything about her threw me off. I knew I couldn't trust her— not completely—but a small part of me wanted to.

Truth be told, I admired her. She was so calm, so collected, so rational. My emotions felt like a stone tied around my neck. I had no idea what to do, where to go, while she seemed to have plan after plan ready to go. And there was a small nagging voice inside me reminding me that I was all alone, and I needed help.

She was offering me a hand up. I felt torn and conflicted. I wished Viggo were awake—he would have an opinion on what to do.

"You stupid idiot," I whispered to him, stroking my hand over his. "We were almost even."

"Even with what?" came Desmond's voice from the door.

I glanced at her, turning around to face her. "It doesn't matter. What do you want?"

"You've been in here for hours, Violet. I came to check on you."

I stared at her and she sighed. She moved into the room and sat down on the desk. "Ask your question."

"Is it that obvious?"

There was a flash of a smile. "I was a pretty good spy, once upon a time."

"Fine. Did you do this to Viggo? Is this your way of trying to control me?"

She shook her head, her mouth tightening. "No, Violet. I can understand why you would think that, though."

"How do I know you're telling me the truth?"

Leaning back, she sighed. "You don't. I can only try to earn your trust from here on out. Step one of doing that is to do everything in my power to help Mr. Croft here get better."

I watched her closely. "What's step two?"

She didn't say anything. Instead, she stood up and went back to the door. Reaching down, she picked something up and carried it in.

It was my backpack, the one I had left with Tim. She held it out to me, and I took it. Opening it up, I saw all of my belongings and the false egg inside. She had even returned my gun.

"I leave control of the egg to you, although I do ask if you will allow my scientists to study it. However, it is up to you. Keep it, throw it away, destroy it—whatever you want."

I stared at her for a long moment, baffled by the woman in front of me. "I don't understand you," I whispered, clutching the bag to my chest.

Desmond gave me a look of sympathy. "I bet. Lots of people have tried to use you, Violet, so your distrust is perfectly understandable. But I don't want to use you. I want to help you and I want you to help me."

"How can you help me?"

She ran a hand through her hair. "Well, for starters, I can help you get what you need to save Mr. Croft's life."

I scoffed. "For my help?"

"I would like your help—your willingness to help— but I won't blackmail you into it. That doesn't bode well for any continued relationship."

I frowned, not anticipating her reaction. Every time I thought I could predict how she wanted to use me, she proved me wrong. It was weird, but I was beginning to like her. I still wasn't sure what I wanted to do though.

"So even if I don't help you, you'll still help me? Free of charge?"

She laughed, and the sound reminded me of wind chimes—bright and beautiful. "Nothing is ever free, Violet. I would, of course, ask you to accompany Owen on any expedition to steal the equipment needed, but I assume you would want to go along anyway."

I frowned. Again, that blunt information, freely given with an intense sincerity. For good or for bad, she didn't pull a punch.

"Why are you so…" I waved my hand, trying to pick a good word that wouldn't insult her.

"Blunt?" she offered, a small smile playing at her lips. I nodded and she shrugged. "Honesty is an undervalued commodity. Keeping secrets is the cancer that is slowly killing Matrus and Patrus. Given enough time, and lies, both places would fail, and the last vestiges of humanity would disappear from this earth. I don't have time for it. And also, I have found that honesty can inspire people. I won't let my people go into any situation against their will, and I won't lie to spare them uncomfortable truths about what they are getting into. It builds trust, and separates me from Matrus and Patrus. I don't have time to be anything but honest."

I stared back at her for a long time, wrestling with my indecision. Everything she said struck a chord in me. I wanted to believe her. I chose to believe her.

"Okay," I said. "So, if I helped you, what would you want me to do?"

She shot me a beatific smile, her face lighting up from within as she replied, "I'd want you to help me win a war."

READY FOR THE NEXT PART OF VIOLET AND VIGGO'S STORY?

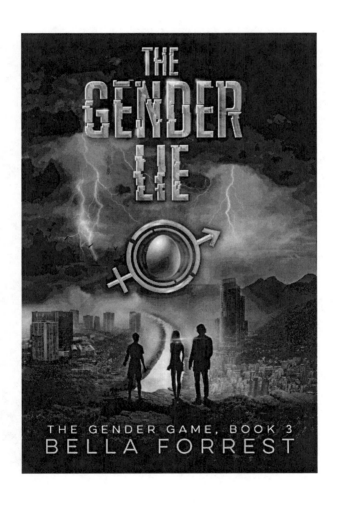

Dear Reader,

Thank you for reading! I hope you enjoyed *The Gender Secret*.

The next book in Violet's journey, Book 3, *The Gender Lie*, releases the last day of the year: December 31st 2016!

If you visit WWW.MOREBELLAFORREST.COM and join my email list, I will send you an email as soon as *The Gender Lie* is live.

You can also visit my website for the most updated information about my books: www.bellaforrest.net

Until we meet again between the pages,
—Bella Forrest x

ALSO BY BELLA FORREST

THE GENDER GAME
The Gender Game (Book 1)
The Gender Secret (Book 2)

A SHADE OF
VAMPIRE SERIES

SERIES 1:
Derek & Sofia's story

A Shade of Vampire (Book 1)
A Shade of Blood (Book 2)
A Castle of Sand (Book 3)
A Shadow of Light (Book 4)
A Blaze of Sun (Book 5)
A Gate of Night (Book 6)
A Break of Day (Book 7)

SERIES 2:
Rose & Caleb's story

A Shade of Novak (Book 8)
A Bond of Blood (Book 9)
A Spell of Time (Book 10)

A Chase of Prey (Book 11)

A Shade of Doubt (Book 12)

A Turn of Tides (Book 13)

A Dawn of Strength (Book 14)

A Fall of Secrets (Book 15)

An End of Night (Book 16)

SERIES 3:
Ben & River's story

A Wind of Change (Book 17)

A Trail of Echoes (Book 18)

A Soldier of Shadows (Book 19)

A Hero of Realms (Book 20)

A Vial of Life (Book 21)

A Fork of Paths (Book 22)

A Flight of Souls (Book 23)

A Bridge of Stars (Book 24)

SERIES 4:
A Clan of Novaks

A Clan of Novaks (Book 25)

A World of New (Book 26)

A Web of Lies (Book 27)

A Touch of Truth (Book 28)

An Hour of Need (Book 29)

A Game of Risk (Book 30)

A Twist of Fates (Book 31)

A Day of Glory (Book 32)

DETECTIVE ERIN BOND

(Adult mystery/thriller)

Bare Girl

Write, Edit, Kill

CPSIA information can be obtained
at www.ICGtesting.com
Printed in the USA
LVOW08s0036160518
577261LV00005B/1044/P